MW01679953

Trials of Faith

Crystal Ratcliff

PublishAmerica
Baltimore

First printing

ISBN: 1-59129-519-x
PUBLISHED BY PUBLISHAMERICA BOOK PUBLISHERS
www.publishamerica.com
Baltimore

Printed in the United States of America

For Him

1

Cassandra sat on the floor in the bathroom of her apartment wiping the tears from her eyes. She had just made the biggest mistake of her life. Things had been going bad for some time now, but this topped it all. She was feeling more guilt than ever before and there was tightness in her chest that wouldn't go away. *What is wrong with me? Am I going to die? Oh God, please don't let me die. I promise I'll change. I will do things right from here on out. I remember what the Bible says about my body being the temple of God. I know it was wrong. I'm sorry.* As she prayed she felt the tightness around her heart relaxing. She stood up and decided she needed some air. She left the party that she and her friends were throwing undetected. She did not want to explain herself right now.

As she walked along the sidewalk just below her second floor apartment, her best friend and roommate spotted her. "Cassie, where are you going?" she called after her from an open window.

"I just need some air. I'll be back in a little while." In truth, she wouldn't be able to return to the apartment until morning if she wanted to avoid the party. Cassandra and her roommate had decided to throw a party just before everyone went home for Christmas break. Now she regretted it with all of her heart. *How could I have done that? I've always been so against drugs, and now... Well, I'm a hypocrite. But I will never do it again,* she thought to herself while continuing down the sidewalk.

Cassandra was not sure where she was going and the more she thought about it, she just wanted to get in her car and start the trip home. Her parents lived two hours from the university she had chosen to attend. When she had selected Kansas University, the distance from her parents had been a big influence in the decision. She wanted her space, her freedom. Now she wished she had chosen the local junior college and stayed at home.

Cassandra and her best friend, Elizabeth Monroe, moved to Lawrence in July and found a great apartment to share. Her first semester in college started out very well. She enjoyed all of her classes and was meeting new people. College was very different than her small town high school though. In high school, it was popular not to drink and smoke, and certainly not to do drugs. Cassandra and Beth had quickly found out that to fit in here they were going to have to get a little wild. They started drinking only a few weeks after their arrival when they attended their first college party. From there everything started to spiral downward for Cassandra. She was now drinking at least every weekend and had taken up smoking. She knew it was wrong. She had been raised in church all of her life, but she didn't want to be labeled a 'weirdo.' The guilt after each episode was quickly fading away and her heart was getting harder and harder. But every time she did something new, she was stricken with guilt. Tonight was the worst guilt she had experienced and she was ready to go home.

Cassandra turned back toward her apartment. She figured she could sneak into her apartment, grab the bag she already had packed, and head home. She just needed to let Beth know so she wouldn't worry about her.

"I'm heading home," she told Beth after dragging her into her bedroom.

"Why? Are you okay?" her friend questioned.

"Yes. I just…I just want to go home."

"It's awfully late."

"I know." Cassandra paused. "Do you ever feel guilty for the things we've started doing?" She could see her friend looked confused. "The partying and everything."

"No," Beth said simply. "Be careful going home, Cass. Your dad is going to kill you."

Cassandra nodded her agreement and said good-bye to her friend. She pondered over how they had changed so much in a few short months. She felt sick to her stomach thinking about how disappointed her family would be if they knew the person that she'd become. Cassandra pushed the thoughts away as she started the drive home. *I'll feel better when I get home.*

Cassandra quietly walked into her parents' home. She didn't want to wake anyone, especially since she wasn't sure how she would explain coming home at four in the morning. She climbed up the stairs of the two-story ranch style home and made it to the door to her bedroom door before she was stopped by the sound of her brother's voice.

"Cass, what are you doing?" he whispered, looking very groggy yet concerned as he peeked out his own bedroom door.

"I'm sorry, Chris. Did I wake you? I decided to come home a little early, that's all."

"It's four in the morning, Cass. Are you okay?" There was no missing the concern in her younger brother's voice.

"I'm fine. Just a little tired that's all. I'll talk to you in the morning."

She retreated to her bedroom and enjoyed how it was the same as it always had been. *At least something is the same, even if I'm not.* She crawled into her bed and began to think more about the party and found that she couldn't sleep.

She went over to her desk and grabbed the Bible that was in the bottom drawer. She was ashamed that she had not even taken it with her to Lawrence. Cassandra flipped through her Bible and found an old study guide from her youth group. 'Salvation Assurance' was the title of the lesson and she knew it was exactly what she needed. *Dear Lord, am I saved? If I'm saved, why do I sin so much? Help me understand what I'm reading.*

She turned to the first Scripture listed, Ephesians 2:1-10, and started to read and pray. *Help me to accept your gift and to put these doubts out of my mind. I'm sure it is Satan causing me to doubt. Forgive me for my sins and help me to do better. I know that I'm saved. How could I not be? I've gone to church all my life.* She felt a little better, but there was still something nagging at her. She lay awake for some time before she was able to close her eyes and fall asleep.

"Cassie, are you going to join us for lunch?" her mom was saying as she opened the blinds in Cassandra's room. Cassandra responded by covering her head with her blanket and groaning her refusal.

"Honey, when did you get in? You know your father doesn't like you driving too late at night, so I'm assuming you got here right after we went to bed. Around 11:00?" Marlene Smith had a way with her daughter. Cassandra immediately felt guilty.

"It was a little later," Cassandra mumbled as she peeked out from under the covers. She knew she would be getting a lecture from her father about her poor decision to drive home in the middle of the night.

Her mother gave her a disapproving look, but said nothing. "Do you want some lunch?" Marlene asked as she gave her youngest daughter a kiss on the top of her head.

"Yeah. I'll be down in a minute."

Marlene left the room and wondered exactly what time her daughter did get home last night. She didn't really want to, but she knew she would have to tell her husband, Curtis. He would be upset with Cassandra, but he would handle it well. He always did. Marlene stopped in the living room and had a quick conversation with her husband before heading to the kitchen. She went into the kitchen and got out the bread, turkey, mayonnaise, chips, and paper plates. It wasn't too long before two of her four children and her husband came to join her.

Cassandra was the first to come in. Her youngest daughter was still looking pretty tired. She had made an effort to look presentable though. She had slipped on a pair of jeans and a sweatshirt, her long blonde hair pulled back in a ponytail. She came over and hugged her mother. "Can I help with any thing?"

"Of course not, Dear. I'm so glad you're home. You just sit down and I'll make you a sandwich."

Chris, the youngest of the Smith children, made his entrance next. "Chris, why don't you get some pop out of the fridge for everyone?"

"Sure, Mom. I suppose Cassie doesn't have to do anything," he joked, rolling his eyes at his sister.

Cassandra was just a year older than Chris and the two had always been close. "Just because we haven't seen her in two months doesn't mean we can't put her to work," he said, winking at Cassandra.

"You're just jealous." Cassandra shot back. "It will be your turn next year. Have you decided where you're headed?"

"I thought maybe I'd follow my big sister around at KU. What do you think?"

"That would be fine with me, assuming you didn't tell anyone we were related." She turned and saw her dad enter the kitchen and hurried over to give him a hug, "Hi Dad."

"Well, hello. I didn't know you were coming home last night. What time did you get in?" Curtis Smith asked easily. He had already talked to his wife and knew that it was later than he would have liked.

Cassandra looked at Chris. She knew Chris wouldn't say anything. They had covered for each other many times. "It was pretty late," Cassandra confessed. "I was just in such a hurry to start my winter break and I couldn't wait until today to make the trip home."

"Honey, you know I don't like you driving home so late at night by yourself. It could be dangerous. Will you keep that in mind next time you are so antsy to come home?"

"Okay, Dad. I'm sorry."

"Let's have some lunch!" Chris said, bringing the pop to the table, followed by his mom with the sandwiches.

The family bowed their heads as Curtis prayed over the food. Cassandra was glad to be home. She was enjoying her family so much she didn't realize it was getting so late in the afternoon until her older sister, Melissa, burst into the kitchen, dropping her bags and throwing her arms around her mother. "Hello everyone. I missed you all so much!"

Melissa was now hugging their father before turning to Cassandra and Chris. "What are you doing here already? I thought I would beat you home." This question was directed to Cassandra, but Melissa didn't wait for an answer. "Chris, how tall are you? You just keep growing and growing!"

Marlene sat back and watched her family as they all greeted each other. Melissa did most of the talking, but then she always did. Melissa was a senior at Colorado State University so seeing her was a special treat for the Smith family. Between her job and school, she was rarely able to make the long trip home. Marlene was happy to have her girls home for the holidays.

As Cassandra sat in church the next day, she listened intently to Pastor Allen. He was talking about salvation and her heart was pounding. She looked for a distraction and spotted her older brother, Michael, and his wife, Shannon, across the auditorium. Michael gave her a smile and a wave. She couldn't wait until Pastor Allen dismissed in prayer so she could go talk to them. At twenty-five, he was seven years older than Cassandra. He had been married for a little over a year and Shannon was expecting their first baby. Michael worked at the local oil refinery and Shannon was a cosmetologist.

Pastor Allen returned to the podium and made a few announcements before closing in prayer. As soon as the Amen was said, Michael and Shannon were on their way over to the other Smith clan. "Hey, guys! How are you girls doing? Let's go have some lunch," Michael said.

"I have a roast in the oven. There's plenty for everyone. I knew you all would have some catching up to do," Marlene explained to her oldest child.

After greeting each other, the group disbursed and headed to the Smith house. The roast Marlene had made was wonderful and everyone enjoyed it. The family spent the better part of the afternoon talking and laughing before

Shannon and Marlene announced they were ready for an afternoon nap. Curtis had already fallen asleep in his recliner, so the siblings decided to head to the driveway for a basketball game. Playing basketball had always been one of the family's favorite activities. The group played for about an hour and then decided to head in for a cold drink.

"So, how's Shannon doing?" Melissa asked Michael.

"She is tired most of the time. She is ready for the baby to be born. I am too, but for different reasons."

"How long does she have left?" Cassandra asked. "A month?"

"About that. She's due January 20th. We're hoping she will have the baby while you girls are home."

"That would be great. I can't believe I'm going to be an aunt," Cassandra said in awe.

"Have you set a date, Mel?" Chris asked.

"For what?" Melissa asked. She honestly had no idea what her little brother was referring to.

"Oh, come on, we can all tell by your letters that you are getting pretty serious with…uh, what's his name? Greg?"

"You don't know what you're talking about, Chris," Melissa said defensively.

"Why do I know nothing about this, Mel?" Cassandra questioned.

"There's nothing to know," Melissa said, winking at her sister. Cassandra took the hint that they would definitely be discussing Greg later.

"I don't care who it is, but I'm ready for someone else to get married. Take some of the pressure off Shannon and I to have babies. People are already asking us when we're having another one and the first one isn't even here yet!"

"Well, it seems that Mel is on her way to wedding bliss."

"I never said anything about getting married in my letters, Chris, so just back off," Melissa said quickly.

"Okay, okay. I'm sorry."

"Come on, Cass. Let's go upstairs," Melissa said, walking from the kitchen towards the stairs in the hallway.

"So tell me about this guy. You've been holding out on me," Cassandra said as soon as they reached the privacy of Melissa's bedroom.

"No I haven't. Greg is just a good friend," Melissa replied smiling, "right now."

"Mel…"

"He's wonderful, Cass. He is so sweet, the sweetest man I've ever known. Not to mention the most gorgeous. We've been getting to know each other for about a year, but we are really no more than friends. I can't tell if he wants more or not. I certainly do, but haven't found the nerve to tell him. I met him at church. He is in the choir and teaches the 2nd grade boys Sunday school class."

"Wow. He sounds great," Cassandra said before her thoughts shifted. "You go to church in Colorado?"

"Of course, aren't you going in Lawrence?" The look on Cassandra's face was the only answer Melissa needed. "You need to have fellowship with other believers. Didn't Mom and Dad find a church for you?"

"Well, they did and I went for awhile, but I just never felt at home there. And I've been really busy with school." Even to her own ears, Cassandra's words sounded lame.

"Sounds like excuses to me. You better get your act together. Do you want to ask Dad for the name of another church there?"

"No! If they knew I wasn't going, they would be so mad. I'll just try the first one again. Maybe I just need to give it another chance."

In truth, Cassandra had only visited the church her father suggested in Lawrence a few times since she was in town. She had gone the first few weeks, but quickly realized that without anyone to answer to it was easier to sleep in or work on homework. Then when she started partying she felt too guilty to attend church. She purposed in her heart to visit there again when she went back for the spring semester.

"Tell me more about Greg."

Cassandra looked up when she heard a knock on her bedroom door. "Come in," she called, watching as her best friend came in her room. "Hi, Beth. When did you get home?" Cassandra had been home a week and Christmas was only a few days away.

"Yesterday. What have you been up to?"

"Not much. Just enjoying the break. I've done some Christmas shopping, but I need to go again. I still need a gift for Shannon. She's hard to buy for because I don't know her very well."

"How 'bout a trip to Wichita? I have some shopping to do too."

"Okay. That sounds great. Let me see if Mel wants to come." Cassandra went looking for her sister and found her in the kitchen with her mom. "Beth and I are going to Wichita to do some Christmas shopping. Do you want to come Mel?"

"No thanks. I've done my shopping and you couldn't pay me enough to get out into that mad house."

"Will you be back for supper, Dear?" her mom asked.

Cassandra looked at Beth who gave a shake of her head. "I don't think so. Maybe we'll catch a movie." Beth smiled hugely. The girls had been friends since childhood and sometimes it was like they read each other's minds.

"Don't be too late. You know your father." Marlene felt the need to remind her daughter.

"Okay. I'll see you later."

"Good-bye, girls. Be careful," Marlene called after them as they headed out the door.

Wichita was the nearest city to the small town where the girls lived. Cassandra enjoyed the small town atmosphere, but it was nice to have a larger city just twenty minutes away. When the girls arrived at the mall, they started their Christmas shopping. Melissa had been right. The place was a mad house, but Cassandra had to find a gift for Shannon. On the drive over, Cassandra and Beth decided to go out to eat and catch the six o'clock movie before heading home so they had plenty of time to do their shopping.

They went from store to store for almost three hours before Beth announced that she was finally finished with her shopping. Cassandra had found what she thought to be the perfect gift for Shannon two hours ago. It was a mother's journal. Shannon could use it to record all of her thoughts, feelings, and frustrations of motherhood. Cassandra was more than ready to leave the crowds and find somewhere to eat. The girls decided on their old favorite, a Mexican restaurant across the street from the mall.

"I hate shopping," Cassandra announced when they were seated.

"I love it! The crowds are a little tiring, but shopping is my favorite sport."

"Oh Beth, you would consider it a sport," Cassandra said, shaking her head. "What are your plans for Christmas?"

"Same old, same old. Visiting my grandparents, spending the day eating and sleeping. What about you?"

"About the same."

"I almost forgot to tell you. We are going to a party on New Year's Eve."

"We?"

"You and me, silly. Wes Armstrong is having a huge bash. It will be great."

"Wes Armstrong?" Cassandra thought her friend had lost it. Wes was in her high school graduating class. Although Cassandra got along with everyone, she had never actually hung out with Wes. He was too wild for her taste. The thought of going to one of his parties made her cringe. "I don't know."

"Why not?"

"Well, he is pretty wild."

"In case you've forgotten Cassie, you aren't so innocent yourself. At least not anymore."

Cassandra didn't know what to say. *She is right, too right. But I don't want anyone around here to know it.* "I don't think I want to go. It would be too weird."

"You've changed, face it. You would fit in perfectly at that party. Are you afraid to let people know you aren't perfect anymore?"

"I've never been perfect. I'm just not very proud of what I've done while I've been away at college and I plan to stop." She paused. "Don't you ever feel guilty?"

"No way. I'm just having fun. There is nothing wrong with having fun."

"I didn't have to drink and smoke to have fun in high school. Why do I have to now?"

"You know as well as I do what the kids in Lawrence are like. Everyone does it."

Cassandra let the matter drop. She could tell she wasn't getting through to her friend. *Wes Armstrong. Maybe it wouldn't hurt to go to the party. He has always been nice and he is gorgeous. Maybe I will go, but I don't have to drink. How will I get my parents to agree?* She thought as she watched her friend pull out her cigarettes and light up. *I need a cigarette.* As if Beth had been reading her mind, she offered one to Cassandra. Reluctantly she accepted it. She had not realized how badly she would miss smoking. She had slipped out one night earlier in the week to get her nicotine fix. It was going to be harder than she expected to quit the habit.

Christmas had come and gone and now Cassandra sat in front of the mirror in her bedroom debating what to do about the party that started in less than an hour. She almost had herself talked out of going when the phone rang. It was Beth.

"Are you ready?"

"No. I don't know if I'm going," Cassandra said nervously.

"You're going. Get ready and I'll be by to get you in a few minutes."

"My parents aren't going to let me go, Beth."

"Why do you have to tell them where you're going? You are in college now. Tell them you're spending the night with me. You are, by the way."

"You're so bossy."

"And you love me for it. See you in a few."

"Beth, wait." It was too late. Beth had already hung up.

Cassandra told herself that it wouldn't hurt anything to go to the party and started to get ready. She quickly applied her make-up and curled her long blonde hair, slipped on her favorite pair of jeans and a shirt. Getting ready was easy compared to the confrontation with her parents that followed. Cassandra chose to approach her mom instead of her dad.

"Mom, Beth's on her way to pick me up. I'm going to spend the night with her tonight."

"Let's check with your father. You know how he doesn't like you out on New Year's Eve when so many are driving drunk." Marlene immediately headed to the living room where Curtis was watching television and included him in the discussion. "Curtis, Cassie has made plans for this evening. She wants to spend the night with Beth."

"Are you going straight to her house?"

Cassandra shook her head.

"What are you going to do?"

"We were going to meet with some of our friends from high school."

"I see. Well, I don't want you cruising around or anything. You need to plan on spending the evening somewhere and staying off the streets."

"Of course," Cassie said, knowing they would be heading straight to the party. She wasn't about to tell her parents that though.

It was on the tip of Curtis's tongue to mention that he didn't want her going to any parties where alcohol would be present, but he was interrupted when they heard the honk of a car horn. He also hoped that he didn't need to remind his daughter of the rules he expected her to live by while in his house. However, Curtis couldn't deny that his daughter had changed in the few months that she had been away from home.

Cassandra's parents watched her leave knowing she had just been less than truthful with them. "What do we do Curtis? We're losing her." Tears filled Marlene's eyes as she spoke.

Curtis put his arm around his wife and gave her a squeeze. "Honey, give her to the Lord. He will take care of her." He spoke more confidently than he felt.

"Have you smelled the smoke on her clothes when she comes back from her walks? At first I couldn't believe it. She has always made such good choices."

"It's a lot easier to make good choices in a small town when you live with your parents than it is when you are out on your own. I think we need to pray for wisdom to talk with her about what is going on. We can't just ignore it. Come on, Dear. Pray with me."

Curtis took his wife's hand and they knelt in the living room and prayed for their youngest daughter. Curtis and Marlene had been fortunate with Michael and Melissa. They had continued their walk with God even when they left the family home. The couple praised the Lord for this, but also asked for wisdom and instruction as they faced their daughter's rebellion.

2

Cassandra had no idea that her parents had seen through her story and was impressed with herself as she walked out the door.

"Did they give you any trouble?" Beth asked as Cassandra climbed in the passenger seat of the car.

"Not really." She felt a little guilty as she thought about deceiving her parents, but she hadn't actually lied. It had been much easier than she expected. She let herself get excited about the party. She hadn't spent an evening away from home since she came back for Winter break. Seeing her old high school friends would be a lot of fun. "Maybe this will be fun."

"Of course it will be. I'm anxious to see Paul."

"Paul? I thought you hated him."

"It just wasn't the right time. That's why we broke up. So, who are you excited to see?"

"Honestly?" Cassandra gave her friend a mischievous grin. "Wes."

"Wes! I thought he was too wild for you?" Beth teased Cassandra. " I remember the way you two were always flirting! I knew you liked him. You just wouldn't admit it because you were too good for him."

"Not too good, Beth. Just too different. I don't think I would have held his interest, if you know what I mean. He only had one thing on his mind."

The girls talked about their high school days as they drove to the Armstrong home. It was a few miles from Cassandra's house and before she knew it, she was headed into Wes Armstrong's house.

It didn't take long for Wes to notice Cassandra. He was surprised to see her. This wasn't usually her type of party. She was gorgeous. He watched her and Beth greet some of their old classmates. Cassandra was smiling and laughing as she talked to her friends. She was wearing jeans and a blue, long sleeved, fitted shirt. The blue shirt accented her deep blue eyes. Wes took in her long legs and couldn't wait any longer to approach her. He was glad that Paul had stole Beth away by the time he reached Cassandra.

"Cassie, you look better than ever," he said, looking her up and down.

"You're not so bad yourself," Cassandra flirted. He was just how she remembered him; tall, dark, and handsome.

"I must say I didn't expect to see you here. How are things going in Lawrence?"

"Great. What have you been doing since graduation?"

"Working mostly. And partying. So, tell me Beautiful, is there a man in your life?" As he asked her this, he put an arm around her slim waist.

"You certainly get right to the point, don't you?" She pushed his arm away.

"You're avoiding my question." He leaned close to her. For a moment Cassandra thought that he was going to kiss her, but he turned and whispered in her ear. "Tell me you're single and we can spend the night together."

"Well, I am single, but there is no way I'll be sleeping with you tonight."

"Listen to you. I just meant that we could be each other's date. I'm hurt that you think so little of me," he said, looking innocent. "Did you say tonight? Does that mean there's hope?"

Cassandra laughed. Wes always had that effect on her. Wes was shocked to hear that Cassandra was still single. He remembered that she didn't date much in high school, but was certain that when she went to college she wouldn't be single for very long.

Beth and Paul came back carrying some beer. "Here, Cass. I got one for you," Beth said as she handed one to Cassandra.

Cassandra took it, all thoughts of her plans not to drink behind her. "Thanks."

She looked back at Wes and saw the look of approval on his face. She was surprised that he didn't give her a hard time about it, but also relieved. It was the first time any of Cassandra's high school friends saw her even hold a beer. She did not realize it at the time, but the testimony for Christ that she had worked to establish all through school was shattered. Beth and Paul kept walking and disappeared, leaving Wes and Cassandra alone again.

"Come on. Let's have some fun," Wes said, taking her hand and leading her through the crowded house. The pair mingled with everyone, but Wes had plans to get her alone before she left the party. Cassandra was one of the few girls in high school that he wanted but couldn't have. He thought since she was drinking, he just might get lucky tonight. Not that he would take advantage of her, but she was definitely not the innocent Cassandra Rose Smith she used to be.

Cassandra was enjoying catching up with her old friends and she was happy to see that she wasn't the only one who had taken up drinking while away at college. *Maybe I'm not so bad after all,* she thought as some of her old girl friends stole her away from Wes. She smiled and waved at him as she disappeared down the stairs leading to the basement. The Armstrong's house was two stories with a finished basement and people were everywhere. Cassandra could see that the real party was going on in the basement as she and her friends descended the stairs. She took in the scene and decided that she wanted no part of things that were going on down there. Cassandra gave the girls an excuse and headed back upstairs.

It didn't take long for Wes to find her again and he suggested they go upstairs to his room where they could talk. Cassandra agreed, glad to have a chance to get away from the crowd and loud music. Wes took her hand and led the way. When they got to his room, Wes shut the door, leaving the blaring music behind them. Cassandra took a look around and smiled. It was almost exactly as she expected his room to look. There were posters of women and music groups hanging on the walls. He had a waterbed, desk, and an entertainment center with a stereo, TV and VCR.

"What are you smiling at?"

"Oh, it is just what I expected. I can't believe your mom lets you hang this stuff up," she said, motioning toward one of his posters.

"Yeah, those are nice, but I would rather have a poster of you." Wes winked at her when he said this. Cassandra laughed, rolling her eyes. Wes chose this moment to put his arms around her and pull her close. "I've always wanted to do this," he said as he kissed her lips softly.

Cassandra was a little surprised, but didn't pull away. In secret, she had often wondered what it would be like to kiss Wes. It didn't take long for Wes to lead her over to his bed. The two sat down and continued to kiss. Cassandra found herself enjoying it and didn't stop him until he slipped off his shirt and reached for hers. "Wes, wait."

"What's wrong?"

"I just don't want to do this. It isn't right. I'm sorry." Cassandra stood up and straightened her clothes.

"Don't you want me? I could tell you liked it," he said softly.

Cassandra thought how much he sounded like someone from a movie with his smooth talking. "I know. That's the problem. I've always been attracted to you, but I can't sleep with you, Wes. I just can't. I'm sorry. Please don't be angry with me."

"I'm not going to pretend I'm not disappointed, but I've always respected you for your beliefs. And I'm not mad at you. Very disappointed, but not mad. Very disappointed."

"You said that already," she pointed out, relieved that he was not mad. Cassandra knew that she should have known better than to put herself in the position she was in.

"Oh, did I? Cassandra Rose Smith, I think you are an amazing girl and you are going to make some guy very happy someday," Wes said as he kissed her on her cheek. He put his shirt back on and took her hand, "Come on. I can't stay in here with you and keep my hands off you."

"Thanks for understanding. I'm sorry."

"Quit apologizing. We have a party to enjoy," Wes said as he led her down the hallway and back down the stairs.

Cassandra had another beer and watched Wes become the center of attention. Just before the clock struck midnight, Wes found her again so he could kiss her one last time. An hour later, she watched Beth stumbling up the stairs with Paul. Cassandra waited an hour before deciding she was ready to go. She climbed the stairs and walked down the hallway. She opened the first door she came to and saw Beth and Paul passed out on the bed. *I don't believe it. Did Beth and Paul have sex?* Cassandra realized that she wouldn't be going anywhere. She walked down the hallway to Wes' room hoping it would be empty. It was, so she slipped underneath the covers on his bed and fell right to sleep.

Cassandra didn't wake up again until eleven o'clock the next morning. She was startled to see that Wes was asleep on the floor. He was rousing up as well. She smiled at him and covered her head with the covers.

"I knew you'd spend the night with me," he joked, sitting up so he could see her reaction.

"Whatever." Cassandra laughed as she crawled out of his bed. "Thanks for letting me use your bed. I wonder if Beth is alive again," she said as she pulled her long hair back in a ponytail and glanced at herself in the mirror.

"I heard Paul got lucky." Wes held out his hand for her to help him off the floor.

Cassandra, at that moment was very happy that she had not made the same mistake with Wes. She certainly did not want her first time to be discussed with anyone. She waited on Wes and the two made their way down the hallway. They stopped at the room where she had seen Paul and Beth the night before, but they were gone. They found Beth in the living room and the two girls started to leave, but not before Wes pulled Cassandra aside and told her that he had enjoyed seeing her and asked if he could come by sometime. She told him yes and that she would be leaving in about two weeks. He said he would make sure to stop by before then.

The girls stopped at Beth's so Cassandra could change clothes before they headed to the Smith house. Beth talked nonstop about her experience, describing it as wonderful and beautiful. Cassandra wondered how much she actually remembered. The way Beth had stumbled up the stairs, Cassandra found it hard to believe that she remembered as much as she said. When Beth dropped her off, she said she would stop by the next day, but Cassandra was hoping she wouldn't show up. She had lost a certain amount of respect for her good friend and wasn't sure what she would say to Beth without letting her know of her disapproval.

Cassandra sat in church the next Sunday and felt nothing. She was desperately trying not to pay attention and it seemed to be working. She didn't need to worry about Beth stopping by for the rest of the break. From what she had heard, Beth and Paul were spending every waking moment together. Cassandra looked across the auditorium to where Michael and Shannon usually sat. They weren't there and Cassandra hoped it was because Shannon was in labor. She really wanted to see the new baby before she headed off to school. She would be leaving at the end of this week, preferably before church on Sunday. After the party last Friday, Cassandra had realized that she felt fine if she didn't think about God or her parents. She had managed to get out of church last week claiming she didn't feel well, but she hadn't been able to come up with an excuse this week.

Marlene watched her daughter fidget through the entire service. She was determined to talk with Cassandra right after church. Curtis and Marlene had planned to talk with Cassandra as soon as she got home from Beth's house last Saturday, but another one of her friends had shown up and stayed for most of the afternoon. Since then Curtis had been busy at work and Marlene didn't want to approach her daughter alone. She had no idea how to handle this. She said a short prayer for wisdom before Pastor Allen dismissed in prayer.

"Melissa, why don't you take Chris out to lunch today? Your father and I would like to have some time alone with Cassie."

"Okay Mom. Are you buying?"

Marlene reached in her wallet and handed Melissa a twenty-dollar bill. Curtis draped an arm over Cassandra's shoulders and led her toward the door. Marlene sent Melissa and Chris on their way and hurried to catch up to her husband and youngest daughter.

"Where are they going?" Cassandra asked.

"To get something to eat. Your mother and I want to talk to you."

Cassandra nodded her head and followed her parents. She acted relaxed, but inside she was scared to death. It wasn't very often that her parents singled one of their children out to have a talk with them. *Have they found out about the party? Maybe Melissa told them I wasn't going to church in Lawrence.* Her thoughts raced with things they might want to talk about. The drive home was only a few blocks, but to Cassandra it seemed like miles. Obviously, her parents weren't going to talk until they got home.

They walked into the house and Curtis and Cassandra sat down at the kitchen table. Marlene started making some sandwiches while Curtis said a silent prayer for wisdom. "Honey, your mom and I are worried about you. We feel like you are doing some things in your life that aren't honoring God. Is there something you would like to tell us?" he began after finishing his prayer.

"What do you mean?" Cassandra didn't know what to say and was trying to buy some time.

"Well, we can see a difference in you. We have smelled the smoke on your clothes when you get back from your walks. Are you smoking?"

Cassandra couldn't lie. They already knew the answer. "Yeah," she said, looking down at her hands, "it just sort of got started and I'm trying to quit, but it is harder than I thought it would be."

"Is there anything else that just sort of got started?" Marlene asked, annoyed at her daughter's reasoning.

"I don't think that everything I do is your business. I mean, I don't mean to sound disrespectful. I am in college now, living on my own. You should trust my judgment." Cassandra was backed into a corner and the only way she knew to react was to be angry. She loved her parents and knew they were right, but she didn't want to hear about it.

"What reason have you given us to trust your judgment, Cass?" her father asked. "You are obviously making some poor choices."

"I don't have to sit here and listen to this. I'm eighteen years old! I don't even live here anymore! I'm just visiting," she yelled as she stood up.

"Cassandra, sit down." Her father's voice was stern. She obeyed. "You may not live here, but you do still have a bedroom upstairs that you call home – if I'm not mistaken. We cannot control what you do when you are away at college, but as long as you are staying in our house, you will obey us. We know you've been lying to us and that hurts us very much. You said you didn't want to be disrespectful, but that is exactly what you are doing. We love you very much and we don't want to see you make mistakes that will hurt you or your future. I think if you were attending church, reading the Bible, and praying, you would be making better choices. God loves you and He will forgive you for your sins. He wants you to turn back to Him. We love you, Cassie. We are just concerned for your well-being. Do you understand?"

She nodded her head. "Can I go now?" Cassandra avoided making eye contact with her parents by concentrating on her hands.

"You understand that while you are here, you will respect our rules?"

Cassandra nodded again.

"Yes, you may go."

As soon as her father granted permission, Cassandra was out the door.

"Oh, Curtis!" Marlene walked over to embrace her husband before bursting into tears. "She is so hard hearted already."

"Honey, it will work out. God is in control. Just remember that. We may not like the path she has chosen, but God knows all about it. I think all we can do is love her and pray for her." Curtis was trying hard to be strong for his wife, but found himself a little shaken by what had just taken place. Never before had any of his children showed them so much defiance and disrespect.

Cassandra glanced back at her parents house before climbing into her car and backing out of the driveway. She wasn't sure where she was going; she just wanted to get away. She decided to drive to the lake a few miles out of town. There was a secluded area there that she liked to go to when she needed to think.

They are right, but I'm not so bad. Everyone drinks and smokes. I'm just having fun. What is so wrong with that? I've been their good little girl all my life. I'm ready to enjoy myself. And I'm sick of hearing about God. I can't have fun if I try to live by the Bible.

Cassandra was so distracted by her thoughts, she didn't notice that the car behind her was trying to get her attention. She reached the turn that led to her favorite spot on the lake. She drove another half mile before she reached the lake and pulled her car to a stop. It was then that she saw the 1966 Ford Mustang pull in behind her. It was Wes Armstrong.

"Hey, crazy driver! I've been trying to get your attention since you left your house," he called to her while getting out. Cassandra got out of her car and watched him approach. "Wow! You look nice. Why are you so dressed up?"

"Oh." Cassandra looked down and realized she had neglected to change her clothes. She still had on the dress she had worn to church. "Church." Cassandra was trying not to let Wes see her face. She didn't want him to know she had been crying.

"Cassie," he said as he positioned himself in front of her. "Are you okay?"

"Yeah, I'm fine. So what are you out doing?"

"Don't try and change the subject." He put a finger under her chin and made her look at him. "Is there something I can do?"

"No. I just had a fight with my parents, that's all. I needed some air."

"It isn't a good day for a swim," he joked. Cassandra smiled. She had not thought through her plan. The lake was not usually a place you would go in the middle of winter. "I guess we could try it, but I didn't bring my suit. I'd have to go in the buff."

"You always make me laugh, Wes. I like that about you."

"So, let's go for a walk." He looked down at her high heels. "Or maybe a drive would be better." Cassandra agreed. They got in the Mustang and started to drive around the lake. "Do you want to talk about it?"

"I really don't. I just want to forget about it. Now, tell me what you are doing today."

"I was coming to see you. I thought we could go to lunch or something. I didn't want you to leave before I had a chance to say good-bye."

"Really? Why would you care, Wes?"

"Because I like you. You're fun to be with." She didn't believe him and it showed on her face. "I'm not going to deny that I would love to get you in bed, but it's more than that. Honest. You are the sweetest girl I've ever met. Your innocence makes me want to take care of you. Don't get me wrong, I know we could never be a couple or anything."

"And why is that?" Although Cassandra knew the statement was true, it made her angry.

"Because you're too sweet. I would never want to hurt you," Wes replied, choosing to ignore the anger he detected in her voice.

"Why would you hurt me?"

"I would never hurt you intentionally, but you know we are different. I want things out of a relationship that you aren't willing to give – at least not right now. That would be very hard for me, especially with you living three hours away."

"Going without? That is what this is about. We could never be a couple because I won't put out. What is with guys and sex? Do you know that I haven't met one guy who hasn't tried to get me into bed within the first few weeks of knowing each other?" Cassandra glared at him.

"Well, I can't speak for everyone, but being around an attractive woman is hard on a man. We don't always think with our heads." He looked over at her and saw the look on her face. "Don't get mad at me. You asked. Now, let me ask you some questions. Why do you always flirt with me?"

"I told you the other night that I find you attractive. I like you. I always have, but I know I couldn't hold your interest," she answered honestly.

"How long do you plan to wait?"

"Till I'm married."

Wes smiled at her. That was exactly what he liked about her. "If you ever change your mind, look me up. I'd be happy to give you some lessons."

Cassandra relaxed again. "Do you ever stop?" she said, laughing.

"You can be sure that no other girls have been special enough to drive my car. How 'bout it?"

Cassandra gladly accepted the opportunity. She loved fast cars and Wes had spent a lot of money making his one of the fastest in town. All thoughts of the fight she had with her parents were behind her, she was having too much fun. After awhile she realized that she hadn't eaten any lunch and Wes offered to take her out. They spent the afternoon laughing and talking and eventually Wes took her back to her car. When they said good-bye, Wes kissed her on the cheek and said he would miss her. He gave her a piece of paper with his phone number on it and told her to call anytime she needed anything.

Cassandra reluctantly started the trip home. She didn't want to face her parents, but thought she should go to evening church with them. She didn't know what her father would do if she disregarded their conversation and disobeyed him while staying there, but she didn't want to take the chance and find out. When she pulled into the drive, her parents' van was already gone. She felt relieved. She went in and climbed the stairs to her bedroom to freshen up. She found a note from her mom on her bedroom door.

Cassandra,

Michael called this afternoon to tell us Shannon is in labor. We left for the hospital at 3:00. We aren't sure if we will make it to church or not. You are welcome to come up to the hospital and wait with us, but if you don't, we expect you to go to church. We will try and call you later. We love you, Honey.

Mom

Cassandra looked at her watch. It was 5:30. She quickly changed into jeans and a sweatshirt before rushing to the hospital. She wanted to be there when her niece or nephew was born. On the drive to the hospital, she worried about seeing her parents. She also worried that she had missed the baby's arrival. Cassandra had been at the hospital only a short while when she realized she didn't need to worry at all. Her parents were not angry with her. They treated her like they always did. As for missing the baby's arrival, she ended up waiting with the rest of her family and Shannon's family in the waiting room until well after midnight.

Cassandra looked lovingly at the baby boy in her arms. She had always liked babies, but this was her nephew and he was the cutest baby she had ever seen. Shannon had given birth to Matthew Lane Smith early Monday morning. Curtis and Marlene had given the new parents a few days to be alone with their baby before asking to come by for a short visit. Cassandra had not held Matthew in the hospital. He was so small, only six pounds, she was afraid she would hurt him. She felt more comfortable here in Michael's living room.

"It's my turn to hold him. Give him up," Melissa said as she took Matthew.

"I can't believe I'm a father," Michael said, shaking his head.

"And I can't believe I'm a grandma!" Marlene exclaimed.

Curtis let Melissa hold the baby for a few minutes before saying, "Well, we will leave so you can feed this little guy and try to get some sleep."

"Try is the key word. He's been waking up every few hours to nurse," Shannon said.

Melissa gave Matthew to his mother and hugged Michael and Shannon. "I guess I won't see you again before I leave. I love you guys. Take care of that precious boy and send me lots of pictures."

"I love you too, Sis. Be careful," Michael said.

"When does your plane leave?" Cassandra asked.

"Seven tomorrow morning. Are you going to drop me off?"

"I can do that and then I'll be heading out too," Cassandra said as she hugged Michael and Shannon and kissed Matthew on the forehead. "I love you."

"Can we go now?" Chris asked impatiently. "This mushy stuff makes me sick."

Cassandra chased him out the door and by the time Melissa and their parents reached the van she had him in a headlock. When he cried for mercy, she let him free and they climbed into the van laughing. Curtis and Marlene took their children out to eat before going home that evening. When they got home, it was late. Everyone decided it was time to go to bed.

An hour later there was a knock at Cassandra's bedroom door. She opened it to see Chris standing there. "I was just packing some things. Come on in," she said.

"Why do you have to leave tomorrow? Your classes don't start until Monday."

"I'm just ready to be back at my own place. It's strange not having anyone to answer to for so long and then come back, and well, you know." Cassandra stopped, not wanting to explain anything further.

"Something has been bothering me, so I'm just going to ask you." Cassandra noticed that her brother's face grew red with embarrassment. "My friend, Steve, he said that you, uh... He said that you slept with Wes Armstrong." Chris spit it out. He hadn't wanted to approach the subject, but after fighting with his friend about it knew he needed to know the truth.

"What? Where did he hear that?" Cassandra was shocked.

"He saw you guys come out of Wes's bedroom at the party the other night."

Cassandra's heart sank. She hadn't even thought of how that must have looked. "I didn't sleep with him. I was in his room with him for awhile, but nothing happened. Wes wanted to, but I stopped him. You believe me, don't you Chris?" She was crushed and didn't want her brother to think poorly of her. It was very important to her that he understand she was being truthful.

"Of course. I didn't mean to be nosy, but I wanted to know the truth. I don't want people spreading rumors about my sister. Why were you there, Cass?" he questioned as he searched his sister's eyes.

"I can't really explain it. I'm just going through a phase, I guess." Chris didn't ask any more questions about the party. The siblings stayed up for another hour talking before Chris went back to his own room.

Cassandra tried to go to sleep but found that she just didn't feel right. Something was bothering her, but she couldn't put her finger on it. She pulled her basketball out of the closet and went out to the driveway to shoot baskets for awhile.

"It's Cass," Marlene whispered to her husband from the window overlooking the driveway. The bouncing of the ball had woke the couple up, but it was not highly unusual for one of their children to be shooting baskets so late. He joined her by the window. "Maybe we're getting through to her."

Curtis put his arms around his wife and held her tight. "Or maybe she's running from God and can't sleep." Marlene looked at him as he continued to stare down at their daughter. She knew he wasn't trying to be negative, but it was so discouraging.

"I'm sorry, Honey. It was the first thing that came to mind," Curtis explained when he noticed the moist brown eyes that stared up at him.

"Should we go to her?"

"I think we've said enough. She'll be on her own again tomorrow and the choice will be hers. Let's just pray that she chooses God." He led his wife to the side of their bed where they knelt and prayed for their children, especially Cassandra.

The next morning, Cassandra woke to the sound of her alarm at 5:30. She took a shower and quickly got ready before going downstairs for breakfast. Her parents and Melissa sat around the table eating French toast, scrambled eggs, and bacon. "Mom, you didn't have to cook all this," she exclaimed.

"It's the last morning I'll have with my daughters for awhile. I wanted to do it. Don't worry. I'll be going back to bed when you leave." Marlene thought it was worth the trouble to be able to visit with her daughters one last time before their departure.

While his girls finished eating, Curtis loaded their bags in Cassandra's car. He was still loading their bags when Marlene and the girls came outside. Melissa and Cassandra hugged and kissed their parents. Melissa climbed into the car, but Marlene laid a hand on Cassandra's arm. "Honey, remember what we talked about and that we love you." Cassandra nodded and got in the car. Marlene's heart ached as she watched her daughter drive away. She was afraid that they had not gotten through to Cassandra and prayed that God would work in her heart.

3

March, 1999

Mac Lugot stood along the wall at the college party his brother had dragged him to. He felt out of place and his brother, Nic, had abandoned him for a cute blonde. He stood scanning the crowd for someone who even looked familiar when he spotted her. She sat on the couch alone looking as lost as he did. He watched her for a few minutes, taking in every feature. Mac decided she was beautiful as he took in her blonde hair, deep blue eyes, and slim figure. He inquired about her to some of the other guests before getting up the nerve to approach.

Cassandra sat on the couch in her apartment, beer in hand, watching as her friends and people she had never met before got drunk. They were all laughing and having a good time. When Cassandra returned to Lawrence from her trip home for the holidays, she had started right where she left off with the exception of doing drugs. She didn't want any part of that. Paul had come to visit Beth only once since she came back to school and Beth was devastated. Cassandra thought she had recovered quickly because she already had another boyfriend who she was being intimate with. Cassandra had been on a few dates, but nothing ever became of them. All the men she had dated had one thing on their mind: sex. And she was still determined to wait until she was married.

Cassandra watched as a handsome man approached her. She thought he looked vaguely familiar. "Is this seat taken?" he asked kindly.

She was in no mood to be hit on and stiffened. "No," Cassandra said, waiting for the line he would give her to try and get her into bed.

The man sat down next to her. “How are you doing tonight, Cassandra?” He hadn’t noticed her mouth, which he found extremely attractive, from across the room. He found that he already wanted to kiss this woman that he did not know.

“How do you know my name?” she asked in surprise.

“I have my sources.” He paused. “No, I noticed you from across the room and commented on how beautiful you were and someone told me your name. You are beautiful by the way,” the man said smoothly.

“Thank you.”

“So, this is your apartment. It’s very nice. Do you have a lot of parties here?”

“Yes.”

“You’re a freshman at KU majoring in accounting. Is that right?”

“You seem to know a lot about me and I know nothing about you. Let’s talk about you for awhile.”

“I thought you’d never ask. My name is Mac Lugot. I am an accountant at a firm downtown. I could probably help you get a job there if you’re looking for one. It would be good experience for you and it would look great on your resume when you graduate.”

“Are you trying to hit on me or give me a job?”

“My main intention is to hit on you, but if I have to get you a job for you to go out with me, I will.”

Cassandra smiled.

“Finally. I knew I could get you to smile. Now all I have to do is get you to say more than a sentence to me.”

Cassandra laughed before voicing what she’d been thinking. “You played basketball for KU from 1993 to 1997. You started your junior and senior year until you blew out your knee in the game against Missouri.”

“Who have you been talking to?” Mac asked, clearly surprised by her knowledge concerning him.

“No one. I just thought you looked familiar and when you said your name I put it together. I’ve always been a big KU basketball fan.”

“Wow. I didn’t know I was a celebrity.”

Cassandra smiled and laughed a little. “What are you doing at a college party?”

“My younger brother is a senior at KU and he dragged me here tonight. It’s his birthday, so I told him we could do whatever he wanted. Now I’m glad I came. What do you say we go get something to eat at the diner around the corner?" Mac suggested. He was already impressed with the young woman who sat in front of him and wanted to know more about her.

Cassandra was instantly on alert. "If you're glad you came, why do you want to leave?"

"I'm glad I came because I met you, but it is kind of hard to get to know someone in this atmosphere," he said, motioning to the people dancing around them.

Cassandra was impressed that he wanted to go to a public place rather than her bedroom and agreed to go to the diner with him. She told Beth what she was doing and Mac let his brother know he would be back to pick him up. The two left Cassandra's apartment and walked a few blocks to the diner Mac had mentioned. They found a corner booth and sat down across from each other. The waitress came over right away and took their order.

"So what happened after you blew out your knee?" Cassandra asked.

He nodded. "Well, it took awhile to recover and you probably know I couldn't play again for the rest of the season. I'm from Houston, Texas. The only reason I came here was to play basketball. I got offered the job at the firm right after graduation. I had done my internship there. My brother and I were living together; we still do. I thought it was a good opportunity for me, so I decided to stay. What made you decide to come here?"

"I just wanted to get away from my home town, but not so far away that I couldn't visit whenever I wanted. I can't believe that I'm sitting here with you. I used to watch you on television. My whole family enjoys basketball. We all played in high school and I think my youngest brother will play in college."

"How many brothers do you have?"

Cassandra was shocked at how interested Mac was in her life. *Maybe he isn't like all the other guys I've met here.* "I have two brothers and one sister. And a nephew who was born in January. What about you?"

"I have one brother, Nic. Do you go home often?"

"Not really. I get busy with school and everything." Cassandra answered. This was not completely true. Since she had been home for winter break she had not gone back because of how guilty she felt when she was around her parents. She had only called once when she got back to let them know she made it okay.

Mac and Cassandra talked for two hours at the diner before the waitress came over and asked them to leave because it was closing. Cassandra looked at her watch. She couldn't believe it was already midnight. Talking to Mac had been so easy and relaxing. There had not been one awkward moment of silence. They walked back to her apartment where the party was in full force and stopped outside the door.

"I really enjoyed talking with you tonight," Mac said. "Could we do it again sometime?"

"I'd love to. It's going to be crazy in there and I probably won't get to talk to you again tonight, so here's my phone number." Cassandra took a piece of paper out of her purse and wrote her phone number on it before giving it to him. They walked in the door and joined the party. Cassandra had been right. It only took a few minutes before they were separated.

"Cassie, how was it?" Beth asked.

"He is very nice! And gorgeous too. He's going to call me."

"Is he here? Which one is he?"

Cassandra scanned the crowded living room until she spotted Mac. "He's the tall one over there with dark hair in the blue shirt."

"Wow! He is gorgeous. How tall is he?"

"I don't know. He towers over me. He played basketball at KU when he went there."

"How old is he?"

"I'm guessing twenty-five or so. I didn't ask him."

Beth's boyfriend, Tom, came and took her hand. "I'll see you later," Beth said before going to her bedroom with Tom. Cassandra didn't like Tom. She thought he was too controlling. He never let Beth hang out with her friends anymore. When he came over, they always went straight to Beth's room and only came out when Tom was ready to leave. Cassandra wondered what Beth liked about him.

Cassandra found a group of her friends to hang out with. She talked and laughed with them for awhile as she watched the crowd begin to leave. Usually everyone was gone by two or three in the morning. She was hoping that everyone would leave soon. She wanted to go to bed, but didn't want to go in her room with a bunch of strangers in her apartment.

"Cassandra…" Mac whispered close to her ear. She turned to face him. "I finally talked Nic into leaving. I wanted to say good-bye. I'll call you soon."

"Okay. Good-bye." Cassandra watched with some regret as he left. She wondered when he would call her and hoped it would be soon. An hour later, she watched the last of her guests leave. She immediately went into her room and crawled into bed.

Monday evening Cassandra sat at her desk studying when the phone rang. It was Mac. Cassandra was surprised. She hadn't expected him to call so soon. It was just two days ago that they had met. "Hi. How are you doing?" she asked.

"I'm fine. I can't stop thinking about you. When can we go out?"

Cassandra laughed. "You don't waste any time, do you?"

"I'll be there in thirty minutes. Bye."

"Wait. Don't hang up. Where are we going? I mean, what should I wear?"

"Dinner and a movie. See you soon."

Cassandra smiled. She really liked Mac. She went and stood in front of her closet debating about what to wear. She decided she needed help and went to find Beth. She knocked on her bedroom door and she heard Tom holler something that sounded like 'go away.' Cassandra apologized, explaining she didn't know he was there, and went back to her room.

Tom is such a jerk, she thought putting on jeans and a nice shirt. She carefully applied her make up and curled her hair. She had just finished before the doorbell rang.

She answered it, surprised to see Mac in a suit. Cassandra started to blush with embarrassment. "You look very nice. I guess I need to change."

"Oh, no. Your apartment is on my way home from work. I thought I'd just stop off and change at my place. Is that okay?"

"Yeah. You had me worried. I wondered what kind of dinner and a movie we had to dress up for," she joked.

"Cassandra, can I talk to you for a minute?" Beth said from in the kitchen.

"Come in. I'll be right back," she said to Mac and walked into the kitchen. "What's up?"

"I'm sorry about before. Tom was just joking around."

"I doubt that. Beth, I'm not mad at you. And I'm not going to accept an apology from you for Tom. I don't see what you see in him anyway. He doesn't treat you right." She started the familiar conversation and then remembered Mac was waiting in the living room. "I don't have time to get into this with you right now. Come and meet Mac," she said excitedly. Cassandra led Beth into the living room where Mac was waiting. "Mac, this is my roommate Beth. Beth, this is Mac."

"It's nice to meet you," Mac said.

"Nice to meet you too," Beth said.

"We're going to dinner and a movie. I'll see you later," Cassandra said before leaving the apartment. They walked down the stairs and Mac led her to a brand new Chevrolet truck. He opened the door for her before climbing in the driver's side.

"My place is only about ten minutes from here," he said, pulling out of the parking lot. "I can't wait to get out of this suit."

"Do you always work this late?" Cassandra asked. It was already seven o'clock.

"I never know what my hours will be during tax season, but the rest of the year I work eight to five. By the way, I found out today there is an opening for a Secretarial Assistant position. It's for a lady named Jenna Howard. She is the secretary for one of our partners and needs a part-time assistant. If you're interested I could get you an interview."

"That would be much better than what I'm doing now. I work on campus in the Financial Aid Office, but the pay is not enough so I work a few nights a week at the Smokehouse Bar and Grill. I'd definitely be interested in finding something different. Do you know how much they pay?"

"No, but I'm sure it is very well. I'll find out for you. Tell me about your day."

Cassandra told him about her day. She was amazed that he was interested. He was definitely different from the other guys she had dated. She decided that she liked Mac very much. Cassandra was still talking when he pulled into the driveway of a large, beautiful house.

"This is your house? I guess I chose the right major," she mumbled getting out of the truck and heading for the front door. "You are going to give me a tour, aren't you?"

"If you want. But first I'm getting out of this suit," Mac said, opening the door. The front door opened to a foyer area with hard wood floor. "You can wait in there," Mac said, motioning toward the living room before disappearing up the stairs that were directly in front of the door.

When Mac came back downstairs he gave her a tour of the four-bedroom house. Cassandra was very impressed and surprised at how nicely decorated the house was considering two bachelors lived there. It was also immaculate. She wondered who did the cleaning, but didn't think it was any of her business. If she were to guess, she thought he probably hired a house cleaning service. After the tour, they went to an Italian restaurant that Mac thought Cassandra would like.

They enjoyed a nice dinner together before going to a movie. When they got back to Cassandra's apartment building, Mac walked Cassandra to her door. Cassandra had enjoyed herself and told him so. He told her he would call her tomorrow about the job at his firm and said good night. Cassandra let herself in the apartment wondering if she was in love. She had spent two evenings with Mac and he had not even held her hand. She decided that Mac was a true gentleman.

Mac's call could not come soon enough for Cassandra. She had thought about him nonstop since their date the night before. She had also done some figuring to see how much the job would need to pay for her to consider it. Mac called her that afternoon. He told her the pay. It was more than she expected, so she asked what she needed to do to apply.

"I've already set up an interview for you. This afternoon at 4:30. Will that work?"

"Mac! I can't believe you. I don't have any time to prepare."

"You've got an hour. Or I could tell them you're not interested."

"No! No, don't do that. Give me directions and I'll be there."

Mac gave her directions to the firm. He told her that the partner's office she was looking for was on the fifth floor. He said that Jenna Howard's desk was the first desk she would see when she got off the elevator and she would have a short interview with Jenna before meeting the partner. If Jenna liked her, she would probably get hired.

Cassandra hung up, suddenly very nervous. She got out her suit that she only wore to interviews and quickly got dressed. She checked her hair and make up before rushing out the door. She found the firm easily with Mac's directions and sat in her car a moment trying to compose herself. She noticed a sign in front of the building that read Wilson, Jensen, and Lugot Tax and Accounting Service. *Mac's last name sounded like it would be spelled like that. Lugot. It can't be. He didn't say he was a partner.*

Cassandra went in the building and found the elevator. She took it to the fifth floor where she immediately found Jenna Howard.

"Hi. My name is Cassandra Smith. I have a 4:30 appointment."

"Hello Cassandra. I'm Jenna Howard. Just have a seat in the waiting area and I will be right with you."

"Thanks." Cassandra took a seat in the waiting area to the left of Jenna's desk and waited. She hoped she wouldn't have to wait too long because she was getting more and more nervous as time went on. Before she knew it, Jenna joined her in the waiting area and conducted what Cassandra thought was a very informal interview. She told her what the job included and how many hours she would need to work. Cassandra told her she was a student at the university and Jenna said that would be no problem. Jenna told Cassandra to wait a few more minutes while she spoke with the partner. Cassandra was very excited. She thought the interview went well.

A few minutes later, Cassandra sat in a huge office waiting for the partner to ask her a few more questions. *I wonder if I could find out where Mac's office is and stop by before I go home. Maybe I could ask Jenna.* Cassandra's thoughts were interrupted when the door to the office opened. She turned to see Mac come in the door. "Mac, I was just thinking about you. I thought I'd try and find you before I went home."

"I'm glad to hear that you've been thinking about me. How did the interview with Jenna go?" he asked as he approached her.

"I think it went well. At least I hope so. She is very nice. I hope she liked me." In an effort to feel less small, Cassandra stood. Mac still towered over her.

"I don't see how anyone could not like you." Mac barely made it through his sentence when he noticed Cassandra was wearing a skirt and found himself staring at her long legs. "I'm sorry. You look very nice." He recovered quickly.

Cassandra blushed and looked down at her hands. "So, how did you know I was in here?"

"Jenna told me I needed to come and interview my new Secretarial Assistant," Mac said as he walked around the desk and sat in the big leather chair.

"What? You're the partner?" Cassandra sat back down in shock.

He smiled smugly, obviously proud that he had pulled off keeping the secret. "I don't make it a habit to tell people I'm a partner here. I don't want to seem full of myself. Besides the look on your face just now was worth keeping it a secret."

"You could have told me. I've been sick with nerves."

"I'm sorry. But Jenna liked you, so you're hired if you still want the job."

"Did you just create this job when you met me?" Cassandra asked, suddenly very tense.

"No. Jenna's assistant quit yesterday and I thought of you. I knew you would be perfect."

"What if things don't work out between us? Will you fire me?" she asked seriously.

"Cassandra, that isn't the way I do things. I want things to work out between us personally, but if they don't, that won't change our professional relationship. Besides, if I fired you for that, you could sue the firm and I would lose my job. I certainly wouldn't take that risk. So, what do you say? Do you want the job?"

"Yes. Is the salary negotiable?" she asked jokingly.

"No way. I already requested that you get the highest part-time salary the firm offers. You ask more questions than anyone else I know. It drives me crazy, but I like it." He pushed a button on his phone. "Jenna, could you come in here? We need to figure what Cassandra's schedule will be and then you can go over the new employee paperwork with her."

"I'll be right there," Jenna said.

Jenna came in and the three of them figured the hours that Cassandra would work. Cassandra only had classes Monday through Thursday and she was always finished by noon. They set her schedule for Monday through Thursday afternoons and all day on Fridays. After her schedule was set, Cassandra followed Jenna back out to her desk. Jenna had her fill out the new employee paperwork. By the time she was finished, it was six o'clock. Jenna buzzed Mac and asked if Cassandra could go.

"Not yet. Send her in please," Cassandra heard Mac say.

"You know, I haven't seen him this happy in months," Jenna said, shaking her head. "Go on in."

Cassandra wasn't sure what Jenna meant, but she hoped it meant that Mac liked her as much as she liked him. She walked back into Mac's office. "You wanted to see me?"

"Yes. I have to admit that I made your interview so late because I wanted to have an excuse to ask you over for dinner. Nic's going out with some friends and I thought I'd pick up a pizza on my way home. What do you think?"

"That sounds like fun," Cassandra said enthusiastically. For some reason she didn't even worry about spending the evening in this man's home alone. There was something about Mac that made her relax and enjoy herself when she was with him.

"I have some things to finish up here. I'll pick you up at seven."

"I can drive over. That way you don't have to get back out," Cassandra offered.

"Okay. Be there shortly after seven. Bye Cassandra."

Cassandra said good-bye and drove back to her apartment. She couldn't wait to tell Beth the news about her job. She would need to put her two weeks' notice in at her other jobs tomorrow. Jenna wanted her to start as soon as possible. Beth was not home when Cassandra got there. She was disappointed. She wanted to tell someone her news. After debating about it for awhile, she dialed her parents' number.

"Hello?" Chris answered.

"Hi! It's Cass."

"Cass? Who's that?" he joked. "We haven't heard from you since right after you left."

"I know. I'm sorry. I've been busy. Guess what? I just got a job at a major accounting firm here in town. It's only a secretarial position, but it will be good experience for me."

"That's great, Cassie. Mom wants to talk."

"Wait… Guess who I met the other night?"

"Who?"

"Do you remember the name Mac Lugot?"

Chris was silent for a moment. "No way!"

"Yes and he's my boss."

The two talked a little bit about Mac before Chris handed the phone to Marlene. Cassandra talked to her mother for awhile before her father got on the line. She told them both about her job and about Mac. They were happy for her and congratulated her. "Honey, does this mean you won't be home for Spring break?" her father asked.

"Probably not. I'll try and come for a weekend soon. I promise. I love you, Dad. I've got to go now."

"I love you too. Take care."

When Cassandra hung up, she changed into jeans and a T-shirt and waited anxiously until seven o'clock to leave. When she got to Mac's house, he led her into the dining room. He had already lit some candles, and had champagne and pizza waiting for her. "I've never had a candlelit pizza dinner before. This is wonderful," she said, taking her seat. "You're just full of surprises."

"I want to keep you interested," he smiled.

"Oh, I am definitely interested," she flirted.

They ate their pizza with little conversation before settling in to watch a movie Mac had rented. Cassandra sat on the couch and when Mac was finished starting the movie, he joined her. He sat next to her and took her hand in his. At that moment, Cassandra decided he was the sweetest man she had ever met. The movie was one she wanted to see so she really enjoyed it. She also enjoyed being close to Mac.

"How 'bout a little one-on-one?" he asked when the movie ended.

Cassandra was taken aback. *Maybe he isn't such a gentleman.* "What?"

Mac was amused, "You did say you played basketball, right?"

"Oh, yes," she paused. "It's pretty late. What about your neighbors?"

"They won't mind. Come on." Mac took her hand and led the way to his garage where he picked up a basketball on their way outside.

"Will this bother your knee?"

"No. I'm supposed to wear a brace, but surely you won't be too rough on me," he said as he winked.

"I could get it for you. Where is it?"

"You worry entirely too much." He handed her the basketball. "I'll give you a five-point lead."

"No you won't," Cassandra objected. "I don't need it," she continued hotly as she shot a long jumper from beyond the three-point line. It sailed through the net.

Mac laughed and the game began. Cassandra could tell that he was going easy on her and this just made her angry. She was a competitive person and loved to play sports. She hated it when guys thought that they needed to give her some sort of advantage.

"Are you going to play or not?" she asked after he had let her score again. The score was now 7-2.

"You are really something," he said before taking the ball. In the next ten minutes, Mac came back from five points behind to win the game 10-9. "Was that better?" he asked as he sat down on the concrete in front of the goal.

"Much better," she said as she joined him on the ground.

"You lost."

"Yes, but at least it was fair." She smiled. "Now we'll have to have a rematch. I hate to lose." They rested a few minutes before starting another game. They hadn't played for even ten minutes when Mac glided past her and jumped up for a lay-up. He came down hard and fell to the ground. "Are you okay?"

"Yeah," he said as he tried to get up. Cassandra saw him wince with pain when he put his weight on his left knee. "I think we'll have to finish this another time."

"Let me help you." When they entered the house, she helped him to the couch. "Do you think you re-injured it?"

He shook his head. "I just need to put some ice on it and I'll be fine." Cassandra disappeared into the kitchen and reemerged with an ice pack and a glass of water. "Thank you." He paused, trying to read her facial expression. "Go ahead and say it."

"Say what?"

"I told you so."

"Oh, no. I wasn't even thinking that. I just feel bad. Let me get you some pillows so you can keep it elevated."

"There's some in the linen closet upstairs. Second door on your right." He called after her. When she returned, the two visited while Mac iced his knee.

"I should probably get going."

"I'll walk you out," Mac said as he stood.

"No you won't. You just relax."

Mac didn't argue, but he remained standing. "When can I see you again?" he asked.

"Unfortunately, the rest of the week I work at the Smokehouse every evening. I could call you next week sometime," she offered.

"I guess that will have to do, but I will miss you. I've really enjoyed getting to know you Cassandra."

"I've enjoyed getting to know you too. You're very sweet."

"There is something I've been wanting to do since the first time I saw you. Cassandra, would you mind terribly if I kissed you?" Cassandra shook her head no and Mac leaned down and gave her a soft kiss on the lips. "That was nicer than I imagined. Be careful going home. Good-bye, Cassandra."

"You can call me Cassie. I'll call you soon," she said before leaving.

I think I'm in love. He is the sweetest man alive. Cassandra's heart was racing on the drive home. She was falling for Mac Lugot. When she got home she was too excited to sleep. She sat in the living room watching TV waiting for Beth to come home so she could share her excitement. She had only been home for a half-hour when the phone rang.

"Hello?"

"It's Mac. I wanted to make sure you got home okay."

"I did. Thanks for being concerned."

"I really just wanted to hear your voice again before I went to sleep."

"I'm glad you called. I think I needed to hear your voice too." She paused. "I hope your knee feels better."

"Good night, Cassie."

"Good night, Mac." Cassandra hung up the phone and went into her bedroom. She lay on her bed staring at the ceiling and thinking about Mac until she finally went to sleep sometime after one o'clock.

4

The next few days Cassandra was very busy. She went to her classes in the morning and then worked in the Financial Aid office. From there she went to the Smokehouse and waited tables until midnight. Friday she worked all day at the Financial Aid office before heading to her second job.

On Saturday she spent the day catching up on her studying before going in to work at the Smokehouse. She had tried to call Mac earlier in the day, but there was no answer. She figured he was working at the office.

The Smokehouse was very busy. It always was on the weekends. Cassandra was going from table to table, taking orders and refilling drinks. The rush was beginning to die down when she heard a man say, "Excuse me, Miss. Could you take our order?"

She turned around. "Mac! What are you doing here?"

"Would you believe me if I said I came to eat?" he said, smiling at her. "I really came to see you," he said, winking. "This is my brother, Nic. Nic, this is Cassandra."

"Hello Nic. What can I get you guys?" Cassandra took their order and disappeared into the kitchen.

"What do you think?" Mac asked his brother.

"She's gorgeous. She seems nice, too. Are you sure she's not too young for you? I think I'd be the perfect age for her."

"Whatever. I really like her. She doesn't seem to mind that I'm a little older."

Cassandra returned to their table with the drinks they ordered and explained that she was very busy and couldn't talk. She continued waiting her tables and barely spoke to Mac and Nic while they ate. She was embarrassed that Mac had seen her this way. She was a mess. When they were finished, she took them their ticket.

"Can you get a break?" Mac asked.

"No. We're just too busy," she admitted regretfully.

"What time do you get off?" Mac asked as he stood.

"Midnight."

"I'll be back to pick you up. You look great tonight," he whispered. "Keep the change."

Cassandra watched him and Nic as they left. *What was he talking about? I look terrible*, she thought. She looked down at the bill he had pressed in her hand. It was a fifty-dollar bill. *A twenty-dollar tip. Is he crazy?* Cassandra reluctantly got back to work. She hoped that midnight would come quickly.

The rest of the night she had her mind on Mac Lugot. She tried not to look at the clock for the next few hours as she waited her tables. Business had started to slow down and that made the time go even slower. Finally, her manager told her she was free to go. She grabbed her purse and walked out the front door.

She immediately saw Mac's truck and went over to the driver's side window. He rolled the window down.

"Hi. Are you going to get in?"

"Not until you take this twenty dollars back."

"That was a tip for excellent service, Cassandra."

"I see. How many other waitresses have you given a tip like that to?"

"None. I've never had service like I got tonight. Now get in."

"You are so bossy," Cassandra said, shaking her head. "I thought I'd take my car home, if you don't mind. And I'd like to take a shower."

"That's fine. I'll follow you."

Cassandra and Mac drove to her apartment. When they went inside, it looked as if Beth and Tom were having a party, so Cassandra took Mac's hand and led him into her bedroom. "I'll just be a few minutes," she said before disappearing through the bathroom door to take a shower.

Mac sat down on Cassandra's full-size bed. He looked around her room, deciding it fit her perfectly. She had it decorated in blue and yellow daisies. He made a mental note to send her daisies on Monday. She had a desk with several books stacked on it. There were pictures of what he assumed were her family everywhere. *She is so sweet. It just makes me want to take care of her*, he thought.

Cassandra only kept him waiting about fifteen minutes before emerging from the bathroom. Mac thought she looked beautiful and told her so.

"You are too kind. So what are we doing?" she asked.

"How 'bout we hit some bars?" he suggested. "Oh, I guess that won't work."

"No, it's fine. I have a fake," Cassandra explained. Shortly after she and Beth had moved to Lawrence, they met a guy who made fake I.D.'s. They had both got one, deciding it was a necessity since they were in college. Mac and Cassandra spent the next two hours bar hopping and drinking.

Mac suggested they go to his place to relax. Cassandra agreed. She was tired from working all evening. When they got to his house, Mac flipped on the TV and not even ten minutes later Cassandra was asleep on his shoulder. He got up and laid her down, trying not to wake her. He got a blanket from the hall closet and covered her up before turning off the TV and going up the stairs to his bedroom. It didn't take him long to go to sleep either.

The next day Cassandra woke with a terrible hangover. She looked around and had to think about where she was and how she got there. *Mac. He must be upstairs.* She looked at the clock and was shocked to see that it was after one in the afternoon. *Maybe he isn't still asleep.* She got up and walked around the first floor of the house. Not finding anyone, she started up the stairs. The door to Mac's room was open but he was not there. She continued down the hall to the office and knocked softly on the half open door.

"Come in," Mac said. She opened the door wider. "I'm glad you finally woke up. I hope you slept okay."

"Too well, I think. You should have woke me sooner."

"I didn't want to bother you. Besides I had some work to do."

"Do you always work so much?"

"Tax season. You'll learn when you start working. It is the busiest time of year. How about some lunch? I've got some stuff I can throw together in the kitchen."

"That sounds interesting."

"Good afternoon, Cassandra," Jenna Howard greeted her new employee. "I'm so glad you're here. Things are getting backed up since Stephanie left us. She didn't even bother to give us some notice. Let me show you where you'll be working." Cassandra followed Jenna to a cubicle next to her own. "You can arrange it however you like. There's some drawers for your personal things over here."

"This is very nice. I've never had my own desk before."

"Well, I hate to put you right to work, but I do have something I need done right away. Mac needs this report typed up and copied for a meeting he has in one hour."

"Okay. How many copies?"

"Twelve. Make sure there aren't any errors in it. He hates that. Sometimes I want to tell him to type it himself," Jenna said, smiling. "Don't misunderstand me. He really is easy to work for."

Cassandra went right to work and finished her task in a half-hour. "Here you go, Jenna."

"Oh. You're done already? Take it in to him, would you?" She pushed a button on her phone. "Mac, Cassandra has those reports for you." She turned to Cassie. "Go on in."

"Hello. I've missed you," Mac greeted her.

"You just saw me the other night," she said, smiling. "Here's the report you needed."

"Thank you. How's your first day going?"

"Fine. I've never had my own desk before." Mac smiled. He was finding out that Cassandra was not hard to please. "I better get back. Jenna said that she had a lot for me to do."

"Can I see you after work?"

"If you're lucky," Cassandra flirted before leaving his office.

Mac and Cassandra pulled into her parents' driveway. She was nervous about seeing them after so long. It was the weekend after tax season ended. Mac had been right. Once Cassandra started working for him, she began putting in lots of overtime and there was no way she could get away to visit her parents for the weekend until now.

Mac and Cassandra were together every chance they got and when she said she was going away for the weekend, he asked if he could come along. He said he would love to meet her family and couldn't stand to be away from her for that long. She was happy to have him come. She wanted him to meet her parents, but she knew they would not be happy that Mac didn't share their faith.

"They're going to make us go to church on Sunday," Cassandra said.

"Cassie, it's going to be fine. I don't mind going to church every once in awhile. Don't worry about it. If you found something in me to love, surely they will at least like me, right?" Mac joked. After seeing each other for almost two months, she knew he made jokes to relax her. "Should we go in?"

"I guess so," Cassandra said, getting out of his truck. Mac grabbed their bags and together they walked to the front door. Cassandra peeked her head in and said, "Hello? Where are you guys?"

"Cassandra! I've missed you so much, Honey," Marlene said as she came to the door and hugged her daughter. "Hello," she said, turning to Mac, "you must be Mac. Welcome to our home."

"It's nice to finally meet you, Mrs. Smith," Mac said.

"Well, come on. Everyone is waiting for you guys. Your father is grilling some steaks and chicken and I'm making some things to go with it," Marlene said, walking toward the kitchen.

Cassandra was surprised to see Michael, Shannon, and Matthew were there too. "Hi everyone. I want to introduce you to Mac."

Cassandra began the introductions and hoped that Mac was not being overwhelmed. When she got to Matthew, she went and took him from Shannon. "And this is little Matthew. I can't believe how much he has grown. He is so big!"

"Tell me about it. He has really put on weight," Michael said.

"Cass, I think you should take Mac out back to introduce him to your father," her mother said.

Cassandra handed Matthew back to Shannon and took Mac's hand. They went out the patio door, where her father was grilling on the deck. "Hi Dad."

"Hi Honey!" Curtis said as he hugged his daughter.

"Dad, this is Mac."

"Nice to meet you, Mac."

"I've heard a lot about you, Mr. Smith," Mac said.

"So, you've taken a liking to my daughter?"

"Dad! Be nice," Cassandra stopped him before he could interrogate Mac. "Is supper almost ready?"

"Not quite. You have time for a game if that's what you mean."

"A game?" Mac asked, obviously intrigued.

"She hasn't told you? It's tradition at our house to play basketball before the meal."

"Now we're definitely speaking my language," Mac said.

"He played at KU," Cassandra explained before turning to round up her brothers.

Michael and Chris gladly accepted the challenge. The group had time to play one game before Marlene called them in for supper.

The Smith family enjoyed all of the great food and fellowship. Mac was the center of attention as everyone asked him all sorts of questions. Chris asked lots of questions about what it was like to play college basketball. Michael asked questions about Mac's partnership at the firm, and Curtis and Marlene asked about his upbringing and family life. Mac handled all of their questions very well, not being the slightest bit annoyed with the interrogation. After supper, the family played card games until late since no one had to get up early the next morning.

Michael and Shannon left when everyone was ready to retire for the evening. Marlene had Cassandra show Mac the guestroom where he would be staying. "Was it terrible?" she asked when they were alone.

"No. Your family is great. I can tell how much they care about you."

"Well, I'm sorry they asked so many questions."

"Cassie, they just want to get to know the man you're falling in love with," Mac said, pulling her close.

"I should go. I'll see you in the morning," she said before he kissed her. "Let me know if you need anything."

"Good night, Baby," Mac said as he watched Cassandra leave his room.

He changed before crawling into the bed. He lay there thinking about Cassandra and her family for a long time before falling asleep. He had never been around a family like the Smiths'. They were certainly different than his family.

The next morning when Mac woke up, he took a shower and got dressed. He went downstairs in search of Cassandra. She and her mom and dad were in the kitchen eating breakfast. "Good morning, Mac. Did you sleep well?" Marlene asked.

"Great. Thank you," he spoke to Marlene before turning and smiling at Cassandra.

"What would you like in your omelet?" Marlene asked.

Mac told her and sat down next to Cassandra. "Two home cooked meals in a row. I haven't had this much home cooking in years!" Mac said.

"It's what I love to do," Marlene replied.

"When did you graduate from the university?" Curtis asked Mac.

"1997." Mac watched as Cassandra's father's eyebrows rose. "Sir, I want you to know that I genuinely care for your daughter and would never do anything to hurt her. I realize I'm a little older than Cassie, but…"

"Mac, I think Curtis is forgetting that he is ten years older than I am and we met when I was in college." Marlene smiled at Mac and then turned her eyes to her husband. "Did you forget that, Dear?"

"I guess I did. My apologies, Mac. But it is definitely different when we're talking about my daughter. No wonder my father-in-law didn't like me." Curtis chuckled, remembering the reaction he had received the first time he met his wife's father. "Honey, I'd say I took the news much better than your dad. Wouldn't you agree?"

"Yes. At least you didn't yell and throw things at the poor man."

"Grandpa did that?" Cassandra asked.

"He sure did. He threatened to get his rifle too. But your dad handled it all in stride. He won him over with Scripture. 'Thou shalt not kill,' he quoted before Grandpa started laughing. Then Curtis explained that we had met in church and that he was in love with me and planned to ask for my hand in marriage."

"Looking back, it sure was funny," Curtis said, laughing.

"It sounds like it," Mac said. Marlene handed him his omelet. "Thank you, Mrs. Smith."

"You're welcome," Marlene said.

They sat around the table talking for about an hour. Chris came down and Marlene made him an omelet before making herself one.

Cassandra was pleased that everyone was getting along with Mac so well. She thought his good manners and politeness were making a good impression on her parents. When she had come down that morning, her mother and father told her how nice they thought he was. They asked her if he was a Christian and Cassandra answered honestly. She really didn't know. They had never talked about it before. Her parents had frowned at that, but said nothing further.

After breakfast Cassandra took Mac for a tour of her hometown. She showed him her school, church, and other places that had significance to her. Mac was glad to have a chance to be alone with his girlfriend. "I missed you."

"What do you mean? You've been with me since yesterday morning."

"I know, but I haven't got to love on you," he said, putting his hand on her thigh. "Is there somewhere we can go just to be alone?"

"Yeah," Cassandra said and gave him the directions to her favorite spot by the lake. They sat by the water in each other's arms talking for a long time. Cassandra and Mac had gotten close over the last two months and she was certain she was in love with him. Mac felt the same way, but the two had never actually said the words to each other. They had also spent a lot of time alone, but Mac never pressured Cassandra to have sex with him. He figured it would happen when the time was right.

"I really like your family. They are all very nice. When do you think I will be able to meet your sister?"

"Mel will be home for the summer, I'm sure."

"You're not planning on going home for the summer, are you?" Mac asked in panic.

"I've been thinking about that. I can't. Not if I want to keep my job. Isn't that right, Boss?"

"Very true. I forgot about that. I would miss you too much anyway."

"I would miss you too." They sat in silence for a few minutes, both thinking of what it would be like without the other.

"Cassandra Rose Smith, I love you." Mac broke the silence and Cassandra's heart melted. She thought it was safe to assume he was in love with her, but it was wonderful to hear the words.

"And I love you, Mac Wayne Lugot."

The next morning, Cassandra sat in the pew that her family always sat in at church. Pastor Allen was speaking on the resurrection of Jesus Christ in honor of Easter. Cassandra listened to the terrible account of Christ's crucifixion and felt convicted. *They were so cruel to Him. If Christ died on the cross for my sins, I could at least live the life He would want me to.* She looked at Mac sitting next to her. He looked very interested in Pastor Allen's message and for the first time she wondered if he was saved or raised in church. Pastor Allen went on to speak of the resurrection and the hope that it gave.

Cassandra sat very quietly listening to Pastor Allen. Her palms began to sweat and her heart began to beat so rapidly in her chest she could feel it in her ears. *Lord, I can't go to the altar with Mac here. He'll think I'm weird. I'll deal with this at home. I know I need to stop drinking and smoking. I know that. It is just so hard. Please forgive me for my sins. Amen.*

Cassandra felt a little better after saying the short prayer, but she was still feeling very convicted. *I'm just feeling bad about drinking and smoking, that's all*, she thought.

Pastor Allen concluded his message by giving the salvation plan beginning in Romans 3:10. Mac looked over at his girlfriend. She had a very serious look on her face, one he had never seen before. He watched as people began going to the front of the church and kneeling at the front pew. *What are they doing? Praying? This church isn't like any I've ever been in. I've never heard about Jesus Christ rising from the dead. And for me? I doubt that. Why has Cassie never talked about this? Does she believe all of this? She's no different than me. She drinks with me all the time. I know she smokes even though she tries to hide it. This is all so confusing.* Mac's thoughts were interrupted by the Pastor dismissing in prayer. He bowed his head and closed his eyes like everyone else, but inside he was full of turmoil. Something just didn't feel right.

Mac and Cassandra were both happy to leave the church, each for their own reasons. The two walked in silence to Mac's truck and quietly drove back to Cassandra's house. When they got there, they were both happy to have the distraction of the family celebrating Easter. Mac met some of Cassandra's grandparents, aunts, uncles, and cousins. They spent the afternoon eating, playing games, and hunting Easter eggs.

That evening when Mac and Cassandra said good-bye and left for Lawrence, they were both happy to be alone. Cassandra was the first to speak. "I can't wait to get home. I am so tired."

"Me too," Mac said, trying to think of how to ask some of the questions that were on his mind. "Cassie, can I ask you something?"

"Sure."

"Well, it's about your church. I had never heard all that. About salvation, I mean. Do you believe in that?"

Cassandra sat silently for a moment before saying, "Yes, I do." She felt so terrible that Mac didn't already know that answer.

"Why have you never told me about it?"

"I don't know. I know I'm doing some things I shouldn't be right now."

"Are you saved?" Mac's question was enough to make Cassandra break down into tears. "Honey, I didn't mean to make you cry. Are you okay?" Mac said as he pulled off to the side of the road.

"It's just that I'm ashamed. I've never told you about Jesus and I'm certainly not living the way I should. We've always gone to church. I don't know what happened to me when I came to Lawrence. I just became too concerned with what others thought. I'd never taken a drink before I came here."

"Or smoked?"

"Or smoked." Cassandra was embarrassed. "I knew you didn't like it. I didn't want you to know."

"Cassie, I think everyone goes a little crazy when they get away from home. You don't need to feel bad."

"But I do. It's wrong. My parents are disappointed in me. I feel so guilty all the time. This morning I was convicted about it in church. I can't do it anymore, Mac, I just can't. Will you break up with me?"

"Of course not. I don't care if you drink or not. I love you for you, not what you do. I don't understand your beliefs, Cassie, but it's not going to stop me from loving you."

"Oh, Mac. I love you so much."

"I love you too," he said, drying her eyes with his t-shirt. She smiled at him. "Can you tell me what this salvation thing is? I'm just really confused."

"Well, it's when you accept Christ as your Savior."

"Accept. What do you mean by that?"

"You believe that Christ died on the cross for your sins and rose again so that if you accept him, you will have eternal life. You pray and ask forgiveness for your sins and ask Him to come into your heart and save you."

"Then what?"

"You're saved. If you ask, He will save you. It says that in the Bible."

"And what if you don't accept Him?"

"When you die, you will go to Hell."

"You've done this? Asked him to save you?"

"Well, I'm sure I have. Like I said, my parents have always gone to church and until this year, I did too." Cassandra didn't tell him that she couldn't actually remember a specific time when she had accepted Christ as her Savior.

Mac nodded. He wasn't sure he understood Cassandra correctly. He decided to let the matter drop. They got back on the highway and it didn't take long for Cassandra to lay her head in Mac's lap and go to sleep. Mac thought about what he had heard that day, from Cassandra and her church.

I don't understand any of this. The Pastor talked about a personal relationship with Jesus Christ. When he talked about salvation it sounded as if you would know for sure if you had gotten saved, but Cassie sounded unsure. Almost like she was saved because she went to church. And that isn't the way I understood the Pastor at all. He decided he just didn't understand it, but he thought since it was important to Cassandra he would try. When they got into Lawrence, Mac drove to Cassandra's apartment.

"Wake up, Honey. We're at your place," he said waking Cassandra. She woke up and Mac carried her bag up the stairs to her apartment. He tucked her in bed before letting himself out.

Mac drove home and tried to sleep. He couldn't get the day's events out of his mind. He crawled out of bed and went down to his storage room in the basement. He wanted some answers.

"Mac, what are you doing?" Nic asked, turning on the light to the basement stairs.

"Oh, I'm looking for a Bible."

"A what? Why in the world do you want a Bible?"

"I went to church with Cassie and her folks this weekend and the Pastor was talking about some stuff I had never heard before. I wanted to check it out."

"What kind of stuff?"

"Well, a lot of different things really. God sending His Son to die on the cross and rising again three days later. Did you know that is why people celebrate Easter? And something called salvation. It was really confusing to me."

"I've heard of salvation. You have to be really good and you can't do anything fun. You don't want any part of that, Mac."

"Maybe you're right," Mac said as he climbed the stairs. He tried to believe Nic's explanation of salvation, but he couldn't shake the horrible feeling that Nic was very wrong. He took one more look in his office on the bookshelves for a Bible, but was unsuccessful. He settled for watching TV with Nic until very early Monday morning.

5

Mac stood in front of the Bibles at the Christian bookstore baffled at how many there were to choose from. He had decided earlier in the week to buy a Bible when he couldn't find one at his house. The problem was that he didn't want to ask Cassandra for help. He didn't want anyone to know what he was doing. Nic had already made it clear that he thought salvation was a bad thing. Mac didn't want to risk receiving flak for being interested in what he had heard at Cassandra's church. He thought if he bought a Bible and started to read it, he would find out that the whole thing was just a hoax.

Mac picked up and flipped through several of the Bibles on display, looking for one like Cassandra had used on Easter. After spending almost an hour looking, he finally found one that looked exactly like the one she had used. He thought the study guides would help him understand what he read. He took the Bible to the register and laid it on the counter.

"Did you find everything okay?" the cashier asked.

"I guess so." Mac sounded unsure.

"You've made a good selection. Sometimes buying a Bible can be very overwhelming. They have so many different kinds these days," the older lady said reassuringly.

"I can agree with that."

"Would you like to have your name engraved on this?"

"Oh, no. I don't think so," Mac said politely. *I'm not planning on keeping the thing anyway. I'm just going to make sure what Cassandra said isn't true and get rid of it.*

Mac paid for the Bible and quickly left the store. He had a long drive back to the office. He had purposely gone to a store on the other side of town because he didn't want to run into anyone he knew.

Cassandra stood in front of the mirror in her bathroom getting ready for her date with Mac. The couple had not been on a date since they got home from visiting her parents. Once they returned, Cassandra had started studying furiously for her finals and she had really only seen Mac at work. He came over a couple of nights offering to help her study, but Cassandra found it too difficult to concentrate when he was there. Finally, her finals were over and her summer vacation had officially begun. She was anxious to start spending more time with Mac.

The doorbell rang, breaking into her thoughts. She answered it, but it was only Tom. "Come on in. She is in her bedroom," Cassandra said, forcing herself to be nice.

"You look sexy. Maybe we could go to your room instead," Tom slurred. He was obviously drunk.

"I don't think so," she said before raising her voice. "Beth, Tom is here to see you."

Cassandra turned back to her bedroom to finish getting ready. *He gives me the creeps.* She was actually looking forward to when Beth went home for the summer just so she wouldn't have to see Tom anymore. *Maybe they will break up over the summer.* Cassandra finished her hair and makeup and waited in her room for Mac to come. When the doorbell rang, she jumped up and bolted for the door.

"Hi!" she said, swinging the door open and throwing her arms around Mac's neck. "I've missed you so much."

"I missed you too, Baby," he said, returning her embrace. "Are you ready?"

"More than ready. Tom's here."

"Oh. So that's why you're so happy to see me," Mac said teasingly. "I'm just a reason to get away from Tom." Mac knew how much Cassandra didn't like Tom and from what he had observed, she had reason not to.

"You know that's not true," she said, shutting her apartment door and taking his hand. "You won't believe what he just did. I answered the door and he was hitting on me. Talking about wanting to go to my room instead of Beth's. What a jerk!"

"He what? Maybe I should go back up there and have a talk with him."

"Oh, no you don't. I'm not going to let him ruin the first date we've had in weeks! Although, I'm flattered that you would defend me," Cassandra said as the two reached Mac's truck.

"Of course I would. What do you want to do? I thought we'd go out to eat and then to a movie. Does that sound okay?"

"Let's go to the zoo!"

"The zoo?"

"Yeah. I haven't been to the zoo in months. We could get something quick to eat before we go. I don't think they close till nine. And then we can rent a movie and go to your house."

"Okay, if that's what you want to do," Mac said as they got into his truck. "You're always surprising me."

Mac drove to the closest fast food place and they ate before going to the zoo.

Mac hadn't been to the zoo since he was a kid and didn't think he would enjoy it, but he would do anything to please Cassandra. They walked around the zoo hand in hand talking and laughing. They spent almost three hours touring the grounds and watching the animal exhibits. Mac really did enjoy himself, but he decided he would enjoy almost anything, as long as he was with Cassandra.

After they were finished at the zoo, they rented a movie before going back to Mac's house. Nic was gone so the couple was there alone. Mac started the movie and offered Cassandra a beer. She turned down the beer, but asked for a Coke instead. Mac returned a few minutes later with her soda and some popcorn.

"How have you been doing on quitting?" he asked.

"Pretty well, really. I haven't had a drink since we got back from my parents' house. Smoking is the hard part. I was so stressed during finals that I didn't do too well with that, but I'm working on it."

Mac cuddled in next to her on the sofa. "That's great." Cassandra turned her attention to the movie, but Mac was still looking at his girlfriend. She was the most beautiful woman he had ever dated. He found himself thinking about how much he wanted to make love to her.

"Why are you looking at me like that?"

"Because you're beautiful," he said as he kissed her softly.

"That's sweet, but I thought we were going to watch the movie."

"I would rather watch you."

"Mac," she said, shaking her head. Mac kissed her again and again. Before she knew it, they were going too far. "Mac, stop." She pushed him away.

"What is it, Cassie?"

"I'm just not ready for this. I'm sorry." Cassandra stood up. "I need some air." She rushed out of the living room and through the kitchen to the back door. She went out the door and stood on the deck. *He makes me feel so good, but I can't have sex with him. I just can't. I owe it to him to explain my intentions to wait until I'm married, but I don't want to lose him. What will he think? Will he break up with me?* Cassandra felt a hand on her shoulder.

"Cassie, are you okay?" Mac asked. "I'm sorry I upset you."

"It's not your fault, Mac. It's mine. I should have discussed this with you before, but I'm scared," Cassandra said as she turned around to face him.

"Scared? Scared of what?"

"I'm afraid of losing you." Cassandra's eyes filled with tears.

"Baby, don't cry," Mac said, hugging his girlfriend. He held Cassandra at arm's length so he could look into her eyes. "If you're not ready to have sex, we don't have to. That isn't going to make me leave you. I love you and I'm willing to wait."

"Till marriage?"

Mac was shocked. He didn't know anyone who was waiting until they were married. *Is she serious?* Mac looked into her eyes. *She is serious.*

"Cassie, I must admit I'm surprised, but I admire your determination to do what you feel is right. I'm not going to pretend I'm not disappointed. I love you and would love to show you that physically."

"I want you to know it isn't easy for me either. I am attracted to you and would like to have that closeness with you, but I think it should be saved for marriage."

"You should know that I haven't waited, Cassie."

"I figured that."

"Does it bother you?"

"Sometimes. I'm jealous that another woman has had that intimate relationship with you and I want it, but I can't have it. But I don't think any less of you, if that's what you mean. I love you, Mac. I'm sorry that I didn't discuss this with you sooner. Things have moved so quickly for us and you mean so much to me. Since I moved to Lawrence, not one guy that I've dated has been willing to wait. None of them stuck around for more than a couple of weeks. I was just afraid of your reaction."

"I don't want you to feel that way. You can tell me anything and it's not going to change my love for you. Even if it does make me angry or upset, we will work past it. Okay?" Cassandra nodded. Mac pulled her close and hugged her before kissing her softly on the lips. "I love you, Cassie."

"I love you too."

"What do you say we go watch that movie?" Mac asked as he took Cassandra's hand and led her back into the living room.

They cuddled on the sofa together as they watched the movie. Mac tried to pay attention, but his mind kept wandering. *I don't deserve her. She is too sweet. Maybe Nic is right about salvation. Cassie thinks drinking, smoking, and sex are wrong. I need to start reading that Bible so I can try and understand her. I've never felt this way about anyone. I can see myself married to her, but when? I don't know if I can wait that long. Maybe she will change her mind as we get closer. What if she doesn't?* He tried to turn his attention back to the movie.

"Are you ready to go home?" he asked when the movie ended.

"Not really. I'm sure Tom is still there. He has been spending the night a lot lately. I know the only reason he is letting Beth go home for the summer is because he is going back to Nebraska. Otherwise, I'm sure she'd be staying."

"When will she leave?"

"On Monday, I think. I've been meaning to talk to you about that. Do you think I will get any overtime this summer? With Beth gone, I'm going to be responsible for *all* of the rent and utilities. I'm worried I won't make it."

"I don't know about the overtime. We are usually pretty slow in the summer. But I could pay Beth's half of things for you."

"Absolutely not! You spend too much money on me as it is. I'll think of something."

"You're not getting another job."

"I'm not?"

"No. I won't ever get to see you."

"You are so bossy." Cassandra shook her head. "But I might not have a choice."

Mac thought for a minute before coming up with what he thought was the perfect solution. "You can move in with Nic and I."

"No. I'm not going to take advantage of you. Besides, my parents would freak."

"Okay. I'll charge you rent. Then you're not taking advantage of me."

"What about my parents?"

"You'll have your own room and it will only be temporary. Just until Beth comes back."

"I don't know. I'll have to think about it."

"Come on. I'll show you your room," he said, grabbing Cassandra's hand.

"Mac!" she objected.

"I mean, for tonight. You said you didn't want to go home." He smiled at her.

"Cassie, I don't know if that is such a great idea. Things seem to be moving rather quickly between you and Mac. We don't want you to put yourself in a position where you would be tempted to make a mistake." Curtis Smith was talking to his daughter over the phone. She had just asked him what he thought of her renting a room in Mac's house.

"I know what you mean Dad. But I've told Mac that I'm waiting until I get married and he respects that."

"That may be true, but things can happen when you continually put yourself in a tempting situation. Not to mention how it looks. What kind of testimony would you have to Mac's neighbors?"

Cassandra didn't tell her dad that she had spent the night at Mac's house several times and nothing happened between them. "Maybe you're right."

"Your mother and I aren't going to tell you what to do, Cassandra. But we want you to know that we would not approve of the situation."

"Okay Dad. I don't know what I'll do yet. When do you and mom want to come for a visit?"

Curtis and Marlene gave Cassandra a date when they would be visiting before she hung up the phone. She still didn't know what to do about her living situation. Beth had moved out a few days ago and Cassandra had to make a decision soon. Her lease agreement ended May 30th and that was only a week away. She picked up the phone and dialed Mac's number at the office. He answered and Cassandra told him what her parents had said.

"Actually, I've been thinking about an arrangement that might make your parents feel better. Jenna is single and I know she would love to have some company. Since her husband died a few years ago, I know she has been lonely. Her children live in California and Texas so they don't visit much. She said she would love to rent you a bedroom for the summer. That way you have a place you can call yours but if you want to stay at my house, that's fine too. Would that make your parents feel better?"

"I'm sure it would. But I don't want to impose on Jenna."

"She already told me it would be fine. You can move in whenever you want."

"Mac, thank you. That would be wonderful. It would be no different than what we do now. I would feel much better with this arrangement than staying with you. I'll call my parents and let them know. They are coming to visit in two weeks."

"I'll tell Jenna that you're going to start moving on Saturday."

"Okay. That sounds good."

"I love you."

"I love you too. Bye."

"Bye, Cass."

Cassandra hung up the phone and called her parents back. They were happy to hear that she had chosen not to move in with Mac. They made arrangements to meet in two weeks at the accounting firm. Cassandra was excited because Melissa would be coming too. She hadn't seen her since Christmas.

On Saturday morning, Mac rang Cassandra's doorbell. Cassandra was still sleeping so she didn't hear the bell. Mac was suddenly worried about her. He realized he didn't like her staying by herself. He was glad she was moving today. He rang the bell again. Cassandra jumped out of bed. When she saw it was Mac she opened the door rubbing her eyes.

Mac put his arms around her and pulled her close. "I rang twice. I was worried about you," he said as he hugged her and then, realizing she was still in her pajamas, took a good look at her. "I wish you would have agreed to stay at my house. I could get used to seeing you like this. You're so cute when you wake up."

"I don't know who you are looking at."

"I guess you aren't quite ready to start moving."

"Well, after you dropped me off last night, I stayed up late putting my things in boxes. I must have slept through the alarm. I'll get ready," Cassandra said, turning back to her room. "Where's Nic? I thought he was going to help us?" she called.

"He's coming. He saw some girl in the parking lot and was distracted," Mac said as he looked around the place. Cassandra had rented a storage unit for the furniture and things that wouldn't fit into the room she was renting from Jenna.

Nic came in and they started loading up the truck. When Cassandra was ready, she came out and supervised. The group took one load to the storage unit before loading up again and driving to Jenna's house.

Jenna lived a few miles from Mac's house. Cassandra had never seen Jenna's house so she was kind of curious to see where she would be staying for the summer. Mac pulled into the driveway of a two-story blue house.

Jenna came out to meet them.

"Come on, Cassandra. I'll show you your room." Jenna led Cassandra up the stairs to the second floor. Her room was at the end of the hallway and the bathroom was just across the hall. "If you want to change anything around, you're welcome to."

"This is great." Cassandra looked around at the bedroom. There was a full-size bed, dresser, and a desk. The room was nicely decorated with a floral pattern on the walls that matched the bedding. It reminded Cassandra of her room at her parents' house. She opened the closet doors to find a huge closet.

"This will be perfect. I won't need to change a thing. Thank you so much for letting me stay here, Jenna."

"It's no trouble. It will be nice to have someone around. Don't worry, though, I won't be checking up on you or anything."

"Are you sure you don't want more rent money? You are giving me a great deal."

"No, no. I wouldn't have charged you anything, but Mac said you wouldn't stay here unless I charged you rent."

While Jenna gave Cassandra a tour of the rest of the house, Mac and Nic carried the boxes of her clothes and personal belongings up to her room. "Well, I guess that's everything," Cassandra said. "Jenna, I'll be back a little later to unpack. Mac is going to take me back to my apartment so I can get my car and pick up my deposit from my landlord."

"That's fine. Here is a key to the house and you're welcome to make yourself at home here."

Mac dropped Nic off at their house before taking Cassandra back to her apartment. "Do you want to get together later?" Mac asked.

"Sure. I just want to get my room situated and then I could come over. Thanks for helping me today, and for getting this arranged with Jenna."

"No problem. I guess I'll see you later. I love you." Mac kissed her.

"I love you too. I'll try and be there before supper. You can make me some of your famous spaghetti," Cassandra said as she winked at him.

Cassandra went up to her apartment one last time. She was going from room to room to make sure she hadn't forgotten anything when the doorbell rang. She assumed it was Mac so she flung the door open. "What?" she said before looking up and seeing Wes Armstrong standing in the doorway.

"Is that how you greet everyone?" he said, stepping inside and hugging her. "I don't know, but I think it is kind of rude."

"Wes." Cassandra was shocked. She could barely find words to say. "How are you?"

"I'm okay. I wanted to surprise you."

"You definitely surprised me. What are you doing in Lawrence?" she asked, pulling out of his grasp.

"We're doing a job here starting Monday. I decided to come up early and visit you. Chris gave me your address after Christmas. I intended to come sooner." He looked around the living room. "Is your apartment always this bare?"

"No. Actually I moved out today. I just came back up to make sure I hadn't forgotten anything."

"Are you going home?"

"No. I rented a room from my boss where I work. Come on. I need to get my deposit back from my landlord." Cassandra and Wes walked to the office. Cassandra couldn't believe he was here. *How will I explain this to Mac?*

"You look great," Wes said.

"Thank you."

"I noticed you hadn't been home to visit very much. Is it because of the job you were talking about?"

"Yeah. I got a part-time job at an accounting firm. It's really nice because I'm gaining some experience in my major." Cassandra chose not to tell Wes about Mac. He had came early specifically to visit her and if she told him about Mac, he might feel he had to leave.

Cassandra and Wes did some catching up while they waited at the office for Cassandra's landlord to get the check ready for her. Cassandra's mind was racing on how to handle this. She decided to take Wes back to Jenna's so she could call Mac. She would have to cancel their plans for the evening. When Cassandra got her money, the two left. Wes followed Cassandra to Jenna's house.

"Cassandra, you don't have to knock. You live here now," Jenna said, opening the door. "Oh, hello."

"Jenna, this is my friend, Wes. He is visiting from El Dorado. Wes, this is Jenna."

"Nice to meet you, Ma'am."

"You can call me Jenna. Come on in. Would you like something to drink or anything?" Jenna led Wes to the living room.

Cassandra excused herself and went upstairs to her room to call Mac. He answered. "Mac, its Cassandra."

"Are you coming already? I haven't even started the spaghetti."

"No. I've got to cancel on you. I went back up to my apartment to make sure I hadn't forgotten anything and a friend from high school showed up."

"That's okay. I get to see you all the time. Have a good time."

They said good-bye and hung up the phone. Cassandra went back downstairs where Wes and Jenna were talking. "I was going to try and put my things away before supper. Do you mind, Wes?"

"No, not at all."

"Come on. You can keep me company."

Cassandra and Wes went to her room and Cassandra started unpacking her things. She felt guilty she hadn't told Mac that her friend from high school was male. She was afraid of how he would react. When Cassandra was done putting her things away, she decided to take Wes to one of her favorite restaurants. They said good-bye to Jenna and left. Cassandra and Wes went out to eat and then decided to go to a movie. When the movie was over, Wes drove Cassandra back to Jenna's house.

"I enjoyed spending the evening with you, Cassie," Wes said. "I've thought about you a lot since Christmas." Wes took Cassandra's hand in his and looked into her eyes. He leaned in to kiss her.

"Wes. I'm seeing someone. I didn't tell you earlier because I didn't want you to feel like you had to leave. I'm sorry."

"Have I ever told you that you apologize too much? You don't have to apologize to me. I should have called. I'm sorry I put you in this position."

"No. I should have told you earlier. It's not your fault."

"We have to admit our relationship is a little weird. I could tell you weren't flirting with me like you used to, though. So, who's the lucky guy you've fallen in love with?"

Mac sat in his office reading the Bible he had bought weeks ago. This was the first time he had opened it. He wasn't sure where to begin, but he knew that some of the Scriptures Cassandra's pastor had read were in Matthew and Luke. He decided to start in Matthew.

Although at first he found it difficult to understand, he continued to read. Since Cassandra had canceled their date, he had all evening to himself. Nic was out with friends. Mac read in his office for quite some time before going to his bedroom. He read the entire book of Matthew before turning out the light. He found chapters twenty-seven and twenty-eight particularly interesting.

So, it's true. Jesus did die on the cross and rise again three days later.

I don't think he died for me, though. I'm not as good as Cassie. I've done lots of things that she thinks are wrong. I guess I need to keep reading.

6

On Monday morning, Mac sat in his office fuming. "What? Her friend was a guy?"

"Mac, I'm sorry. I didn't know that you didn't know. I assumed she told you about him," Jenna stammered. "I shouldn't have said anything."

"She told me about her friend, but she conveniently left out that he was male. And it's not your fault. You didn't march in here and tell me on purpose. I can't believe her. Do you think it was a boyfriend or something?"

"I'm not getting in the middle of this," Jenna said, turning to leave Mac's office, "but I think they're just friends," she said before closing the door behind her. Jenna regretted the conversation terribly. Mac had said that he couldn't wait to see Cassandra because he hadn't seen her since Saturday and a friend had come to visit. Assuming Cassandra had told Mac about Wes, Jenna said he was a really nice guy. Now she felt horrible. She could tell it was going to be a long day.

When Cassandra came in to work that afternoon, she said hello to Jenna and then went into Mac's office to say hello like she always did. She didn't stop long enough for Jenna to warn her about the conversation that had taken place earlier that morning.

"Hi Mac. I missed you."

"Hello. I'm very busy, Cassandra. Please don't disturb me for the rest of the afternoon." Mac knew he was being cold, but he didn't know what to say to Cassandra at that time. He needed time to think and he didn't want to discuss it at the office.

"Okay," Cassandra said slowly. "Sorry I bothered you." She felt like she was going to cry as she turned and left his office. He had never been so short with her. She knew something was wrong. "Jenna, what is wrong with him?

Did I do something?"

"I tried to tell you before you went in. Mac said something about your friend being in town and I told him he was a really nice guy. I'm sorry, Cassie. I assumed he knew."

"Oh no." Cassandra sighed. "I should have told him. I was going to tell him. I was just afraid of how he would react." She sat down in front of Jenna's desk and dropped her head into her hands. "I messed up. Mac has told me before to tell him everything, even if I think it's going to upset him. He was so mean just now. I think he is really angry with me." She let the tears fall.

"Go back in and talk to him. I'm sure it will be fine."

"He told me not to bother him the rest of the afternoon."

"Well, I've got plenty of work for you to do. Maybe it will keep your mind off of him. Then after work you can talk to him," Jenna said, handing over a basket full of papers Cassandra needed to file and sort.

Jenna meant well, but nothing could keep Cassandra's mind off of Mac. She knew she had really messed up. She tried to concentrate on her work, anxiously waiting for five o'clock to come. Cassandra rehearsed in her mind what she would tell Mac, but nothing sounded good enough. She saw Mac come out of his office around 4:30. He said something to Jenna before getting on the elevator. Jenna looked at Cassandra across the room compassionately.

"Is he leaving? For the day?" Jenna nodded her head. "He didn't even say good-bye."

"You could go after him."

"No. He obviously doesn't want to talk to me."

Cassandra finished what she was working on and left for the day. She went to Jenna's to eat some supper and decide what to do about Mac. She spent most of the evening thinking about him and wondering if he was going to break up with her. Jenna tried to keep her busy with conversation and then helping her do some things around the house. Finally at nine o'clock, Cassandra couldn't take it anymore. She drove to Mac's house. She sat in the car for a long time before finding the courage to go up to the door. She had almost decided it was better not to know than for him to actually break up with her. She knocked on the door and waited.

"Hi. Can I come in?" she asked timidly when Mac answered.

"Yeah. We need to talk," he said as he walked into the living room and sat down in his recliner.

Cassandra noticed that he sat where she couldn't sit next to him. "Mac,

I'm so sorry. But Wes really is just a friend. There is nothing going on between us. I promise you that."

"Why didn't you tell me?"

"I was afraid of the way you would react. I know you told me before that I could tell you anything and I'm sorry." Cassandra walked over to where Mac was sitting and knelt down in front of him. "I know I should have told you and I really was going to tell you when I saw you today. When I was telling Wes how wonderful you are, I realized that I needed to tell you. I'm very sorry, Mac."

"Cassie, I don't want to have to doubt you. I want to be able to trust you."

"And you can. I promise that I will be completely open and honest with you from now on, no matter what. Even if I'm afraid of your reaction, I will be honest with you. I realized today how important you are to me. I don't ever want to lose you. I love you and I'm sorry that I hurt you. Will you forgive me?"

"Yes. And I'm sorry I didn't tell you good-bye today. I was angry and I didn't know what to say."

"You don't need to apologize to me. You had every right to be mad at me. Now let me tell you about Wes," Cassandra said as she crawled into Mac's lap. She spent the next few minutes telling Mac about her complicated history with Wes and what they had done that weekend. "And Sunday night when I got back to Jenna's, I thought about how I would feel if you did those things with another woman. I mean, going to the movies and all that. I would hate it. You can never do that."

"Oh really? You did. It's only fair that I get one last date with another woman too." Cassandra tried to figure out if Mac was teasing her. "I'm just kidding. I don't want to go on a date with anyone but you." They sat in the recliner for a long time silently. They just enjoyed being close to one another.

"Why don't you guys get a room?" Nic teased as he came in the front door. "I mean really. You have four to choose from. Make that three. You can't go in my room."

"Hi Nic," Cassandra said.

"Hey. I've been trying to catch you. When did you say you were going to Mom and Dad's?" Mac asked.

"I'm flying out on Wednesday, remember? You were going to take me to the airport. Is that soon enough for you? Do you guys want the place to yourself?" Nic teased again. Mac claimed that he and Cassandra weren't sleeping together, but Nic didn't believe him. Nic did wonder why they never went up to Mac's bedroom together, though. And when Cassandra stayed the night she slept in the guest bedroom.

"Do you ever stop?" Cassandra asked, smiling. She really liked Nic. He was funny and charming.

"I'll be glad to get rid of you for awhile, but not because we want the place to ourselves. Besides, Cassie's parents will be here on Saturday. Who all is coming again?"

"Mom, Dad, Chris, and Melissa."

"Melissa? You have a sister? Maybe I should stay another week or two."

"Sorry. She's very much involved. I wouldn't let her date you anyway," Cassandra said. Nic put his hand over his heart and pretended to fall onto the sofa.

"You can all stay here with me. There's plenty of room, especially with Nic gone," Mac said.

"That's a good idea. I didn't want to impose on Jenna. I'm sure my parents will offer to stay at a motel, though."

"Well, I will insist then," Mac said.

Cassandra laughed. One of the reasons she loved Mac was his persistence. "When will you be back, Nic?"

"Never," he joked. "No. I don't know. I'm done with school so I need to find a job. I'd like to find one closer to my folks, not that I don't love my brother."

"Well, I'll miss you."

On Wednesday morning, Cassandra woke to the phone ringing. It was Mac asking if she could take Nic to the airport in Kansas City. He was swamped at the office and wouldn't be able to get away. She agreed. She hurried to get ready before driving over to pick up Nic. He loaded his bags into the trunk of her car and they started the long drive. Kansas City was about an hour away.

They made small talk for awhile before Nic turned the conversation to a more serious topic. "I want you to know that I've never seen Mac so happy. It's kind of weird. He doesn't cuss anymore, he hardly drinks, and he claims that…well…never mind. But he is happy, very happy."

"What makes that weird?"

"Well, I know he has you and you're a great girl, but why has he given up so many things he enjoys?"

"I never asked him to give anything up. I guess if you really care about someone, you are willing to give up things that you know that person doesn't like. When Mac and I first started dating, I was smoking. I knew he didn't like it, so I cut down considerably. I haven't had a cigarette in a couple of weeks now."

"You used to drink too."

"I know and I was miserable with guilt. I wasn't raised that way. When Mac and I went home for Easter, I realized that I didn't want to feel that way anymore. I'm not going to judge anyone or try to pass my own convictions onto anyone else, though. That's between them and God."

Nic changed the subject then. He didn't like talking about God. He didn't even know if he believed there was a God and he didn't want to get into a debate with Cassandra. Nic was relieved when they pulled into the airport parking lot. Cassandra had not mentioned God again, but that one time had put Nic into a bad mood. *Why? Why did that ruin my day? I guess it just made me uncomfortable talking about something so personal with her.* They walked into the airport and checked in his luggage and found his flight. Nic told Cassandra that she didn't need to wait until he left, but she insisted.

When it was time for him to board the plane, Cassandra hugged him. "I think I'm going to miss you. I know Mac will."

"He has you. I figure I'll be back before too long for the wedding."

"The wedding?"

"Yours and Mac's. I told you I've never seen him this way with anyone else. He is definitely in love with you. He's a lucky guy. Thanks for bringing me and I'll miss you guys too," Nic said before walking down around the corner to board the plane.

Cassandra stood there and watched his plane as it left. She thought a lot about what Nic said about her and Mac getting married. She had pictured her future with Mac several times, but they had never talked about marriage. She wondered if Nic was right about his prediction. *Is Mac really thinking about marrying me?* Cassandra decided that it was too soon for him to be considering that. They had only been dating for three months. *Nic must be mistaken.*

"Mac, we appreciate your offer, but we don't want to impose. We are going to be staying a week," Curtis Smith replied to Mac's offer for them to stay with him.

"I insist, Mr. Smith. I would enjoy the company. My brother flew back to Texas last week and I must admit, I miss him."

"Are you sure?" Marlene asked. "We can be a pretty messy group."

"I want you to stay with me. There's plenty of room. If you like, I can take off right now and take you there to get settled in."

"No. That's not necessary. It's almost five o'clock. We can just go then," Curtis said.

Cassandra's parents had just arrived at the accounting firm and Mac was already asking them to stay at his house. Cassandra and Melissa were talking excitedly while Chris rolled his eyes at them. "Cassie, he is handsome," Melissa whispered.

"I know. And he's wonderful. I'm in love. What's the status with Greg?" Melissa answered by holding her left hand in front of Cassandra's face. Cassandra shrieked drawing everyone's attention to them. "Sorry," she said before turning her attention back to Melissa. "When? Why didn't you tell me? I can't believe you. Do Mom and Dad know?"

"I wanted to surprise you. He asked me a week before I came home and I called Mom right away. We've set a date in August and then I will be going back to Colorado. He's coming to visit next month. You have to come and meet him."

"Oh, I will. I can't believe you're getting married. I'm so happy for you!" Cassandra said as she hugged her sister. Their attention turned to their parents, Chris, and Mac. The group was evidently making supper plans. Mac was volunteering Cassandra to help him make supper for them. "What's that? Are you volunteering me, Honey?"

"I was just saying that you would help me make supper tonight. How 'bout spaghetti?" Mac asked.

"I should have guessed," Cassandra said before turning to her sister. "That is all he *can* make."

"We'll wait in the lobby so you guys can finish your work," Curtis said, herding his family from Mac's office.

After her father had closed the door, Cassandra ran over and hugged Mac. "I can't believe how much I've missed them, especially Melissa. I'm so glad they're here. Melissa is getting married in August. I can't believe it!"

"So that's why you were screaming."

"He's coming to visit in July so I will have to go home to meet him. He's going to be my brother-in-law and I've never even met him. I'm sure he's nice. Mel has always had good taste. I'm too excited to work."

"I can tell. You're rambling," Mac said teasingly. "Why don't you take your parents over to Jenna's so they can see where you live? You can pack some things to stay at my place with them. By the time you get done, I'll be finished here and you can bring them over to my place."

"That sounds great," Cassandra said as she kissed him on the cheek. "Thanks, Boss. I'll see you after while," she called from the door to his office. Mac watched her disappear from his office, thinking how much he loved her. Cassandra told her family her plans and they followed her to Jenna's house. Melissa and Chris rode with her. The siblings talked mostly of the upcoming wedding. Melissa asked Cassandra to be her maid of honor and Cassandra gladly accepted.

When they arrived at Jenna's house, Cassandra gave them all a tour of the house. She had introduced her parents to Jenna when they arrived at the firm and Cassandra could tell that they really liked Jenna. She packed a bag of some things to get her through the week while she stayed with her family at Mac's house and the group traveled to his house.

"This is his house?" Melissa asked in awe. "He must be loaded."

"We don't really talk about it, but I think he gets paid very well at the firm. Wait until you see the inside," Cassandra said as she got out of the car.

"No wonder you like the guy. Nice truck, nice house," Chris commented.

"That has nothing to do with it, but it is an added bonus," Cassandra said as she winked at Chris. From the look on her parents' faces, she could tell that her parents were thinking the same thing as Melissa. "Are you ready to go in?" she asked, leading the way. She knocked on the door and waited for Mac to answer.

"Come on in," Mac said as he opened the door. "I'll show you where you can put your things." He led the way upstairs. He showed Chris to what used to be Nic's room and then showed Melissa and her parents to the other two guest rooms. "Melissa, I guess you will have to share with Cassie. Will that be okay?"

"That's fine. We have a lot of catching up to do."

"Great. I'm going to go down and start supper while you guys get settled in. Cassie, when they're done, you can show them around if you want. Then you have to come and help me. I don't want to mess up when I have such important guests," he said, winking at her.

When Mac disappeared down the hall, Melissa whispered, "He is very charming. Does he make everyone feel so important?"

"I think so. He is very sweet. I'm so glad you like him," Cassandra said.

"Mom and Dad told me he was very likable. I was excited to see for myself."

"I probably feel the same way about meeting Greg. He's going to be my brother-in-law and I've never even met the guy."

"You will next month. You'll like him."

Cassandra's parents and Chris reappeared in the doorway of the room Melissa and Cassandra were sharing. "Are you ready for the grand tour?"

"Yeah. I got lost finding my way back," Chris joked.

Cassandra showed them around Mac's house, ending the tour in the kitchen where she began to assist Mac with the spaghetti. Marlene offered to help, but Mac politely declined. She sat down at the kitchen table with the rest of her family, amused at Mac's insistence. While Cassandra finished preparing the meal, Mac set the table in the dining room and ushered the Smiths to the dining room table. Cassandra could see that he enjoyed entertaining even though he rarely did so.

When everyone was seated, Mac asked Curtis to bless the food. Cassandra was surprised, but pleased that he remembered. They never prayed over their food when they ate together. The family enjoyed their dinner and made plans for the next day. After dinner, they played card games until everyone was ready for bed.

Sunday morning, Mac and Cassandra sat in the pew at Grace Community Church with the Smith family. Cassandra had only sat in the church once before when she had first moved to Lawrence. After her visit home for Easter, she had intended to start going to church again, but it had not happened. Sunday was the only day that she and Mac could sleep in and relax.

Marlene Smith glanced at Cassandra and her boyfriend. Mac looked as if he was listening very intently. She wondered if he had any questions about what he was hearing. Marlene decided to have Curtis talk with him after the services and she planned on talking with her daughter. From what she could see, Mac and Cassandra were becoming very close.

"Read with me in I Corinthians 10:31," the pastor said, bringing Marlene's attention back to where it needed to be: on the sermon.

"'Whether therefore ye eat, or drink, or whatsoever ye do, do all to the glory of God.'" He paused before continuing. "This verse was a wake-up call to me this week. God is telling us that no matter what we're doing, it should be bringing glory to Him. I wonder if we can say that what we watch on TV brings glory to God. What about what we read? What we say? What we listen to? The list could go on and on. The verse says that even what we eat and drink should bring glory to God."

The pastor continued, but he had lost Mac. He glanced at the Smiths. *I just don't understand. These people are so willing to do whatever the Bible says. What do they understand that I'm missing? And why haven't I heard any of this before? Maybe I wasn't willing to listen.*

After the Pastor closed in prayer, Curtis and Marlene went to say hello to him. "Honey, I think that Mac was really interested today. Maybe you could see if he has any questions or anything."

Curtis glanced back at the young man. "I'll see what I can do."

Mac was still sitting in the pew. He decided that he needed to keep reading the Bible he had bought. He had to figure out how Christ's death and resurrection applied to his life. Ever since the trip to Cassandra's parents' house, he had a bad feeling. He couldn't figure out what the problem was, but he knew the answer was in that Bible. Mac looked over at his girlfriend. *I wish I could talk to her about this. I'm just not ready. Would she even have the answers I'm looking for? I think she is a little confused about it too.*

"Honey, are you okay?" Cassandra's voice interrupted his thoughts.

"Oh, yeah. I'm fine. Where are we going to go eat?"

Cassandra answered him, but he wasn't really listening. He was preoccupied with what the Pastor had preached about. Her parents joined them again and the group left for the restaurant that Cassandra had suggested. When they arrived, Marlene found a moment alone with her youngest daughter.

"Honey, should we be expecting an announcement from you and Mac?"

"What? What makes people think we're planning to get married?"

"I take it I'm not the first to ask."

"No. His brother said something about it before he left."

"Cassie, I can see the love between the two of you. It's in the way you look at each other."

"Mom, I do love him. And I would be thrilled if he proposed, but I don't think we are that serious yet."

"Well, I'm glad to hear that. I would like to see him get saved before you consider marriage. Has he shown any interest?"

"He asked a few questions after Easter, but he hasn't said anything since then," Cassandra said before joining the rest of her family at the table. She didn't want her mom to start questioning her about her own faithfulness.

After lunch, Mac and the Smith family returned to Mac's house. They changed clothes and played a few games of basketball before settling in to relax for the afternoon. Marlene, Melissa, and Cassandra all retreated upstairs for an afternoon nap. Curtis and Chris settled in to watch TV while Mac went upstairs to work in his office.

Mac had only been working a few minutes when there was a light knock on the door. "Come in."

"Working today?" Curtis asked.

"Cassie says I'm a workaholic. But I just like to stay on top of things. Come on in and sit down."

Curtis took a seat before saying, "I noticed you seemed pretty interested in the message today."

"Honestly, I was. I've never heard the things that he preached or the things I heard at your church on Easter. My family wasn't exactly religious. We only went to church occasionally."

"I see. Do you have any questions or anything?"

Mac sat quietly for a moment. He was tempted to ask the questions that had been racing through his mind, but decided against it. He didn't feel like he could talk to Cassie's father before talking with her. "Well, I bought a Bible shortly after Cassie and I got back from visiting you. I've been reading it."

"If you ever have any questions, I'd be glad to try and answer them for you." Curtis could tell that Mac did have questions, but was reluctant to discuss them.

"I'll keep that in mind. Thanks, Mr. Smith."

"You can call me Curtis. Do you mind if I ask you a few questions about my daughter?"

"No, not at all," Mac said even though the question made him nervous.

"I can see that Cassandra loves you. I love my daughter very much and don't want to see her get hurt. You understand, don't you?"

"Of course, Sir."

"I guess what I would like to know is your intentions."

"My intentions, Sir?"

"Call me Curtis. Do you have any plans concerning my daughter?"

"Well, we've only been seeing each other a few months. And although I love your daughter very much, I don't want to rush into anything. We are still getting to know each other. She's young. I don't know that she is ready for anything beyond that. If I thought she was, I'd marry her tomorrow."

"Well, I'm happy to hear that you are serious about her. Marlene and I think that you are very nice and we can see that Cassie loves you very much. We want her to be happy. I will admit that you not sharing our faith does concern us, but you've made me feel better about that today. Anyone who is willing to search the Scriptures is going to find their way to salvation. Thank you for talking with me, Mac," Curtis said as he stood to leave.

"Curtis, I can finish this tomorrow. How 'bout we grab Chris and we go play a game of golf?"

"Golf? I've never played."

"It's time you learn. Let's go." Mac left a note for Cassandra before they loaded his clubs into Curtis's van and drove to the golf course that Mac frequently visited.

7

Cassandra drove into her parents' driveway. She saw the forest green Chevy Tahoe and decided that her sister's fiancé had very good taste. She parked the car and headed toward the front door. Chris opened the door. "Hi, Cass. Do you have anything that needs brought in?"

"No, I think I've got it," she answered, holding up the bag she was carrying.

Chris took it from her. "He is really nice. You'll like him."

"I'm so excited to meet him. How is everyone?"

"We're doing fine. Everyone is in the living room," Chris said as they walked in the house.

They entered the living room and Melissa jumped up to hug her sister. "Greg, this is my sister, Cassie. Cassie, this is Greg," she said, releasing Cassandra.

Greg stood up to shake Cassandra's hand. "It's nice to finally meet you. I've heard a lot about you."

"Likewise," Cassandra said, looking up at Greg.

"Cassie, it's good to have you home," Michael said.

"Oh, Michael. I haven't seen you guys in forever! Where's Matthew and Shannon?"

"She's feeding him. She'll be done in a few minutes. Mac decided not to come this time, huh?"

"Yeah. Where is Mac?" Chris asked.

"He is pretty busy at work. Besides, he'll be coming for the wedding next month."

"Cassie, come help me in the kitchen. Supper is almost ready." Melissa took her sister's arm. "What do you think?" she whispered as they left the room.

"He seems very nice. He's cute too. I love his green eyes."

"I know. That's my favorite characteristic." The girls continued to talk as they set the table. Marlene Smith was busily finishing the supper she had prepared.

"I'm going to call Mac. He wanted to know I made it okay. I'll be right back." Cassandra took the cordless phone and walked up the stairs to her room. She dialed Mac's number and waited for him to answer. "I miss you already," she said when he answered.

"I miss you too, Babe."

"I just got here a few minutes ago."

"How is everyone? Did you meet Greg?"

"Everyone is fine and Greg seems very nice. He is pretty cute."

"Oh, really?"

"Not as cute as you, though. They were just getting supper on the table, so I should probably go."

"You'll be back in a week, right?"

"Right. Friday. It's going to seem like forever. I'll call you tomorrow."

"I love you."

"I love you too." Cassandra hung up the phone. She was really going to miss Mac. This was the first time that they had spent any considerable amount of time apart. She went back to the kitchen to eat supper with her family.

Mac sighed as he hung up. The week was going to go by so slowly without Cassandra around to keep him company. He decided it would be a perfect time to read some more in the Bible he had bought almost two months ago.

Mac grabbed the Bible from the nightstand by his bed and took it downstairs to the living room. He settled in to his recliner and opened to the book of Mark. Mac paused after reading a few chapters. *It's all so interesting, but it doesn't apply to me. It's history. What does it have to do with the present? Why do the Smiths believe this so strongly? Maybe I should pray, but how and what would I say?* Mac decided against praying and went back to reading.

"Hi, Cassie. Come on in," Beth said.

"How are you doing?" Cassandra asked. She had been busy helping Melissa with wedding plans since she got home, but she had slipped away to visit Beth the day before she would be leaving. They needed to make plans for finding another apartment before school started again in August.

"I'm okay. I've stayed pretty busy. I miss Tom terribly."

Cassandra was disappointed to hear that Beth was still seeing Tom, but said nothing. "I can understand. I've been home about a week and miss Mac already."

"When are you going back?"

"Tomorrow morning. I wanted to check with you about apartment hunting. Do you know when you could come up for a visit?"

"Oh. We should definitely be looking. Everything will be taken soon. Maybe I could go back with you."

"I could call Mac and have him set up some appointments for us. But how would you get home?"

"Good question. I'll think of something. Do you want to go for a swim? You can borrow one of my suits," Beth said, leading the way to her bedroom.

"Sounds great. You're so lucky to have your own pool. I haven't been swimming all summer. Maybe when I get back, I can talk Mac into taking me sometime," Cassandra said, following Beth. The girls changed and went out the patio door that led to the pool. They spent the afternoon swimming and talking.

"Hi girls," Beth's mother said as she joined them on the patio. "How are you doing, Cassandra?"

"I'm fine, Kathy. I just came for a visit before I leave tomorrow."

"Oh yeah. We need to start apartment hunting and I thought I could ride back with Cassie, but I wouldn't have a way back," Beth said.

"Your father has to go to Kansas City on Monday. Some business meeting or something. I'm sure he could make a detour and pick you up. Would that work?"

"That would be great! I can spend the weekend with you," Beth said, turning to Cassandra.

"Sounds perfect." Cassandra thought the plan sounded fine until she spoke to Mac on the phone that evening.

"I'm not mad, Honey. I've just missed you so much. I was looking forward to having you to myself," Mac said.

"I guess I was looking forward to that too. I just didn't think about it. She was so excited to come. I think she has been bored and she misses Tom."

"She's still with Tom?"

"Yeah, I know. I wasn't too crazy about that either."

"I'll set up some appointments for you. You want one close to the university and two bedrooms, right?"

"Yes. You're so wonderful."

"Well, you're going to have make it up to me when she leaves. Maybe I can take a couple days off or something. I've got to go. Come see me no matter what time you get back tomorrow. I love you."

"I love you, too. Bye." Cassandra hung up the phone. She went down the stairs to spend the evening with her family before leaving for Lawrence early the next morning. She picked Beth up and the girls started their trip to Lawrence. Beth slept most of the way and was still asleep when Cassandra pulled into Mac's driveway. Cassandra roused Beth up long enough to explain where they were and that she was going in to see Mac.

Cassandra ran to the door and rang the doorbell. She waited, but there was no answer. She tried the door and it wasn't locked. She went in and looked in the kitchen before walking up the stairs. Mac's bedroom door was open so she peeked in. She looked around the room and saw that he was in the bathroom. "Mac," she called. He didn't answer. *He must be in the shower.*

Cassandra sat down on the edge of his bed. She looked around the room. Her eyes stopped when she saw a Bible on the nightstand. She picked it up and flipped through it. There was a bookmark in the book of John. *Why does Mac have a Bible? Has he been reading it?* Her thoughts were interrupted by the sound of the water being turned off. She quickly put the Bible back where it was. She didn't want Mac to think she was snooping.

Mac came to the bathroom door and stopped. "Cassie, you scared me." He walked toward her.

"Come here," he said, taking her in his arms. The couple hugged for a long time. "I can't believe how much I missed you."

"I wanted to surprise you."

"You did. But now I'm not going to want to go to work."

"Beth is with me. She's asleep in the car." Cassandra felt she needed to remind him.

"Oh, I almost forgot." He slumped down on the bed. Cassandra sat down next to him. She saw him glance at the Bible on the nightstand with an alarmed look on his face.

"I saw your Bible. Have you been reading it?" she asked timidly.

Mac felt uncomfortable when Cassandra called it *his* Bible. "I bought it after we got back from Easter. I didn't tell you about it and I'm sorry."

"Why do you need to apologize? I was just curious why you had it. I didn't think you were interested in the gospel."

"I bought it intending to prove your church wrong, but I haven't been able to. Now I'm trying to figure out how it all applies to my life."

"I'm glad," Cassandra said.

"Cassandra, I realized something this week while you were gone." Mac changed the subject. "I don't want to be separated from you ever again. I'm not proposing. I don't think we're ready for that, but you need to know that I want to spend the rest of my life with you. I want to marry you someday."

"I don't know what to say." Cassandra paused. She continued when she saw Mac's disappointed look. "I mean, everyone has been asking me about us getting married, but I had no idea you felt this way."

"How do you feel?" he asked, suddenly uncertain.

"I love you." Cassandra paused.

"But you haven't thought about marrying me?"

"Yes, yes. I've thought about it. I just didn't realize you were thinking about it. Hearing you say all this makes me so happy," she said, hugging him. "I love you so much."

"I love you too. I guess I need to finish getting ready for work. Is Beth staying with you at Jenna's or do you want to stay with me?"

"I think we'll stay with Jenna. I don't want Beth to feel like a third wheel."

"Do you think she ever thought of that when Tom stayed over at your apartment?"

"No, but that's different. This is your house."

"Maybe," Mac grumbled. He stood up and continued to get ready. "Will I see you at all this weekend?"

"I'll see what I can do. I promise."

Mac and Cassandra went down to the kitchen where Mac had a list of apartments. She took the list and the couple said good-bye. Both of them were disappointed that Cassandra's visit had been so short.

Cassandra and Beth drove to Jenna's house. After she gave Beth the grand tour, Cassandra snuggled into her bed to take a nap. When she woke up the girls went to the pool for the afternoon before returning to Jenna's for supper. Afterwards, Beth suggested they go to what used to be their favorite bar.

"Oh. Well…I…"

"Don't tell me you're still not drinking. Come on, Cassie. Let's have some fun."

"Beth, I don't think I have to drink to have fun. I'll go with you if you want, but I'm not going to drink or anything."

"That sounds like fun," Beth said sarcastically.

Even though Beth was disappointed that Cassandra didn't want to get drunk, the girls did go to the bar. Cassandra watched as Beth drank and smoked. Beth also danced with several guys, but Cassandra politely declined the offers she received. "I'm having so much fun. Tom never lets me have any fun."

"If that's true, why do you stay with him?" Cassandra asked, taking advantage of the opportunity Beth had given her.

"Because I love him. Why aren't you dancing? Afraid Mac will find out?"

"No. I started doing something after Wes came for a visit. If I wouldn't want Mac to be doing it with another woman, I don't do it with another man."

"That's so sweet."

Cassandra didn't like the tone in Beth's voice. "At least Mac treats me well."

"What's that supposed to mean?"

"I don't want to fight with you, Beth. But you know how I feel about Tom."

"Oh, so he's not perfect like Mac?"

"I didn't say that. I just think that you deserve better, that's all. But as long as you're happy I guess I don't need to worry about you."

"Well, I am happy. I'm getting another drink."

Cassandra watched Beth walk away. She didn't believe that Beth was happy, but she wasn't going to say that. It was going to be a long weekend, especially if the girls were fighting. Cassandra watched as Beth sat down at the bar and ordered another drink. A man sat down next to her and she started flirting with him. Cassandra decided this was her chance to get some air. She went outside. All the smoke was making her want a cigarette. She wanted desperately to call Mac. She found a pay phone and dialed his number, but there was no answer.

Cassandra was just about to turn around and go back into the bar when she saw Mac with a group of men from the firm walking into a bar across the street. She crossed the street and debated on whether she should go in or not. Eventually, she decided to go in. She stood by the door searching the room for Mac and his friends. It took her a moment, but she spotted them at a table in the corner.

She started to make her way to the table, but stopped when she saw another woman approach Mac. The tall, slender brunette gave Mac a hug and a kiss on his cheek. Cassandra felt sick to her stomach. *Mac's cheating on me. But how could he after all that he said today? What do I do? Should I leave or let him know that I saw him?* Cassandra decided to leave, tears streaming down her face. She had reached the door when she heard Mac calling her name. She continued to walk outside.

"Cassie, hi," he said as he put a hand on her arm. She turned around to look at him. "Are you okay? Why are you crying?"

"Leave me alone."

"What's wrong?" He waited for Cassandra to answer but she was silent. "I think I know what's going on. You saw me with Danielle."

"I can't believe you, Mac," Cassandra said, shaking her head. "Just leave me alone. Please," she said before crossing the street to go back to the bar where Beth was waiting.

Mac ran after her and stopped her before she went in. "Cassie, let me explain. Dani is my ex-girlfriend."

"Oh, really? It didn't look to me like she was an *ex*-girlfriend."

"If she had her way, she wouldn't be. Cassie, you know I love you. I would never cheat on you." Mac searched Cassandra's eyes. They were full of hurt and anger.

"And what would have happened if I hadn't shown up?"

"Nothing. Nothing," he repeated. "Cassandra, you're the only woman I'm interested in. You have to believe that."

Cassandra wanted to believe Mac, but she couldn't. Mac reached to wipe the tears from her cheeks, but Cassandra pushed his hand away. "I can't believe that, Mac, because I know I'm not satisfying you." Mac started to object, but Cassandra stopped him. "I've got to go find Beth."

Mac stared at the door through which Cassandra had disappeared and wondered what had just happened. He stood there for a minute before walking back across the street to the bar where his friends were. He told Luke that he was going home and left. Mac wanted to talk to Cassandra some more, but felt like it wouldn't do any good. She wasn't ready to listen.

Cassandra went back into the bar and found Beth dancing with yet another guy. She wanted to leave, but Beth wanted to stay. Beth had run into some of her friends from school, so she told Cassandra she would catch a ride back to Jenna's with them. Cassandra was relieved to be alone. She drove back to Jenna's in tears. When she went in the front door, Jenna was waiting for her.

"Mac has called three times in the last hour. He's made me worry myself sick about you. You should call him and let him know you're okay."

"I won't be doing that," Cassandra replied defiantly.

"Do you want to talk about it?"

"Oh, Jenna. I don't even know what happened. I saw him with some friends and I followed him. And this girl was hugging him and I got upset. He saw me and came after me and I was just so hurt. He says that it was his ex, but I don't know."

"Come on over and sit down. You're rambling. Slow down and tell me what happened," Jenna said as she handed Cassandra a tissue. Cassandra told Jenna the whole story. "So, why didn't you believe him? Was it a romantic kiss?"

"No. She just kissed him on the cheek, but I'm sure it would have led to more."

"Why?"

"Because…well…" Cassandra was embarrassed and she could feel her cheeks warming. "I know you might think this is silly, but I'm saving myself for marriage."

"Cassandra, that's wonderful. It is so nice to hear that there are still some girls who realize how precious their purity is. Now I understand why you're worried. You think that since you won't have sex with Mac, he must be getting it from someone else."

"Well, I didn't until tonight. I know that it must be hard for him. I mean, he knows what he's missing. I don't."

"I can understand your insecurity, but I really don't think Mac is that type of guy. I know he loves you and I don't think he would do anything to jeopardize his relationship with you. I think you really need to discuss this with him."

"I don't know if I can. He may not even want to talk to me."

"I know that's not true. Like I said, he called three times already." The doorbell interrupted the women and Jenna went to answer it. "Cassie, its Mac. He wants to know if you'll come outside and talk with him," she said as she returned to the living room.

"What will I say?"

"Tell him what you told me. He'll understand."

Cassandra went out the front door and closed it behind her. She looked up at Mac before looking back down at her hands. "Cassie, I'm glad you agreed to talk to me. Do you want to sit down?" She nodded and they sat down on the porch swing. "Honey, I love you and I'm sorry about before. I should have stopped Danielle from hugging me."

"No. It was an innocent hug, Mac." She paused. The couple was silent for a moment and Cassandra looked down at her hands. After a moment Mac placed a finger under her chin to force her to look at him. She could see the confusion in his eyes. "I overreacted. Seeing you with another woman made me insecure. It made me think that since I wouldn't have sex with you, you were getting it from someone else," she blurted out.

"Oh, Baby. I would never do that. I love you and I respect your decision to wait till you're married. Yes, it's hard for me sometimes. I won't lie about that. But because I love you, I will wait for you."

"I'm sorry I doubted you."

"It's okay. I understand why you did. Can I kiss you?"

"Of course."

"Well, you did push me away before," Mac said, smiling.

"Come here," Cassandra said, pulling him close. "I love you."

"I love you too."

The couple sat on the porch swing for a long time talking and holding each other. They were still sitting there when Beth came stumbling up the sidewalk. Cassandra excused herself and helped a very drunk Beth up to her room. After Beth was sound asleep in Cassandra's bed, Cassandra went back outside to say good night to Mac.

"No offense, but what exactly do you and Beth have in common?" he asked when she returned.

"I'm not sure anymore. When we were in high school, we were a lot alike, but now..."

"Are you sure you want to live with her again?"

"After tonight, I thought that it might be a mistake. But when Tom gets back, it will be fine. I'm at your house most of the time and she will be with him. Let's not talk about that. I don't want you to leave, but I need to go to bed. You made our first appointment for nine in the morning. If I go to bed now, I could get a few hours sleep."

"I'll call you tomorrow. Good luck with the apartment hunting. Make sure there is good security and lighting at night."

"Okay, okay."

"I want you to be safe, that's all. I love you and good night."

"You mean good morning," Cassandra joked. She watched Mac drive away before going inside. She went to her room and fell asleep as soon as her head hit the pillow.

The next morning the girls set out to find an apartment. The morning started out poorly because Beth had a terrible hangover and was being a grouch, but by noon the girls were getting along great. Cassandra was starting to remember why she wanted to share an apartment with Beth. They visited three different apartment buildings before finding one that they liked and could afford. They paid the deposit and agreed to move in the first of August.

Mac slipped into the last pew of the church. He sat by himself and listened to the pastor preaching about Saul, who later became known as Paul. Mac was floored that God would forgive someone who took part in persecuting His people. Mac had decided to go to church after reading more in his Bible on Saturday. Cassandra was still busy entertaining Beth, so he was sure the day would go by slowly.

He listened intently as the pastor applied the lesson about Saul's forgiveness to his life. Then the pastor gave an invitation. Mac was used to watching others go forward to kneel and pray at the altar, but this was the first time he felt compelled to go forward himself. Mac's heart was pounding and he felt very uncomfortable. *I'm not going up there. I've got to get out of here.* In Mac's rush from the sanctuary, he bumped into someone.

"Oh, I'm sorry. Excuse me," he stammered.

"That's okay. I'm Richard Walker. Is this your first time with us?" Richard noticed that the man who had run into him seemed very nervous, but chose to act naturally.

"Uh, no. I've been here once before with my girlfriend's family."

"Did you meet the pastor?"

"No." Mac looked around nervously.

By this time, the invitation had ended and the pastor was making his way to the back of the sanctuary. "I'm sure he'd love to meet you. Come with me." Mac couldn't really explain why he did as the man requested, but he did. As he followed Richard, the feeling of being uncomfortable faded. "This is Pastor Wentworth. Pastor this is…Oh, I didn't get your name."

"Mac Lugot," Mac said, extending his hand to shake hands with the pastor.

"It's very nice to meet you, Mac. You came with Curtis Smith and his family last month, didn't you?" Pastor Wentworth asked.

"Yes Sir. I'm dating their daughter, Cassandra."

"Oh, yes. She's a lovely girl. Curtis and I are old friends. Tell me, Mac. What did you think of the services this morning?"

"I found it particularly interesting, Sir. It's hard to believe that God could forgive someone like Saul and then use him in His ministry." For some reason Mac had no problem opening up to Pastor Wentworth and Richard Walker.

"Yes, it is. But if you really think about it, Paul was the perfect choice to preach about God's forgiveness because his sins seemed unforgivable," Richard said.

"I've been reading the book of John, but I'd like to read more about Paul," Mac said, surprising himself. He would not even talk to Cassandra about what he had been reading and now he was telling strangers.

"Richard leads a men's Bible study here on Tuesday evenings. Do you think you would like to come, Mac?" Pastor Wentworth asked.

"We're studying about King David right now. It's very interesting," Richard said.

"I don't know. I've only been reading the Bible a little while. I don't know very much."

"That is the perfect reason to come. We are all learning together," Richard said.

"I'm not sure..." Mac hesitated.

"It starts at seven o'clock. You're welcome to join us. It was nice meeting you, Mac. There's someone I need to speak to," Pastor Wentworth said, shaking Mac's hand again before walking away.

"Do you have any plans for lunch? My wife makes a terrific roast beef," Richard offered.

"Thanks, but I don't think so."

"Okay, then. I hope to see you at the Bible study," Richard said as he shook Mac's hand.

Mac said good-bye and walked out to his truck. He sat in the driver's seat thinking for a long time before driving home. *Me in a Bible study. I don't know. I can't go this week. Tuesday will be the first evening I have with Cassie since she got back. Maybe I could go the next week. It won't hurt anything.*

8

"So, how are you doing on that Bible reading, Mac?" Curtis Smith had found an opportunity to talk with Mac alone during the busy weekend of his oldest daughter's wedding.

"Very well. I've been going to a men's Bible study at Pastor Wentworth's church. I've only gone a few times, but I'm really enjoying it."

"That's great. What are you studying about?" Curtis tried not to show the true extent of his excitement. He was thrilled to hear that his daughter's boyfriend was getting involved with church. He couldn't wait to tell Marlene.

"King David. It's very interesting."

"I'm sure it is. The story of David is wonderful. How did you find out about the study?"

"When Beth was visiting Cassie, I was pretty bored. I went to church that Sunday morning. I met the leader of the study, Richard Walker, and the pastor that day, and they invited me to come. I was reluctant at first, but now I'm glad that I started going."

"Mac, I've been looking all over for you," Cassandra said, joining them on the deck. "You've got to see this dress I have to wear tomorrow. It's purple! I can't believe that Melissa would do this to me. I'm not interrupting anything, am I?"

The men looked at each other and smiled. "Mac was just telling me about the Bible study he's been going to."

"Oh. Come see this dress, Mac," she said, taking Mac's hand. "It really is terrible."

"Yes, Dear." Mac followed Cassandra up to Melissa's bedroom where the dresses were laid out on the bed.

She grabbed the dress and held it up to her. "Do you see what I mean?

Purple!"

"Cassie, it's not purple, it's lilac. I think it is a beautiful dress. Why don't you try it on for me?"

"I just took it off. You'll have to wait until the wedding. I'm not sure that I look very good in it. It's not my color."

"You would look good in a gunny sack, my darling."

Mac and Cassandra were interrupted by a frantic Melissa wondering why they weren't ready for the rehearsal dinner yet. They went to their separate rooms to get ready and then they drove to the church in Mac's truck. The rehearsal went as planned and the dinner was delicious. Cassandra had planned a very calm bachelorette party for Melissa, and Mac went with Chris to Greg's bachelor party.

Mac did not see Cassandra again until the next afternoon as she walked down the aisle in her lilac dress. He thought she looked beautiful. Once she reached the front of the sanctuary, she searched the crowd until she spotted Mac and smiled at him. Mac found himself thinking how much he wished this was their wedding day. *I just don't think she's ready yet, but hopefully soon. Hopefully soon.* Mac's thoughts were interrupted by the processional and the crowd standing as Melissa walked into the sanctuary.

Cassandra and Mac sat in church the next morning. Cassandra was feeling convicted again, but she didn't know why. *I haven't been drinking or smoking or anything. Why do I feel so bad?* Cassandra was so absorbed in her own thoughts she didn't notice as Mac slipped out of the pew and left the sanctuary. *Maybe I need to start going to church more often.* Her father getting up and leaving the sanctuary distracted Cassandra. It was then that she noticed Mac was gone also.

Mac had fled the sanctuary in an effort to escape the conviction he was feeling. He just couldn't make himself go to the altar. He hadn't counted on Curtis Smith following him.

"Mac, is something wrong? You look a little pale."

"No. I mean, I don't know," Mac stammered.

"Do you want to talk about it?"

"Yes. I think I do," Mac said, surprising himself. Curtis led the way to an empty classroom and the men sat down. "Something just doesn't feel right. My heart is racing and I just feel bad."

"I think what you're feeling is probably the conviction of the Holy Spirit, Mac."

"I figured so. But I guess I was too embarrassed to go to the altar."

"Why did you want to go to the altar?"

"I need to get saved. I've been reading the Bible for so long and wondering how it applies to my life. I see now that Jesus died on the cross for everyone's sins, including mine."

"I'm so happy to hear you say that. Let me show you a few Scriptures that should help you understand even more." Curtis opened his Bible to Romans 3:10. "'*As it is written, there is none righteous, no, not one,*'" he read aloud. From there they turned to Romans 3:23 and asked Mac to read them.

"'*For all have sinned, and come short of the glory of God,*'" Mac paused while Curtis turned to Romans 5:12 and Mac read this aloud too: "'*Wherefore, as by one man sin entered into the world, and death by sin; an so death passed upon all men, for that all have sinned,*'".

Curtis explained the verses after Mac read them and they continued to go through the 'Romans Road.' Curtis turned to Romans 6:23. "'*For the wages of sin is death but the gift of God is eternal life through Jesus Christ our Lord...*' Curtis, I'm a sinner. I don't know that I deserve God's gift."

"Here..." Curtis said as he turned back to Romans 5:8. "'*But God commendeth his love toward us, in that, while we were yet sinners, Christ died for us.*' You see? God knows we are sinners and loves us anyway. No one person is more deserving of the gift of eternal life than another."

"What do I need to do?" Mac questioned.

"Read this," Curtis said, turning to Romans 10:9-10.

"'*That if thou shalt confess with thy mouth the Lord Jesus, and shalt believe in thine heart that God hath raised him from the dead, thou shalt be saved. For with the heart man believeth unto righteousness; and with the mouth confession is made unto salvation.*'"

"Would you like to pray now and ask God to save you?"

"I've never prayed before. I don't know how."

"When you pray, you're talking to God. All you need to do is confess that you are a sinner, ask for forgiveness for your sins, and acknowledge your belief that God sent his Son to die for your sins and rose again. It doesn't have to be fancy, just a simple prayer. Look at verse thirteen. *'For whosoever shall call upon the name of the Lord shall be saved.'* God will not turn away anyone who asks to be saved."

Mac and Curtis bowed their heads and Mac said a simple prayer and accepted Christ as his Savior. Curtis went over some more Scriptures with Mac to explain what God expected of one of his children. Mac was very excited and couldn't wait to tell Cassandra. He felt like a weight had been lifted off his shoulders. When the men were done talking, they emerged from the classroom to find that everyone had already left the building.

They walked outside to Mac's truck where Cassandra was waiting. "Mom went home to start dinner. So I guess you're stuck riding with us, Dad."

"That's fine," Curtis said as he climbed in the passenger seat and shut the door. He assumed Mac would want to tell Cassandra about his salvation.

"Cassie, wait," Mac said, stopping her from climbing in the truck. "I have some good news. I got saved."

"That's great! I'm so happy," Cassie said as she threw her arms around his neck. "I wondered what you guys were doing."

Mac and Cassandra got in the truck and they drove to the Smith house. Over lunch, Mac told everyone that he had accepted Christ as his Savior. Everyone was very happy for him. Cassandra listened to Mac talk about how great he felt and how excited he was to start serving God. She was happy for him, but there was something nagging at her. She just couldn't put her finger on it.

After dinner Mac and Cassandra drove back to Lawrence. They had time to go to Mac's house to freshen up before heading out the door for Sunday evening church. Mac was excited to tell Richard Walker and Pastor Wentworth about the decision he had made. He knew they had been praying for him.

Mac reread the verses in the seventh chapter of I Corinthians. *"It is good for a man not to touch a woman." Oh, Lord. I've failed miserably in this area. Not only before Cassandra, but even now. Cassie and I are too close. We may not be having sex, but the intimacy we have should be for marriage. Please forgive me. Help me to slow down, Lord. Help us both to slow down until we have said our vows before You. Give me the strength I need.*

Mac continued with this line of prayer for some time before taking a shower. He had started waking early in the morning to spend time with God before work each day. On this day he knew that he would need to talk to Cassandra about the seriousness of their relationship.

Mac's opportunity came as soon as the workday ended and Cassie knocked on his office door. "Come in," he called to her.

"Hi. I've got a test tomorrow so I need to get home."

"I'll walk you out," he offered, knowing he had some work to finish up. The couple made small talk as they made their way to Cassandra's car. "I want to talk to you about something," he said as he climbed in the passenger side.

"Is something wrong?" she asked, turning to look at him.

"Yes. I don't even know how to begin. I've been reading in I Corinthians and today I read chapter seven. Do you know what it says?"

"Not really."

"Well, it talks about purity and saving intimacy for marriage."

"That's what I thought it was."

"The Lord convicted me this morning about the seriousness of our relationship. I think we need to slow down some."

Cassandra was silent for a moment before nodding. "I agree with you. Sometimes I feel like we go too far, even though we aren't having sex."

"I'm glad you feel that way. It's going to be hard to change, I'm sure. But I think that it's right. And as much as I enjoy having you stay at my house, I don't think that it is appropriate." Cassandra was surprised by this, but allowed him to continue. "I just want you to expect some changes, Cass. I'm not the man I used to be."

"I know. Whatever you think is best is fine with me."

"I better get back up. I don't want to be late for Bible study." Mac leaned over and kissed Cassandra on the cheek. "Good luck on your test."

"I love you."

"I love you too."

Cassandra watched Mac as he walked back inside. She had a very strange feeling. *I should be the one to know these things. I should be the one to know what is appropriate. Mac just recently got saved and I've been saved since…well, forever.* She turned her attention to the road as she left the parking lot wondering why she felt so bad.

"Mom, I know you're disappointed. But we're flying back on the twenty-sixth and we'll drive straight to your house. Mac really wants me to meet his parents." Cassandra was talking to her mom on the phone.

"I can understand that. I'll just miss seeing on you Christmas."

"We'll be there the day after, I promise. I'm kind of nervous. What if they don't like me?"

"Oh, Cassie! Of course they'll like you."

"I don't know, Mom. They aren't too happy about Mac's decision for Christ. What if they blame me and hold that against me?"

"You'll just have to pray about it. God will take care of it. When do you fly out?"

"We're leaving on Thursday after my last final. Mac hasn't visited them for a long time, so he's using some of his vacation time. I've got to go, Mom. Tell everyone hello for me. I love you." Cassandra and her mother said good-bye before hanging up.

Cassandra returned to her studying. She had to prepare for her finals that started the next day. The phone interrupted her again. It was Mac.

"Do you want me to swing by and pick you up?" Mac asked

"I'm not going. I've got to study for my finals."

"You're not going to church?" Mac questioned.

"I told you this morning that I needed to study," Cassandra said defensively. Mac said good-bye and they hung up.

Cassandra was glad that Mac had gotten saved, but was getting tired of his enthusiasm for attending church. They often argued when Cassandra refused to go with him. She knew she needed to go, but Mac had started going three times a week and he was always going to activities and other things at the church. Cassandra always felt uncomfortable at church. Every time she went, she left doubting her salvation. She tried to convince herself that the doubting came from Satan as a way to attack her, but the peace never lasted. It always resurfaced.

Cassandra turned her attention back to her studies and tried to concentrate. She hated arguing with Mac. She watched the clock continuously until she thought Mac would be home. She tried to call him but there was no answer. She tried several more times as it got later that evening. She gave up and went to bed around eleven o'clock. *He must have stayed for one of those fellowships again. I wish I could talk to him.* Cassandra woke up to the alarm clock the next morning. She got up and got ready to go to her first final. She decided to call Mac and make amends.

"It's me," she said when he answered. "I tried calling you last night."

"I went out to eat with Richard and his family after church."

"I missed you."

"I missed you too."

Cassandra could tell that Mac was still upset with her. "I'm sorry that I got defensive last night."

"That's okay. I just don't understand why you don't go with me. It's how you were raised."

"I know. But I really needed to study last night." It sounded like an excuse even to Cassandra's ears. "I'll be done with finals before lunch. Do you want to meet me somewhere?"

"I'm meeting Richard. I'm sure he wouldn't mind if you came."

"No, that's okay." Cassandra's feelings were hurt. She felt as if Mac wasn't including her in his life as much as he used to. She wasn't his only focus of attention anymore. "I'll be in for work this afternoon. Maybe I can see you there."

Mac and Cassandra said good-bye and hung up. She knew she wouldn't get to spend any time with him at work either. He was getting ready to take two weeks vacation for their trip to Texas. And she knew better than ask about meeting with him that evening because Tuesday evenings were Men's Bible study at the church.

"Don't be nervous. They're going to love you," Mac whispered to Cassandra as they emerged from the plane.

"I hope so," Cassandra said before they were interrupted.

"Mac! Cassie! Over here." Nic was waving his arms and calling to them. Cassandra was relieved to see that Nic was the one to pick them up, but then she saw the older couple standing behind him. She was so nervous. "It's so good to see you," Nic continued as he hugged Cassandra and then Mac.

Mac introduced Cassandra to his parents as soon as he had the chance. Mr. and Mrs. Lugot seemed nice, but Cassandra felt inadequate. They were obviously very sophisticated. Cassandra could see that Mac had gotten his height from his father. Mr. Lugot towered over everyone, including Mac.

"It's nice to meet you, Mr. and Mrs. Lugot," Cassandra said, trying to sound confident.

"We've heard a lot about you, Cassandra. That's a lovely name," Mr. Lugot said.

"Oh, thank you."

"Well, are we just going to stand here?" Nic asked impatiently.

Cassandra was glad for the interruption. The group walked out the door of the airport and Cassandra watched in shock as her bag was loaded into a limousine. Cassandra couldn't help but wonder what the Lugot house was going to look like. It was the first time she wondered what they did for a living. She made a mental note to ask Mac when they were alone.

The ride to the Lugot house went by quickly. The family chattered nonstop about things that had happened in their lives since the last time they were together. Cassandra listened and tried to remember tidbits that she could bring up later when she needed to make conversation.

The driver turned into the driveway of a house that Cassandra would describe as a mansion. She wondered now what Mac thought of her parents' house. It was a large house, but definitely not extravagant like this one. Cassandra looked at Mac. He was still talking about something going on at the firm. Mac had never talked about his parents' money. *Why would he? He doesn't talk about his money either.*

When they walked in the front door, Cassandra looked around at the modern décor. It was very nice, but Cassandra certainly didn't feel like she was in a home. It felt more like a business office. She watched as a man came and took her bag from Mac and disappeared up the large staircase. She hoped her awe did not show on her face.

"Mac, do you want to show Cassandra around? Our lunch should be ready soon," Mrs. Lugot said.

"That's a great idea. Are you ready for a tour?" Mac asked. Cassandra nodded and he took her hand and led the way. The next several minutes were spent touring the Lugot house. Cassandra was impressed, to say the least. When Mac showed her the indoor pool, she couldn't hold it in any longer.

"How come you never told me your parents were rich?"

"It's not something I like to talk about."

"What do they do?"

"Well, they own Lugot Industries. My dad works the business and my mom is a lawyer."

"I can't imagine what you think of my parents' house...or me, for that matter."

"You know what I think of you. I'm in love with you," he said, pulling her close, "and your parents' house feels like a home. I like that. I've never understood why my parents like this place. It's so big sometimes we didn't see each other for days when I lived here. Between you and me, Nic and I are closer to the staff than to our parents. Don't get me wrong. I love my parents, but to them money and possessions are what matter. That's why I've had such a hard time witnessing to them. They think they have everything they need."

"I guess I never thought of that. I've always looked at the rich as fortunate."

"Not many people realize the baggage that comes with it. I like the way I live now. My house is large and comfortable, but not showy."

"I like your house too."

"Well, that's good because you'll be living there someday."

"Oh, really?" Cassandra teased. "Do you know something I don't?"

"I know I want you to be my wife. That's all." Mac continued showing Cassandra around the house and grounds ending in the dining room where the rest of the Lugots were waiting.

Cassandra tensed up as soon as she walked in the room. She felt intimidated by the formality of the room, not to mention Mrs. Lugot. She was so prim. Mr. Lugot seemed more laid back and had made an effort to make conversation with Cassandra at the airport. Mac must have felt her tense up because he took her hand and ushered her to their seats. After they were seated, he kept a hand on her leg. She was thankful for the sense of security.

"I hope you found the place suitable, Cassandra. Mac tells us that you are studying accounting. Do you plan on being a CPA?" Mrs. Lugot asked as the staff brought their lunch out.

"Thank you," Cassandra said to the older woman who brought out her meal. She turned her attention back to Mrs. Lugot who looked none too pleased at her politeness. "I think so, but I'm not sure. It just depends," she said, glancing at Mac. Mac had made it clear that when they got married, he wanted her to stay home and take care of the house and children. Cassandra had no problem with that. She liked the idea of being a homemaker.

"Depends on what?" Mrs. Lugot questioned.

Cassandra felt her cheeks flush. "Well, um..." She didn't want to share her and Mac's plans and knew that Mrs. Lugot would think they were foolish.

"I think what Cassandra means is that she plans on becoming a CPA unless her circumstances somehow change," Mr. Lugot filled in. "Plans do change sometimes, Dear."

"I would like to say prayer, Father. Is that okay? Or would you rather I do it silently?" Mac asked. Cassandra was surprised at Mac's boldness. His father looked at him and granted Mac permission to say grace. Mac took Cassandra's hand and said a short prayer of thanksgiving. When Mac was finished, Cassandra could see the look of disgust on Mrs. Lugot's face. It was then that she realized how lucky she was to have godly parents.

Over the next few days, Mr. and Mrs. Lugot seemed to accept that Mac prayed before the meal. Cassandra could tell that they did not really like it, but tolerated it. They had been surprised when Mac and Cassandra requested that Cassandra have her own room. And they seemed to notice that Mac no longer drank or cursed. Things were fine until Mac announced on Saturday night that he and Cassandra would be going to church the next day and that his parents and Nic were welcome to come along.

Mac's mother was the first to speak. "Mac, I thought we made it clear to you that we don't want any part of your religion. We can't stop you from this…this…religion, but give it a rest. You don't have to go to church all the time and I don't want to hear anymore about it."

"I don't *have* to go to church all the time. I want to. And it isn't a religion, it's a way of life. I simply invited you to come with us, that's all."

"I'll go with you, Mac," Nic said, surprising both Cassandra and Mac.

"Not you too," Mrs. Lugot muttered.

"That's great, Nic. I'm sorry that you're so upset about this, Mother. But tomorrow is Christmas Eve and I can't think of any place I'd rather be than in the Lord's House," Mac said. "I think maybe I should say good night." Mac took Cassandra's hand and they left the living room. Cassandra noticed that Mr. Lugot had said nothing. She wondered if it was because he disagreed with Mrs. Lugot on the issue. Mac walked her to the door of her bedroom. "I'm so angry. I had to leave before I said something wrong. Do you think I handled that right?"

"Oh, Mac. I admire your boldness and determination. To be honest, I think you know more about all that stuff than me anyway."

"Why is that, Cassie?"

"I don't know. I just don't know."

"Well, good night. I love you," Mac said as he hugged her.

He worried about Cassandra. There was just something wrong. She didn't seem to have the same zeal for Christ that he did. *Maybe it wears off. But Richard and Pastor Wentworth, they're like me. What aren't you telling me, Cass?* Mac didn't even hear Cassandra say good night because he was engrossed in his thoughts. He released her and went across the hall to his own bedroom. Mac lay awake for a long time thinking about his parents, Nic, and Cassandra. He prayed for all of them and decided that he needed some advice from someone more knowledgeable. He decided that he would call Richard Walker the next morning.

"It's going to take time, Mac. Remember how long it took you to realize your need for a Savior. The best thing that you can do is live the Christian life and take advantage of witnessing opportunities when they come up. Eventually your family will see the difference in you and ask questions," Richard said.

"Nic has agreed to go to church with Cassie and me today."

"That's great. Let the Holy Spirit do the work. Don't pressure him in any way."

"Richard, there is one other thing I wanted your advice on."

"What is it?"

"Cassie. I don't understand her sometimes. She doesn't seem to want to whole-heartedly serve the Lord. I mean, she just doesn't want to get involved at church. She agrees to go on Sunday mornings, but anything beyond that is a fight. Shouldn't she want to be in the Lord's house?"

"Well, yes. But sometimes Christians harden their hearts to the Holy Spirit and the Word. Do you love her?" Richard questioned.

"Of course."

"Do you plan to marry her?"

"Yes. Hopefully soon."

"I'm going to be completely honest with you, Mac. The first thing you need to do is make sure that it is God's will for you to marry her. If God gives you peace about that, you need to have a serious talk with her. Now is the time to work out things that could later cause problems in your marriage. Tell her what you expect of her now and after you're married."

"I think you're right. I probably better go. Thank you for the advice, Richard. You've been a big help." Mac and Richard said good-bye and Mac knelt by the bed to pray.

Dear Heavenly Father, thank you for another wonderful day. My parents and Nic are heavy on my heart. I pray that You would give me an opportunity to share You with them. Help them see You through me. Be with Nic today as he goes to church with me. Open his heart and mind, Lord. Help him realize his need for a Savior. Lord, I want Your will for my life. If it's Your will, give me peace about marrying Cassandra. I love her so much. I pray that You would soften her heart and draw her closer to You. Give me Your guidance and direction in that situation. Mac at that moment knew it was God's will for him to marry Cassandra and he knew he would have to talk to her. *Give me the words to say and allow her to be open and receptive to what I have to say.*

Mac's prayer was interrupted by a knock at the door. "Mac? Are you decent?" Cassandra called.

"Come in," he said after murmuring a quick Amen. "You look beautiful," he said, hugging her. "Is Nic ready?"

"Yeah. You should see him. He looks pretty nice in a suit and tie."

"He's wearing a tie?" Mac was shocked. It was not like his little brother to wear a tie. Cassandra nodded her head, smiling. "I want us to have some time alone today. Maybe this afternoon we can get away for awhile."

"Why?"

"I have a gift I want to give you."

"What is it?"

"It's a surprise. Now, go on down. I'll be down in a minute."

Cassandra walked down the stairs and waited in the foyer for Mac. Nic had disappeared somewhere, so she waited alone. She was startled by the sound of Mrs. Lugot's voice. "I know you're responsible for this."

"For what?" Cassandra asked innocently.

"You've turned Mac into a religious nut. What I don't understand is why he is willing. You're not even sleeping together," Mrs. Lugot said coldly. Cassandra was so stunned, she didn't even know what to say.

"You know he's had lots of other girlfriends. They didn't try and change him and they certainly weren't prudes." Mrs. Lugot stared at Cassandra. Cassandra was unable to stop the tears that sprang to her eyes. "Don't you have anything to say? I suppose it doesn't matter. He'll be through with you soon enough. You're certainly not suitable for him to marry."

"Mother, I can't believe what I just heard," Nic said as he entered the foyer. "I think you owe Cassandra an apology." Mrs. Lugot let out a sarcastic laugh before leaving the foyer.

"Cassie, I'm so sorry." Nic grabbed a tissue and handed it to Cassandra. She was still so shocked that she didn't speak. "I'm sorry. My mother has never met anyone like you. Of that, I'm sure. I think she feels threatened by you or something. Please don't let it bother you."

Tears continued to flow from Cassandra's eyes. Not knowing what else to do, Nic awkwardly tried to hug her. It was then that she let out a giggle.

"You act like you've never hugged a girl before," she said, trying to pretend that what Mrs. Lugot had said was forgotten.

"Well, not my brother's girlfriend. There is a boundary you just don't cross," Nic said, embarrassed.

Cassandra dried the tears from her eyes and checked her make up in one of the many mirrors in the house. She didn't want Mac to see that she had been crying. "Don't say anything to Mac, okay?"

"He would want to know."

"It would just ruin Christmas. I'll tell him later." Nic nodded and Cassandra went back to freshening up her eye make-up.

She didn't think there had ever been a time when someone had been so mean to her. This woman, who was probably going to be her mother-in-law some day, did not like her. She had made that very clear. And she certainly would not approve of the marriage. *Not suitable for Mac to marry.* Tears threatened Cassandra's eyes once again, but she stopped them. The last thing she wanted to do was ruin the final two days of Mac's visit with his parents.

9

"Come on. I want to talk to you for awhile," Mac said, pulling Cassandra out of the Lugot's swimming pool.

"This is so cool. It's weird to look outside and see snow on the ground and I'm in here in my swimsuit." Cassandra wrapped up in her towel and followed Mac to a nearby lounge chair. He sat down and motioned for her to sit next to him. "What is it, Honey?"

"Do you think Nic paid any attention today in church?" Mac asked, deciding to put off the real topic he wished to discuss.

"I don't know. He looked interested."

"I'm hoping he'll talk with me about it before we leave. I talked to Richard this morning about Nic and my parents. He gave me some good advice. He said not to pressure them."

"That sounds like a good idea."

"I also talked to him about you," Mac said. Cassandra looked at him in surprise, but waited for him to continue. "Cassie, I love you and God's given me peace that you are the woman I'm to marry. There are a few things that I feel like we need to discuss, though. I'm concerned about your relationship with God. You don't seem to want a close, personal relationship with Him. Can you tell me why?"

"I wouldn't say that I don't want that kind of relationship. I've just never been able to have it." Cassandra looked down and fidgeted with her swimsuit. If Mac hadn't been preoccupied, he wouldn't have been able to concentrate. This was the first time he'd seen her in a swimsuit.

"If we plan to marry, we're going to have to talk to one another. I want you to tell me what's going on in that head of yours. I want to try and understand you." He lifted her chin so she would look at him.

"I don't know what is wrong with me. Ever since I can remember, I've gone through phases. I try and read my Bible and pray, but I just can't stick with it. I guess I'm just not a very good Christian."

Mac nodded and continued. "Why don't you come to church with me all the time?"

"Maybe I'm just burnt out on church. I've gone all my life and you've only gone for a few months," she said defensively.

"Honey, don't get defensive. I'm not judging you. But I've met a lot of people who've gone to church a lot longer than you, your parents included, who are far from being burnt out. Is that really how you feel?"

Cassandra shook her head and tears filled her eyes. "I don't like going to church anymore because…well…I leave doubting my salvation." She looked down and started fidgeting again.

"Oh, Cassie. Why didn't you tell me?" Mac said as he pulled her close and hugged her.

"I just…I'm supposed to know."

"Tell me about when you got saved," Mac said, pulling away from her so he could see her face.

"That's the problem, Mac. I don't remember. I'm sure I got saved at some point, but I just can't remember. I faintly remember going forward and praying with the Pastor's wife and then the Pastor announced that I got saved. I got baptized after that. It was when I was very young. I have an old lesson that my youth pastor did when I was a senior. It talks about two types of doubting. One type of doubt is from Satan so you don't serve God and the other doubt comes from the Holy Spirit trying to make you realize that you really aren't saved. I go over it and over it. I just keep coming back to that day that I went forward. That makes me think its Satan, but then the doubt always comes back." Cassandra was crying as she choked out the final words. It felt good to talk to someone about the doubts she had been having.

"Maybe we should pray that God would reveal to you where these doubts are coming from," Mac said, taking her hand as they knelt at the lounge chair.

Mac prayed and then Cassandra said a simple prayer. "God will answer our prayers. If you aren't really saved, He will let you know because He wants everyone to accept Him as his or her personal Savior. I hope that God will give you the peace you need soon. I wanted to talk to you about some other things, but I think they can wait. I'd like to give you your gift now." He reached for a small flat box hidden beneath his towel. "Merry Christmas," he said, handing it to her.

Cassandra took the gift and carefully unwrapped it.

"I hope you don't take this long with all your gifts or tomorrow's gift opening will take all day."

Cassandra opened the box and stared at the beautiful diamond necklace and earrings set. "Mac, they're beautiful, but...This is too much. I can't imagine how much they cost."

"And you'll never know. It's a gift. You're not supposed to worry about the cost," Mac said. He watched her finger the heart-shaped ruby ring that he had given her for her birthday in July. He imagined that she was thinking he had already spent too much money on her birthday. "That was your birthday. This is Christmas." She looked at him and back down at the necklace and earrings. "You're not making this very much fun for me."

"I'm sorry. I don't mean to be ungrateful. I love them. Thank you very much. Will you help me put it on?" she asked, picking up the necklace. It was a square diamond solitaire that Cassandra had admired at a jewelry store they had browsed in months before. She put on the matching earrings and stood to find a mirror. They were beautiful. *Far too beautiful for someone like me. I'm not suitable for him.* Cassandra thought as Mrs. Lugot's words ran through her mind. Tears sprang to her eyes, but she willed them to stop before Mac noticed.

"You look beautiful. Do you like them?"

"I love them. Thank you," she said as she turned around and gave him a kiss and a hug. "Open yours now." She handed him the gifts she had bought for him. "It's not much." She felt like the Bible concordance and two ties that she had bought for him were not enough compared to the gift that he had given to her.

"Thank you, Honey. I've had my eye on this," he said, flipping through the concordance. "And I can always use more ties." He glanced at the clock on the wall. "I don't mean to rush, but we should probably get ready for the party."

"I can't believe your parents have a business party on Christmas Eve. I think of Christmas Eve as a time to spend with family and friends. Besides, I don't know what I'll wear."

"Wear your dress you wore to church this morning."

"I'm sure your mother wouldn't approve." Cassandra reluctantly followed Mac to the dressing rooms. They gathered their things and went to their rooms to get ready for the party. Cassandra certainly was not excited about the party. She knew the only dress she had brought was not appropriate. She took a quick shower and started to get ready.

Cassandra heard a knock at her bedroom door as she was applying her makeup. She opened the door a crack and peeked out. There was no one there. She looked down and saw a package with a note attached. She picked it up and closed the door. She sat down on the bed and opened the card. She assumed it was from Mac.

Cassandra,

Although I think you would look beautiful in whatever you decided to wear, my wife was worried about your selection for this evening. I guess she thought you might have neglected to pack your formal gown. I did not tell her that I was doing this, so we can keep it between us and she'll never know. I hope it's the right size. However, don't feel that you have to wear it. The decision is yours.

Sincerely,

Mr. Lugot

Cassandra was shocked. She opened the package and pulled out a gorgeous red evening gown. She held the dress up to her in front of the mirror. It looked like it would fit. Cassandra tore off her robe and quickly tried on the gown. She stood in front of the mirror and admired the gown. It was floor length with a tasteful slit up the left leg. It had a square neckline with spaghetti straps. The gown was accented with beautiful embroidery. Cassandra could not believe her eyes. She walked back over to the box and noticed a matching wrap and shoes. She sat on the edge of the bed for a time, debating about whether she should wear the gown or not. She reread the note and decided to wear it.

Cassandra finished applying her makeup and fixed her hair. She decided to wear it up with a few strands hanging loosely around her face. She was careful not to wrinkle the gown. *I guess I'm ready. As ready as I'll ever be.*

She decided that she wanted Mac's support, but didn't want to be seen by anyone in the hallway. She decided to throw her shoe at his bedroom door to get his attention. She waited a few seconds and threw her other shoe. Mac did not come to the door. He had obviously already gone downstairs.

She grabbed her shoes and retreated to her bedroom once more. *Well, I guess I'm on my own.* She took one last look in the mirror before building up the courage to step out of her bedroom and descend the stairs.

Cassandra walked carefully in the high heels Mr. Lugot had chosen for her. The last thing she wanted to do was trip and make a fool out of herself. As she walked cautiously, yet confidently down the staircase, she noticed that several of the Lugots' guests had arrived. One man spotted Cassandra and she saw him nudge another man standing beside him. It didn't take long before all eyes were on Cassandra and a hushed silence fell across the room. She tried not to notice. She searched the crowd for Mac or Nic or anyone familiar.

The silence must have drawn the Lugots into the foyer. No doubt Mrs. Lugot worried that something at her party had gone horribly wrong. Cassandra wished she could have had a picture of the woman's face when she saw the focus of her guests' attention. When Cassandra reached the bottom of the stairs, she crossed the foyer to where the Lugot family was standing. Mac possessively put his arm around her slim waist.

"You look amazing," he said.

"Cassandra, you look stunning. That is a beautiful dress," Mr. Lugot said politely.

"Oh, thank you."

"Yes, Dear. Wherever did you get it?" Mrs. Lugot questioned.

Cassandra looked at Mr. Lugot, who winked at her. "Well, I like to be prepared," she said simply before turning her attention back to Mac. "I looked for you upstairs."

"I'm sorry I wasn't there. I would have loved to have escorted you down those stairs. I don't want anyone getting any ideas."

"Cassie, you look great. When I overheard everyone talking about the mysterious blonde, I knew it had to be you," Nic said, joining the group.

"Exactly what I was saying," Mac said, tightening his hold on Cassandra.

Cassandra woke up in the middle of the night with the strongest conviction she had ever felt. She looked at the clock. It was only two in the morning. She laid there for a minute wide-awake. Her heart was thundering in her ears. *What is it, Lord? What have I done?* Cassandra prayed and then she remembered the prayer that she and Mac had prayed by the pool. She knew this was her answer. *I'm not saved. Oh, Lord. What will people think? I've claimed to be saved for so long.* Cassandra realized that she had to put her pride aside. Salvation was too important to worry about what people would think.

Cassandra rushed from her room and knocked quietly on Mac's door. It didn't surprise her that he did not answer. She quietly opened the door. Mac was sound asleep in the bed. Cassandra shut the door and walked over to the bed. She gently shook Mac to try and wake him. He mumbled something and rolled over. "Mac," she said quietly, shaking him again.

"What? What is it? Is something wrong? What time is it?" Mac was startled.

"It's just after two."

"You can't open any presents yet," Mac said, pulling the covers over his head.

"God answered our prayer, Mac. I know I'm not saved."

"What?" Mac sat up.

"I'm not saved. Will you pray with me?" Mac nodded and the couple knelt beside the bed. It was then that Cassandra accepted Christ as her Savior. "I'm nervous about telling my parents."

"You know they will be happy for you, Cassie."

"I know. It's just that I've lived a lie."

"You believed you were saved. It takes courage to admit that you were wrong. You could have gone on pretending, but you didn't. That takes courage."

"I guess. I'm going to call my parents first thing in the morning."

"That's a good idea."

"What else did you want to talk to me about today?"

"I'm glad you asked. Now's a good time to talk about it. You know I want to marry you. I think we need to talk about what we expect in a marriage. Hopefully, your salvation will change the concerns that I had before, but I'd still like to talk about them," Mac said. "Maybe it would be best if we went downstairs or something. I'm afraid this situation will be too tempting for me. Especially since we're talking about marriage and everything." Mac took Cassandra's hand and led the way to the downstairs living room.

The couple talked for a long time about what they expected from each other. Mac voiced his concerns about Cassandra's church attendance and involvement, and she assured him that she fully intended to become more active. They talked until almost four o'clock in the morning before they fell asleep on the couch.

"Cassie. Cass. Wake up." Mac was gently shaking her. "I'm trying to make breakfast and I need some serious help."

"Didn't we just fall asleep?"

"About five hours ago. Come on," he said before pulling her up. Cassandra woke up and helped Mac make omelets for everyone.

They had just finished when Mr. and Mrs. Lugot made their appearance, followed by Nic. They were surprised to have breakfast ready because they had given the staff the day off. The breakfast went well and when everyone had finished eating, Cassandra took a few minutes to call her parents and tell them the good news. They were thrilled for her and said that they were very proud. Her mother asked about Mac's parents, but Cassandra said she would have to tell her all about it later. She hung up and joined the Lugots around the Christmas tree in the living room.

The family exchanged gifts and Cassandra was surprised that she was included. The Lugots gave her a sweater. She guessed it was cashmere though she had never actually seen one. Nic gave her a tin of candy with a gift certificate to the mall in Lawrence. What surprised her the most was that Mac had more gifts for her. He gave her a sweatshirt, a compact disc, and a book that she wanted. She was embarrassed that she didn't have any other gifts for him, but Mac didn't seem to mind.

Christmas dinner was spent at Mr. Lugot's parents' house. Cassandra was glad for the homey environment after spending almost ten days at the Lugot mansion. She was sure Mrs. Lugot did not feel the same way about the warm house. The day went by quickly. Cassandra was introduced to several members of Mac's family. She was relieved that none of them seemed to be like Mrs. Lugot.

Cassandra had found herself alone with Nic at one point, and he asked about the incident with his mother. Apparently, the only part he had heard had been about her not being suitable for Mac to marry. Cassandra decided against telling him the rest of the story. She didn't want to cause any problems. In fact, she didn't even know if she would tell Mac about the incident. Nic assured her that no one else felt the way his mother did, and that he was sure his mother would warm up to her soon enough. Cassandra wasn't so sure.

"I'm sorry. Am I interrupting anything?" Damon Lugot asked as he entered the room.

"Oh, no. We were just talking," Nic said. "I'm going to go talk to Aunt Diana."

"Mr. Lugot, I…" Cassandra began.

"Please, call me Damon."

Cassandra relaxed a little bit. "Okay. Damon, I wanted to thank you for last night. You don't know how much I appreciated it."

"Sometimes my wife can be…well…Let's just say that sometimes she needs to be proved wrong. Nic told me what she said to you yesterday morning and I'm truly sorry. I couldn't disagree more. You seem to have made Mac very happy."

"Thank you. I needed to hear that. Should I just leave the gown in my bedroom?"

"Oh, no. It's yours."

"Mr. Lugot—"

"Damon. And no arguments. Besides it wouldn't look as nice on anyone else as it did on you."

Nic and the Lugots drove Mac and Cassandra to the airport early the next morning. The couple flew into the Wichita airport and then drove to the Smith house.

They arrived to find all of the family was there. The Smiths had decided to wait and celebrate Christmas a day later when all of their family could participate. Cassandra was happy to see everyone. It was nice to be surrounded by people that she knew loved her. The family had a wonderful dinner and then they exchanged gifts.

Cassandra planned to stay until the weekend, but Mac was to return to work the next day. He left for Lawrence around nine that evening. The couple said good-bye reluctantly, but Mac assured Cassandra that he would be back on Friday evening. She would miss him terribly, even if it was just for a few days.

After he left, Cassandra helped her mom and Melissa do the dishes and clean the kitchen. "So, are you going to tell us about your trip?" Marlene asked.

"Yeah. How'd it go?" Melissa questioned.

"Okay, I guess. You should see their house. It's a mansion with staff and everything. I was definitely out of my element. It was nice to see Nic again and Mr. Lugot is very nice."

"Is there a Mrs. Lugot?" Marlene asked.

"Yes. There is. She didn't like me very much and made that very clear. She said some terrible things to me on Sunday before Mac, Nic, and I went to church."

"What did Mac do?" Melissa asked.

"He doesn't know. I didn't want to ruin his visit or Christmas. Anyway, let me tell you about Christmas Eve." Cassandra told her mother and her sister about the party and the evening gown that Mr. Lugot had given her. Before they all retired for the evening, Cassandra told them about her trip.

She purposely left out the details of the encounter with Mrs. Lugot.

Cassandra enjoyed the time with her family over the next few days, but Friday evening she waited anxiously for Mac to arrive. She missed him terribly. She didn't want to be away from him ever again.

Cassandra decided that she would be happy when they were married. Every time she thought about marrying Mac, Mrs. Lugot's words rang in her ears. She was beginning to wonder if Mrs. Lugot was right about her not being suitable for Mac. They certainly came from different backgrounds and lifestyles. *He says he wants to marry me, but what if he realizes he wants someone more like his mother. Someone sophisticated and professional. What if she is right?* Cassandra decided that it would be at least another hour before Mac showed up, and she couldn't sit by the door that long. She retreated to her bedroom to study her Bible and spend time in prayer.

When the doorbell rang, Cassandra rushed from her room to answer it. She swung the door open expecting to see Mac. It was Beth. "Oh, hi. I didn't know you were still in town. Come in."

"So, how'd your Christmas go?" Beth asked when she had taken a seat on the couch.

Cassandra noticed that Beth seemed upset, but her hair was hanging in her face so she couldn't really see her eyes. "Okay. How 'bout you? Did your parents meet Tom?"

"Yeah."

"Is something wrong, Beth? You don't seem yourself." Although the girls lived together, they rarely spent time together anymore. Cassandra could still tell something was definitely wrong. "Where is Tom?"

"I don't know," Beth said as she started sobbing.

Cassandra sat next to her friend and pushed her hair back. "Beth! What happened?" she exclaimed when she saw her friend's black eye. Beth didn't say anything. "Did he hit you?" Her friend nodded. "Why? Well, it doesn't matter why. Are you all right?"

"It's my fault. I was talking to Paul," Beth said as a fresh burst of tears streamed down her face.

"That doesn't give him the right to hit you. No one has that right. I'm going to get some ice." Cassandra left her friend and went into the kitchen to get an ice pack. *Lord, help me to handle this in the right way. Give me Your wisdom.* Cassandra wished her mother were there, but her parents had gone on a date. "Here. Hold this on your eye."

"Cassie, I don't know what to do. Tom and I fought at the house when no one was home and he stormed off. I don't know if he's going back to my house or not. I don't want to go back without him. My parents will wonder what happened and how am I going to explain my black eye? How could he do this to me here?"

"Here? Has this happened before, Beth?"

"It's no big deal. Most of the time I deserve it."

"Are you listening to yourself talk? No one deserves to be hit. How long has this been going on?"

"Awhile. Look, I didn't come her to be judged or to have you compare Tom to your precious Mac. I'll just go somewhere else."

"No! I didn't mean to make you feel like I was judging you or comparing Tom and Mac. I'm sorry. I just don't think that you deserve to be hit, no matter what you've done." Cassandra searched for the right words. *How could I have not seen this before? I've neglected our friendship. What do I say?* "Do you want Tom to come back?"

"Of course. I love him and he loves me. We just had an argument, that's all." Beth stopped when the doorbell rang. "Maybe that's him."

"How would he know where I live?" Cassandra asked as she walked toward the door.

"I showed him," Beth said simply.

"It's Mac," Cassandra said. Beth slumped back down on the couch and let her hair fall over her face again. Cassandra opened the door and hugged Mac. "I'm glad you're here. Beth is here," she whispered.

Mac walked into the living room holding Cassandra's hand. "How are you doing, Beth?" he asked politely. Mac could tell from the desperation in Cassandra's voice that something was wrong.

"I'm fine. Can I talk to you alone, Cassie?" she asked as she quickly fled the living room. Cassandra reluctantly followed her. "Don't you say a word to him. He doesn't need to know my business."

"Maybe he could help."

"No! He can't help me. I don't need help." Beth was raising her voice and Cassandra knew that Mac would be full of questions. Again, Beth was interrupted by the doorbell and then pounding on the door. "That's got to be him. Tell him I'm in here," Beth ordered.

Not knowing what else to do, Cassandra did as she was told. Beth was right. Tom was the one pounding on the door. "Where is she?" he ordered, rushing past Cassandra.

"In the kitchen," Cassandra said, pointing toward the hallway that led there. Mac was watching the situation and took a place by Cassandra's side. She followed Tom, hoping to prevent him from hitting Beth again if he was still angry.

Cassandra and Mac stood in the opening to the kitchen. Cassandra was disgusted by what she saw. Tom was apologizing and promising it would never happen again and Beth seemed to eat it up. She glanced at Mac who was obviously bewildered as to what had just happened. She took his hand and led the way back to the living room.

"What is going on in there?" he asked, confused.

"I'll tell you about it later," Cassandra said. She sat on the couch and said nothing else until Tom and Beth appeared.

"We'll be going now," Tom said.

"Beth, I'll be here until tomorrow afternoon, if you need me," Cassandra said lamely.

"She won't," Tom said before closing the door behind them.

"What just happened here?" Mac questioned.

"Tom hit her and she thinks she deserved it. She said this isn't the first time."

Mac sat quietly for a moment. "You're moving out of that apartment."

"No, I'm not!" She stood. "The Lord has shown me that I've neglected her friendship, Mac. I've been so busy with you that I didn't even know she was being abused."

"What can you do about it, Cass?" He paused. "She obviously doesn't think she has a problem." Mac could see that he wasn't going to win this battle and decided to let it go for the time being. "Let's talk about this later. I've missed you," he said as he kissed her hand.

10

Mac dropped Cassandra off at her apartment after church. Classes started again the next day so Cassandra wanted to get a good night's sleep. She had not heard anything from Beth since the incident at her parents' house. Cassandra assumed that Beth would show up sometime tonight if she wasn't already here.

Cassandra had talked to Mac about Beth's situation. He said he honestly couldn't offer any advice on the subject. He suggested that they talk to Pastor Wentworth. Cassandra agreed. Pastor Wentworth told Cassandra to let Beth know she didn't agree with the relationship, but to be supportive and understanding when Beth needed it. He told her that there really wasn't much she could do to help until Beth wanted help. Cassandra had been praying for Beth, hoping that she could somehow be a witness to her. She didn't like the idea of waiting for Beth to ask for help, but she knew she couldn't push her.

Cassandra walked slowly up the stairs to the apartment. She wanted to prepare herself in case Beth was there. She decided she needed to make time for her friend. She knew that Tom wouldn't allow Beth to spend very much time with her, but Cassandra thought a little time together was better than nothing.

Mac's initial reaction had been for Cassandra to move out. He didn't like the idea of her running into Tom. He was afraid that Tom might hurt her. Cassandra had refused to move, arguing that Beth needed her right now and that Tom had never shown violence toward her. Mac agreed, but with the condition that if she ever felt threatened by Tom, she would move.

Cassandra opened the door to the apartment and found Beth and Tom sitting on the couch in the living room. "Hi, guys. I wondered when you would be back."

"You're home early," Beth said.

"Yeah. I've got some things to get ready for classes tomorrow. I'm just going to go change. I'll be right back." Cassandra went to her room and changed out of her church clothes, but by the time she got back, Tom and Beth had evidently gone into Beth's bedroom. Rather than retreat to her own bedroom, she decided to get herself some ice cream and sit in the living room to watch television. She hoped that they would come back out, but they never did. Cassandra gave up and went to bed.

The next morning started Cassandra's new schedule. She hated going back to school. She had successfully scheduled all of her classes so that she would be done every day before noon. She would work afternoons at the firm. There was no sign of Beth or Tom when Cassandra left for school that morning. She knew that they scheduled their classes later so that they didn't have to get up early. Her morning classes went by quickly and she was having lunch with Mac before she knew it.

"So, how'd it go last night?" he asked. "Was Beth home?"

"Yeah. They were there. I said hello and went to change my clothes. When I got back, they were in her bedroom. They didn't come out again. The only way I'm going to be able to reach out to her is when Tom isn't around. He's too possessive and controlling."

"I don't like the guy and I hate that you're living there with him."

"I'm not living with him. That sounds bad. I live with Beth. But I guess you could say Tom is a frequent house-guest." Cassandra tried to make light of the situation. Mac did not appreciate the attempt and frowned at her. "Mac, you never worried about this before."

Mac's hand went to the back of his neck and moved to his temple. It was a move Cassandra knew well by now. He was frustrated. "That was before I knew he was a woman beater," he said dryly.

"Let's talk about something else. How's your day gone?" Cassandra didn't want to talk about Tom anymore. She was actually afraid of him now that she knew he was capable of hitting Beth, but she certainly didn't want Mac to notice. She knew he meant well. He was trying to protect her, but Cassandra was sure Tom would never turn his abuse on her.

Cassandra sat at her computer typing her English Composition paper that was due the next day. She had chosen the subject of abusive relationships. She had been praying for Beth and trying to reach out to her for two months with no response. Beth and Tom were planning to leave for Spring Break the next day after their classes.

Cassandra had become more aware of Beth's bruises that were always explained by a fall or running into a door. She didn't want Beth to go away with Tom. She was beginning to fear for her friend's life. *What if he goes too far? It would only take one time. Lord, please give me the opportunity I need to make Beth realize that Tom is dangerous. Give me the words to say to make her understand. Please help her.*

Cassandra continued to write her paper. She had studied the subject extensively and was able to recognize the pattern that had developed in Tom and Beth's relationship. Tom never failed to apologize and promise it would never happen again after each beating. And Beth was quick to forgive because she loved him. Beth's self-esteem had deteriorated and she was a different person than she had been in high school.

Cassandra was interrupted by the doorbell. She went to the door and looked through the peephole. It was Tom. Cassandra opened the door, "Hi, Tom. Beth's not here right now," she said politely.

Tom pushed past Cassandra. She could smell the alcohol on his clothes. "Where is she?" he slurred.

"She's at work. She should be home soon. You can wait if you want, but I have to work on a paper for English," Cassandra said before turning back to her bedroom. She noticed that Tom followed her.

"Wait. Why are you so quick to run off?" he asked, putting a hand on her shoulder. "You are so hot." Tom looked her up and down and tightened his grip on her arm.

"Let go of me." She tried to pull away from him.

"You think you're so high and mighty. I'll show you," Tom spat angrily in her face.

"Let go of me," she repeated.

Tom did not let go of Cassandra. Suddenly he grabbed her hair and pinned her against the wall. "You walk around here like you're so much better than me."

"Tom, I'm sorry if…" she was silenced by a punch to her eye. She let out a scream that was met with Tom pressing his mouth over hers. The pain was unbearable, but she willed herself not to cry. *Oh Lord, please help me.* Tom continued to kiss her as she tried to push him away. She was able to get one leg free and attempted to kick him. "No, Tom. Stop." This caused Tom to smack her across the face. She screamed again and he dragged her into her bedroom. He threw her on the bed, pinned her down, and covered her mouth with his hand. *Lord, please help me. Please.*

The next few minutes were the worst in Cassandra's life. Tom violated her in almost every way. She tried to fight him off and screamed for help. She thought her screams had gone unanswered when the doorbell rang. It was enough to startle Tom out of his trance and cause him to go out the window and down the fire escape. Cassandra had been saved from having her virginity robbed from her.

Cassandra rolled off of her bed and onto the floor. She reached for her phone and dialed Mac's number. "Mac, please come," she said when he answered and then she hung up. She sat on the floor curled up in a ball and started to sob. She wasn't able to think clearly. The events that had just taken place kept running through her mind.

She was surprised to hear the doorbell ring so soon after her call to Mac.

"Open up. It's the police."

"Oh no," Cassandra whispered and finally allowed herself to cry, but she didn't move for the door. She was too sore in addition to the shame and embarrassment she felt. It didn't take them long to come in and find her. Then the questions began.

When Mac saw the police cars and an ambulance in front of Cassandra's apartment, he didn't bother finding a parking place. He slammed on the brakes and jumped out of his truck. He ran up the flight of stairs and down the hall to her door. A policeman stopped him from entering.

"What's happened? Is she okay?" Mac asked as he tried to see inside.

"Who are you?"

"Her boyfriend."

"Got a name?"

"Mac Lugot," Mac replied, his annoyance more than obvious. "She called me."

"Stay here."

The policeman walked away and Mac took a step inside. He looked around, but didn't see Cassandra or anything to explain what was going on. He watched the policeman enter her bedroom. Mac decided he wasn't going to wait for permission and walked toward her room. He stopped in the doorway when he saw her. *Oh, Lord. Oh, Lord. What has happened to her and why? Don't You take care of Your children?*

She was sitting on her bed wrapped in a blanket. Her hair was tangled and her face was bruised with bandages on her eyebrow and cheekbone. Mac could see that she was trying not to cry. Then she saw him. He watched as she looked down and away from him.

"Cassie, Honey…" he said quietly as he entered the room.

"I told you to wait outside."

Mac ignored the policeman and sat down next to Cassie. He hugged her gently and she began to sob. He held her until he heard Beth's voice. "I'll be right back." He got up and went into the living room.

"What's going on?" Beth said.

"Where's Tom?" Mac asked, his anger obvious.

"I don't know. He's supposed to meet me here. What's wrong?"

"Why don't you come see for yourself? Come see what that jerk did."

"Where do you get off? You have no right to call him a jerk," Beth said angrily.

"Come see what he did to *your friend*," Mac said, grabbing her arm. Beth resisted, but out of curiosity followed Mac.

"Oh, Cassie," Beth said softly, staring at her friend.

"What do you think of him now?" Mac asked angrily. "Do you see, Beth? Do you see?"

Beth broke down in tears. "I'm so sorry. I'm so sorry. You didn't deserve this. It's my fault. I'm sorry." She sat down next to Cassandra and put her arm around her and the girls sobbed together before the police began questioning Beth.

The next few hours were a blur to Cassandra. She was going through the motions, but her mind was elsewhere. Mac had been so quiet and the way he was looking at her when she'd first seen him. *What is he thinking? Is he ashamed of me? Does he think it's my fault?* Her thoughts were interrupted by the nurse telling her to get dressed because she could go home soon. Cassie had not wanted to go to the hospital or the exam. She told them that Tom hadn't actually raped her, but they had still insisted on checking her out. She dressed as quickly as she could attempting to ignore the soreness she felt.

"Cass. It's Mac. Can I come in?"

"Yes," she answered quietly.

"They said I can take you home now. Are you ready?"

Cassandra nodded. He put his arm around her and led her to his truck. They said nothing until he pulled into the parking lot at her apartment building. "I'll go grab some of your things so you can stay at my place. Will you be okay by yourself?"

Cassie nodded, but before Mac shut the door she remembered Beth.

"Beth…she can't stay here alone. What if he…what if he comes back?"

"What? She's partly responsible for this!"

"No. Tom is responsible. What if he comes back to hurt her?"

Mac looked into her eyes. She was in so much pain and she was worrying about her friend. He nodded, willing to do whatever she wanted. "Beth can come with us if she wants."

Mac did not feel like being hospitable to the person who had allowed the man access to his girlfriend, but didn't want to upset Cassandra any more than she was already. Beth had followed them back to the apartment and was just getting out of her car. Mac asked her if she would mind packing some things for Cassandra and the two went upstairs.

Beth packed a small bag for each of them and the group left the apartment. Cassandra still had not talked about what had happened to her. Mac wondered if Tom had raped her in addition to beating her, but didn't want to ask while she was so upset. They all sat quietly on the ride to Mac's house.

When they got there, Mac left Beth in the living room and helped Cassandra upstairs to one of his guest bedrooms.

"I want to take a shower," Cassandra said.

"Do you want to talk about it, Honey?"

"No. No," she said, shaking her head. "Please, I just want to forget about it. Please." Tears welled up in her eyes again.

"Okay, okay. Everything should be in that bathroom for you to take a shower." He pointed across the hall. Mac watched her disappear into the bathroom. He didn't want to let her out of his sight, but felt he had no choice. He walked back downstairs and found Beth sitting on the couch. She was nervously chewing her fingernails. "She wanted to take a shower. I don't think she should be alone. Maybe you should go see if she needs anything."

Beth stood up. "Sure. I'll do anything."

"It's upstairs, second door on the left," Mac said as he sat down. When he was alone, he felt compelled to pray. Mac scoffed at the idea. He was angry. He was angry with Beth and Tom. He was angry with himself for allowing her to stay at the apartment, but most of all he was angry with God. He decided to make some dinner to pass the time.

Upstairs, Cassandra had showered for almost an hour. She and Beth were sitting in the guestroom when Beth broke the silence. "Did he…"

"The doorbell rang," Cassandra said quietly. Both girls sat quietly. Cassandra rehashing the scene in her mind and Beth picturing it. "I'd like to see Mac now."

"Sure," Beth said, walking to the door. "Cassie, I'm sorry that I've been so stupid. Can you ever forgive me?" she asked, turning back to face Cassandra.

"I already have."

Mac showed Beth which bedroom she could use and collected an ice pack for Cassandra's bruised face. "I love you," he said quietly as he took her in his arms.

"I love you too."

"Here, let's put this on your eye to keep the swelling down. I made some lasagna. I could bring you some if you want."

"I'm not really hungry."

"I'm not either. I just needed something to do. Would you like me to call your mom?"

Cassandra shook her head. "Not right now. I just want you to hold me." The couple laid down in the bed and Mac put his arm around her. She rested her head on his shoulder and said a silent prayer. *Dear Heavenly Father, I know you allowed this to happen to answer my prayers for Beth. It's not the way I would have chosen, but I know you're in control. Thank you for not letting him take my purity from me. Help me to trust you.*

"Cassie, can you tell me what happened?" Mac asked, caressing her hair.

"I would rather not talk about it right now."

"Okay. But did he…I mean…did he…" He couldn't even say the words.

"He was going to, but the doorbell rang."

Mac felt relieved, but he was still very upset. He held Cassandra until she fell asleep and then he went to call her parents. "Mr. Smith. It's Mac."

"Is something wrong? You don't sound like yourself."

"Well, sir. Actually something has happened. Cassie was attacked. She's okay. She's here with me, but I'm sure she would like to see her mother."

Mac listened as Curtis directed his wife to pick up the other line. "What happened?"

"I'm sorry I don't know more. She's not really talking about it. She called me and asked me to come over and when I got there the police were already there questioning her. I know it was Beth's boyfriend, Tom. I'm sorry, Mr. and Mrs. Smith."

"Why are you sorry, Mac?" Marlene asked.

"Because I knew that guy was bad news and I let her stay there."

"It isn't your fault Mac. Remember that," Curtis said.

"She's resting now. I'm sure she would love it if you were here when she wakes up."

"Of course. We'll leave right away," Marlene said.

"I'm so sorry."

"You can't blame yourself, Mac. We'll be there as soon as possible," Curtis said.

Mac hung up the phone and checked on Cassandra. She was sleeping soundly so he decided to work in his office while he waited for her parents to arrive. At first he couldn't concentrate, but the alternative was to pray and he wasn't ready to do that. He was too angry. When the doorbell did ring, he was shocked that so much time had passed. He rushed downstairs and opened the door to find the Smiths waiting anxiously.

"Where is she?" Marlene asked.

"She's still sleeping. I'll show you," Mac said as he climbed the stairs. Curtis and Marlene both followed.

Mac opened the door and Marlene gasped at the sight of her daughter. "Oh, my." She walked in and stood over the bed. "I'll just sit here with her."

The men exited and Beth peeked out the door of the bedroom she was staying in. "Oh, Mr. Smith. I'm so sorry," she said as she started to cry again.

"Now Beth. She's going to be okay," he said, embracing the younger girl. "It seems as if everyone is trying to blame themselves and that isn't going to help anything," he said, looking over Beth's shoulder at Mac.

Mac awoke to a scream and rushed to Cassie's room. He opened the door and saw Marlene holding her daughter. "It's okay. It's over, sweetie," she whispered. She looked up at Mac.

"Why don't you get some sleep, Marlene? I'd like to sit with her awhile if that's okay."

"That would be fine." Marlene said a few words to her daughter before rising and exiting the room.

Mac took a seat on the bed next to Cassandra. "I had a nightmare," she whispered as he put his arm around her.

"I imagine you might for awhile."

"Are you okay? You've been so quiet since…"

"Why are you worrying about me? You're the one who's been through a terrible ordeal."

"I just…I don't know. You think this is my fault, don't you?"

"No, Cass. No," he said, pulling back so he could look into her eyes. "I think it's my fault. I shouldn't have let you stay there." He looked down as he thought that he really blamed God. He knew Cassandra would not agree.

She leaned back against his shoulder. "You know, I've been praying Beth would see Tom wasn't good for her, but I had no idea God would answer my prayer like this."

Mac chose to ignore the comment. "I love you. I'm so sorry this happened to you. I hate the thought that you went through that."

They sat quietly for a time. "Thanks for calling my parents."

"Do you want me to get you some water? We should probably put ice on your eye again."

"What are *you* doing here?" Mac asked angrily. He was trying to control himself. He had opened the door thinking it would be Cassie's parents and now Tom was standing not four feet away from him.

"I need to see Beth."

"She doesn't want to see you anymore." Mac paused. "You have some nerve showing up here after what you did. How did you get out anyway?"

"None of your business. Now let me see my girlfriend," Tom snapped.

"You may be used to getting your way, Tom, but it's not going to happen this time. You can't push me around." As Mac said this, he started to shut the door.

"What's wrong?" Beth asked as she came into view.

"Beth! It's Tom. Come out here and talk to me."

Mac closed the door completely and locked it. Tom continued to yell through the door.

"Tom. It's over! I don't want to see you anymore. You need to get some help!" Beth called to him before running up the stairs.

Tom continued to yell until Mac flung the door open and threatened to call the police. He finally left and Mac decided to try and talk to Beth. "Beth, can I come in?" He heard her sobbing, but there was no answer. "Beth?" he tried again. This time she answered him and he slowly entered the bedroom. "Are you okay?"

"I'm so stupid," she choked out.

"No. You're not stupid," Mac said slowly. He didn't know what to do. He stood awkwardly by the bed where she sat. "I've been hard on you and I'm sorry. Tom is the one who is at fault here. You were right. He does need help."

"Do you think he'll get it?" she questioned as tears streamed down her face.

Mac shook his head. "I don't know. He will have to serve some time for his actions. I don't know if he'll get any counseling or not."

"I'm scared," the girl admitted. If she had been honest with herself prior to the incident, she would have said that a long time ago.

"I don't think he'll come back. He can't be out on bail for that long anyway. Don't worry, Beth. You can stay here as long as you need to."

"Thanks."

"Sweetie, Mac is really worried about you since you haven't talked about what happened. Do you want to tell me about it?" Marlene asked her daughter when they were alone two days later.

"No. I just want to forget about it. Isn't that okay?"

"Well, yes. But are you sure you're okay?"

"The pain medicine they gave me is really helping my headache."

"I meant emotionally."

"I'm fine, Mom. Honestly. I've done a lot of praying since it happened. I understand that God's ways aren't always our ways. I believe God allowed this to happen to me so that I could reach Beth. And I'm just praying that He will get glory from it by Beth making a decision for Christ. I'm so thankful that He didn't allow Tom to take my virginity. That's a gift for Mac on our wedding day."

"Anything I should know about?"

"Well, no. We have talked about marriage, but nothing official."

"Let me get those bandages changed." Marlene began removing the bandage from Cassandra's left eyebrow.

"Get me a mirror."

Marlene paused. "Why don't we wait until the swelling goes down some more?" she said calmly as she continued to work. "You should probably rest awhile."

"I've been in bed for two days! I'm ready to get up and do something. At least move downstairs to watch TV."

"I suppose that wouldn't hurt."

Marlene helped her daughter descend the stairs and get comfortable on the couch before leaving her to make lunch. She entered the living room a short time later with some sandwiches and fruit. She smiled when she saw that Cassandra had already fallen asleep. She went back into the kitchen and ate her sandwich. The phone rang just as she was finishing. It was Curtis.

"Did you remember what else you wanted me to pick up at the store? I'm headed in now."

"Oh, yes. Eggs. And bubble bath. I think Cass would enjoy a soak in the tub." Marlene smiled as she saw Beth come in. "Now follow the list I gave you. I'm going to make some of her favorite things while we're here."

"Yes, Dear," Curtis said in mock submission.

The two said good-bye and Marlene turned to Beth. "Care for a sandwich?" The young woman looked unsure. "I made it for Cassie, but she's gone back to sleep. Sit down."

"Oh, Mrs. Smith, how can you be so nice to me?" Beth asked as she blinked back tears. "It is my fault. Yell at me or something. Make me feel bad."

Marlene crossed the kitchen and put her arm around Beth as she led her to a chair. "I know you feel bad, but this wasn't your fault. We can waste a lot of energy trying to place blame on someone or we can accept that nothing happens without God's permission."

"Why would God want Cassie to get hurt?"

"I'm not sure. But I've already seen two blessings since the attack. One is that you are no longer with the fellow that did this and another is the change in Cass. I can see that she's drawing closer to God. That puts joy in my heart. I was really worried about her for a time."

"So you're saying God was in this and that good has come from it."

"Well...yes. Don't misunderstand me. My heart aches for what she went through. But there isn't one thing that happens in the world or the universe that God doesn't know about. Did you know that He knows how many hairs are on your head?" Beth shook her head and Marlene felt free to continue. "Romans 8:28 says *'that all things work together for good to them that love God.'* The *'all'* in that verse includes the good things and the bad."

"I think I see what you mean, but I still feel bad." She paused before adding, "This sandwich is good."

Marlene noticed the change in subject and tone. The door was closed for now. *Cassandra was right. Beth just may be searching and her answer is Jesus Christ.* Marlene said a silent prayer for her to be open and receptive to the Word when the time was right.

11

"Are you coming to pick me up for church?" Cassandra asked Mac.

"No, I've got to work. I'll come by and take you, though." Mac heard Cassandra sigh, but said nothing. It had been one month since that horrible night that Tom attacked Cassandra. Mac had not set foot inside the church since and he didn't plan on going back anytime soon. He had decided he didn't want any part of a God who would allow such a terrible thing to happen to one of His own. Mac had not told Cassandra how he felt. He just pretended that he hadn't been going because it was the final weeks of tax season. He was certain she'd be unhappy if she knew.

"I can drive myself. Do you want to meet for lunch?"

"Sure. I'll come over to your place." Mac hated that Cassandra had decided to stay in her apartment again. It didn't matter to him that Beth had made it clear that she never wanted to see Tom again. Mac insisted that they change the locks on the door and was uncomfortable with the idea of Cassandra ever being alone. He had become more protective than he was before.

They said good-bye and agreed to meet at her apartment at one o'clock that afternoon. *Lord, what is going on with him? I know he's busy, but there's something else. Please work in his heart.* Cassandra went to church by herself. She couldn't stop thinking about Mac. The services ran a half-hour longer than usual so she didn't get back to her apartment until one o'clock.

When Cassandra pulled into the parking lot of her apartment building, she saw Mac's truck. He hopped out and rushed to her car. "Where have you been?"

"Well, hello to you too," Cassandra joked. She could see that Mac did not find it amusing. "Church ran a little long today."

"I was worried about you."

"It's just now one o'clock."

"But you usually get home at twelve-thirty," he said, taking her hand.

They started to walk up to Cassandra's apartment. "You can't worry about me every time I'm a half-hour late, Mac. It's not healthy," she said lightly.

Mac sat down on the couch and waited while Cassandra changed her clothes. "I'm not going to let anything happen to you again," he called to her.

"You didn't *let* anything happen to me. Is that what's wrong with you? You think it was your fault." Cassandra stood in the doorway of her room.

"I shouldn't have let you stay here. And I don't want you staying here now."

"Mac, Honey." Cassandra approached him and sat next to him. "You can not blame yourself for what happened. You had no way of knowing what he was capable of. None of us did."

"Beth did."

"So now it's Beth's fault. Why do we have to blame anyone? It happened. That's the end of it. And I'm not going to live the rest of my life in fear."

"It's not the end, Cassandra." Mac stood up. "It won't ever be over. It's always on my mind. I don't understand how you can go on like nothing happened." He was raising his voice now.

Mac had never raised his voice at Cassandra and it brought tears to her eyes. "Believe me. I will never forget that day. But it won't do any good to dwell on the past or what we could have done differently. You have to let this go, Mac."

"Maybe I could if you would just tell me what happened."

"I have told you what happened. I'm not going to give you all the gory details. It wouldn't do any good. You know what you need to know."

"I don't think so."

"What do you want to know? Do you want to know what he said, where he touched me, how it felt? Well, forget it. I don't want to talk about it." Cassandra was also raising her voice now.

"Fine," Mac said before slamming the front door as he left.

Cassandra let the tears flow. They had never had a fight before and she certainly didn't like it. She cried for awhile before turning to her Lord. *Dear Heavenly Father, help us work through this. Help Mac accept the past and move on. Do I need to tell him what he wants to know? I don't want him to know all the horrible details. Should I tell him? Am I handling this the right way? Lord, I just need help.*

After Cassandra prayed, she made herself a sandwich and tried to watch television. She must have drifted off to sleep because she woke up to the doorbell. She peered through the peephole. It was Mac. She opened the door. "I'm sorry about before," he said quickly.

"I'm sorry too," Cassandra said, accepting his embrace. "I don't like fighting with you."

"Me neither."

The couple didn't talk about the fight anymore that day and Mac even agreed to go to evening church with Cassandra. When they got there, Richard Walker approached Mac and said how much he'd missed him and afterwards the Pastor said the same thing. Cassandra noticed that Mac seemed very uncomfortable, but assumed it was because he hadn't been to church in awhile. Mac dropped Cassandra off after church because he had to go in to work early the next morning.

Cassandra decided to call her mother. They hadn't spoken since her parents had visited after Tom had attacked her. "Hi, mom. Sorry it's been so long since I've called. I've just been busy, I guess."

"I'm glad you called. Are you doing okay? How's Mac?"

"I'm fine. Mac is…well, that's why I called. I need some advice."

"Okay, Dear. It doesn't sound good. Is everything alright?"

"Well, Mac's not been himself lately. Tonight was the first time he'd been to church since you left."

"What?" Marlene sounded shocked.

"Exactly. Anyway, we got in a big fight about the attack today. He wants to know everything and I don't really want to tell him all the horrible details. I think Mac is having a hard time dealing with it and I'm afraid that he hasn't been going to church because he's mad at God. He says it's because he's busy with taxes, but I'm not so sure. Do you think it's just a coincidence that this started around the time Tom attacked me?"

"Well, from what you've said, it sounds like you might be right about Mac's anger. Remember, he wasn't raised in church. He may not understand that bad things happen to Christians too."

"I hadn't thought about it that way."

"Maybe you should try and talk to Mac about the way he's feeling and let him know you're concerned."

"I think I will. Thanks Mom. I just want to avoid another argument. That was our first fight." Cassandra and her mother chatted for awhile before hanging up. Cassandra decided she would try and talk to Mac after tax season was over when he could no longer use that as an excuse.

"Do you remember that day at your parents' house when we talked about what we expected from each other in our marriage?" Cassandra asked Mac. The couple had just gotten back to Mac's house from going to dinner and a movie. It was nearly the end of April and it was the first chance they had to go out on a date. Cassandra had spent many hours in prayer preparing for the confrontation. Mac nodded his head that he remembered and Cassandra continued. "Please don't get upset with me. I'm concerned about you. You haven't been attending church and you refuse to pray with me. I'm getting frustrated. It's almost like our roles have reversed from that day we talked. I know it has something to do with…well…you know. Maybe you could try and explain what you're feeling, why you've changed so drastically."

Cassandra waited for Mac to say something. He was quiet for a moment before he began to speak. "You're right. I've been making excuses. I didn't want to tell you how I really felt because I knew you'd be unhappy." He paused and looked into Cassandra's eyes. "The truth is I don't think I want anything to do with a God who would allow that to happen to one of His children."

"You don't mean that," Cassandra said with a gasp.

"Yes. I do. I just can't understand it."

"Mac, I think you've focused on the negative side of the whole thing."

"You think there's a positive?" Mac was shocked.

"Yes. I had been praying for a way to reach Beth and I have. Since the attack, she's gone to church with me a few times and she's starting to ask questions. And although the experience was horrible, it could have been worse. I thank God that the doorbell rang when it did. It was all part of His plan."

"That may be true, Cassie, but why did His plan have to hurt you?"

"I believe it was the only way to get through to Beth. As long as Tom was just hurting *her*, she could overlook it. But when he hurt me, she realized that he was dangerous." Cassandra could see that she wasn't convincing Mac. "I think this is a situation when growing up in church is useful. I've seen lots of Christians suffer in one way or another throughout the years and how they've reacted to the suffering. Some responded in anger and withdrew from God while others, who I admire, drew closer to Him and their faith was strengthened. I've chosen to draw closer to Him. I trust Him with my life."

Mac thought about what Cassandra said and thought that it did make sense, but he wasn't ready to accept it. "That's fine for you, but not for me.

Not right now."

Cassandra decided not to push the issue. The last thing she wanted was to have an argument with Mac. *What if he never accepts it? Then what? I don't want to spend the rest of my life with someone who isn't serving God. I need a man who will be a spiritual leader for me. Lord please work in his heart.*

July 2000

Mac fingered the engagement ring in his pocket. He had decided it was time to ask Cassandra to marry him. He planned to ask her sometime tonight. It was her birthday. The couple had known each other for almost a year and a half. Mac finally felt that Cassandra was ready to make the commitment and he thought there was no better way to make sure she was taken care of. Mac was surprised that he was nervous. He had planned this evening months in advance.

Mac had decided that the best place to propose would be in their future home. He cooked Cassandra's favorite meal and the couple was enjoying it in his dining room. He'd even made her a birthday cake. Cassandra was surprised by all that he had done for her and enjoyed the evening. Now Mac sat watching her, wondering if now was the right time. He decided that it was.

Mac slid out of his chair and knelt down beside Cassandra. "I love you, Cassie, and I want to spend the rest of my life with you. I've known that for a very long time, almost since we met. I guess what I'm trying to say is will you marry me?" he asked as he took the ring out of his pocket and placed it on Cassandra's finger.

Cassandra's eyes filled with tears. "Mac, it's beautiful," she said, trying to think clearly. Her heart was screaming yes, but her mind was saying no. She couldn't marry Mac now. He still had not turned back to God and Cassandra couldn't allow herself to say yes to that kind of marriage. The last few months had been hard enough trying to serve God alone, without Mac's support. There had been a strain on their relationship because of it. "I can't accept it. I can't marry you right now," she said with tears streaming down her face. Mac was shocked. This was certainly not the response that he had expected. "I'm sorry," Cassandra said before standing and rushing from the room. She took refuge in the nearest bathroom.

Oh, Lord. I want to marry Mac. I do. But I know You don't want me to enter a marriage like that. That can't be Your will for my life. I thought that Mac would turn back to You through my testimony, but it hasn't happened. Please give me your guidance in this. What do I do? Is it fair to continue to date him? Am I leading him on? Will he ever turn back to You? Cassandra prayed silently.

"Cassie?" Mac knocked on the door. She unlocked the door and opened it. "I don't understand," Mac said, searching her face.

"I think we need to talk. Let's go to the living room." Cassandra thought her voice sounded calmer than she felt. When they were seated on the couch, she continued. "Of course you don't understand. I've been unfair to you and I'm sorry. Mac, you know that I love you. I love you so much, but I can't marry you. I don't believe that it's God's will for my life to marry someone who isn't serving Him. I was hoping that through me, you would turn back to God. But since that hasn't happened, I think we need to give each other some time." Cassandra could not believe what she had just said.

"Are you breaking up with me?" Mac asked, shocked.

"I guess I am. I don't think that it's fair to either of us to continue in this relationship. At least not the way it is right now. I'm sorry, Mac. I love you. I hope that we can be together again someday." Cassandra was fighting back tears.

"I don't want to lose you. I'll start going to church again if you want."

"I don't want you to do it for me. You need to do it for you."

"I love you, Cassie." He hugged her tightly. Cassandra could tell that he was crying. It was the first time she'd ever seen him cry.

"I love you too." She held on to him for a moment before pulling away. "I've got to go. I'm sorry."

"Wait," Mac called to her helplessly.

"No, I can't." With that Cassandra rushed from the house and drove back to Jenna's house, where she was staying for the summer. *What have I done? What will I do without him?* Once Cassandra got back to Jenna's house, she went to bed and cried herself to sleep. She cried a lot over the next couple of days. She was thankful that she had the weekend before having to face Mac at work on Monday. He sent her flowers on Saturday, but Cassandra had made up her mind that what she had done was right. Until Mac turned back to God on his own, she was going to have to live without him. She knew Mac was the man she was to marry, so she knew it would happen someday.

Monday morning came too soon for Cassandra. She wondered what it would be like to work with him after breaking up. When she walked in, she didn't peek in and say hello to Mac as she usually did. She immediately asked Jenna for something to do. Jenna was the only person Cassandra had told about the breakup. She wasn't ready to tell her family yet. Cassandra had been there only a few minutes when Mac told Jenna he wanted to see her.

"Good morning," he said when Cassandra walked into his office.

"Good morning."

"Sit down for a few minutes," Mac instructed and she obeyed. "I'm going to get straight to the point. I know this is going to be awkward for us both at first. But I'm going to try my best to treat you the same in the office as I did before and I'd like you to do the same. We've never brought our personal life into the office. I'd like to keep it that way. Does that sound okay with you?"

"Yes."

"Now, I've got a few things that I need you to work on this week."

Cassandra wasn't very surprised at Mac's professionalism, but she was saddened by it. She was still very much in love with him. This was going to be harder than she had first thought. She tried to put it out of her mind and focus on the instructions that Mac was rattling off.

The rest of the day went by quickly. After the initial discussion in Mac's office, the two rarely saw each other. By the end of the day, Cassandra was ready to go back to Jenna's and be alone. She sat in her bedroom and tried to concentrate on a book. Jenna came up a little later with a bouquet of flowers.

"These were delivered for you," she said. Cassandra grabbed the card and read it silently.

Cassie,
I miss you already.
Love,
Mac

Tears filled Cassandra's eyes.

"You're doing the right thing. Marriage is a serious commitment. You both need to be ready, emotionally and spiritually," Jenna said.

"Maybe we could still date," Cassandra said quietly.

"Ask yourself this question. Is the relationship strengthening your Christianity? I wish I'd have asked myself that before I married. I spent years agonizing over my husband's spirituality. I see now how things could have been easier the first years of my marriage had I waited for my husband to get his priorities straight."

Cassandra decided that Jenna was right. Mac needed to grow spiritually and he was going to have to do it on his own.

Cassandra walked toward the front door of the church. She was very nervous. She had never been to a church activity without Mac. The second Sunday after their breakup, Cassandra was invited to attend an activity planned for the college students at the church. They were just supposed to have dinner and play some games, but she was still nervous. She had been so wrapped up with Mac that she hadn't really made any friends at the church. Cassandra walked in the door and went into the fellowship hall where the dinner was to take place. She looked around nervously before taking a seat at an empty table. There were several young men and women that she recognized from the church services milling around.

Cassandra watched nervously as a short, little brunette girl approached her. "Hi. My name is Sarah."

"I'm Cassandra."

"It's nice to have you here. Do you mind if I sit with you?"

"No. Not at all." Cassandra was relieved that she wouldn't be eating alone.

"Kyle, over here." Sarah called to a young man across the room. He made his way over to their table and Sarah made the introductions between Cassandra and her boyfriend, Kyle. It didn't take long after that for their table to fill up and Cassandra sat quietly listening to the group's conversation.

"Are you a student at the University?" Sarah made an attempt to include Cassandra.

"Yeah. I'll be a junior next year."

"Me too. I'm a psych major," Sarah said. "I grew up here. Where are you from?"

Cassandra answered her.

"Do you always stay here during the summer?"

"I have been. I was lucky enough to get a job at an accounting firm here in town my freshman year. My boss wouldn't take it too well if I told him I was taking three months off."

Cassandra attempted to make a joke, though it was only funny to her. She didn't include the fact that her boss would probably let her do whatever she wanted.

The rest of the evening went smoothly. Cassandra warmed up to Sarah right away and was able to relax and enjoy herself. When she left that evening, Cassandra made plans to meet Sarah for lunch the next day. Cassandra was glad for the distraction. It would make it easier since she was used to sharing her lunch with Mac in his office. The girls met at a restaurant not too far from the firm.

"So what happened to that guy that used to come with you?" Sarah questioned. Cassandra didn't answer right away and when Sarah saw tears in her eyes, she apologized. "I shouldn't have asked that. It's none of my business. I'm sorry."

"No, it's okay. Mac and I aren't seeing each other anymore. At least for now. He asked me to marry him and the timing just wasn't right." Cassandra couldn't believe how she was opening up to this girl she barely knew. "You're easy to talk to, Sarah."

"Thanks, I guess. How long had you been seeing each other?"

"A little over a year. I can't believe all that we've been through together." Cassandra shared the story of Mac's salvation and then her own.

"What happened?"

"Well…I'd rather not get specific, but Mac is mad at God. I don't want to serve God alone in a marriage."

"That's wise. My parents are like that. My mom attends church by herself and Dad doesn't want anything to do with Christianity. It's been hard on her. I can see that." The girls sat silently for a moment. "Hey, you don't come to ladies Bible study, do you?"

"No."

"Why don't you come with me sometime? I'm sure you'd enjoy it."

"That's a great idea. I need something to take up my time I used to spend with Mac." Sarah told Cassie that she would be by to pick her up for the next week's study. They continued to make small talk and enjoyed a delicious lunch together. They seemed to have a lot in common and Cassandra felt they were going to become friends.

Cassandra listened to the announcements that Pastor Wentworth made Sunday morning before the services. He caught her attention when he asked for a volunteer to teach the five-year-old Sunday school class. *I've been praying for an area of service, Lord. Is this your answer for me?* Cassandra decided to talk more about it with the Pastor after church. She listened to the sermon and when the final amen was said made her way to the front of the auditorium.

"Pastor…"

"Cassandra, how are you?"

"I'm doing fine, thank you. I was wondering if you would be in prayer about the Sunday school class for me. I think the Lord might be leading me to teach."

"That's wonderful. I will keep you in prayer. Let me know soon, okay?" Cassandra nodded in response. "How is Mac doing? I haven't seen him around."

"Well, we're not seeing each other right now – other than at work."

"Is he okay? I've been praying for him."

"He's fine, but he could use your prayers."

"Maybe I'll pay him a visit. Richard is concerned as well."

They said good-bye and Cassandra drove home to Jenna's house. She wondered if the Pastor and Richard visiting Mac would do any good.

"Jenna," Cassie called as she entered the house.

"I'm in the kitchen." The older lady waited for Cassandra to enter. "I've made some lunch. Would you like some?" The two sat down at the kitchen table. "Mac called for you this morning."

"That's strange. He knows that I go to church. Did he want me to call him back?"

"I don't know."

In truth, Mac had told Jenna not to tell Cassie that he had called. He said it was a moment of weakness and wouldn't know what to say to her anyway.

Jenna was in the business of matchmaking. Neither Mac nor Cassandra had been as happy since the break up. She supposed that it could be for selfish reasons because both young people were confiding in her and she was growing weary.

"Will you go to church with me sometime, Jenna?"

"Oh, Cassie. What made you bring that up again? I've told you that I'm a Christian. I just haven't been real faithful to church. Going to church isn't what makes you a Christian."

"I know. I'd just like you to go with me sometime. You would enjoy it." Cassandra couldn't imagine trying to live a victorious Christian life without the support of fellow believers. "I guess I'll try to call Mac." She dismissed herself and went to her bedroom. She was nervous as she dialed Mac's number wondering why he would have called.

Mac stared at the caller ID on his telephone. Either Jenna had told Cassie that he called and she was calling him back or Jenna was calling. He hesitated before answering. He did want to hear Cassandra's voice.

"Hi, Mac. Jenna said you called me."

"I did. Look. I could make up some excuse, but I'm not going to do that. Can I just be completely honest with you?"

"Of course."

"I miss you. I knew you wouldn't be there, but..."

"It's okay. I have to admit I've called your answering machine a time or two."

"If that's true, why are you doing this?"

"You know why." She paused, not knowing what else to say. "How have you been?"

"I'm not going to make small talk with you, Cassandra. I've got to go."

Cassandra hung up reluctantly. She wanted to tell him that she loved him and they could be together again. She could tell she had hurt his feelings when she changed the subject so quickly. Cassie thanked the Lord when the phone rang and it was Sarah.

"You called at the perfect time. I was about to call Mac and beg him to take me back."

"What?" Cassandra gave Sarah a short version of the conversation she'd just had with Mac. "I see. Well, I actually called to see what you thought about the Sunday school class. I was thinking that we should team-teach or something. What do you think?"

"I've been praying about that very thing."

12

Months had passed since Cassandra broke up with Mac and he didn't seem to be budging. She found herself being talked into a double date with Sarah, Kyle, and his friend, Dennis.

"It will be good for you."

"But Sarah, I'm still in love with Mac. I'm not even interested in Dennis."

"He knows about Mac."

"Then why does he want to date me?"

"Maybe he thinks you're fun to be around."

"I don't think it's a good idea."

"It's just a double date. Come on...please."

Cassandra agreed, ignoring the terrible feeling in the pit of her stomach. Sarah gave instructions to be ready in one hour before hanging up. *What have I done? This is a bad idea. I wouldn't want Mac to date someone else.* She reluctantly dressed for the date and put some finishing touches on her hair and makeup.

By the time she heard the doorbell, Cassandra was ready to get the evening over with. She expected to see Sarah when she looked through the peephole, but it was Dennis. He stood there waiting for her to open the door with a bouquet of flowers. Cassandra let out a sigh before opening the door.

"Hi Dennis."

"Hi. These are for you," he said, handing her the flowers.

"Thank you. Come in. I'll just put these in some water." As she did this, she called to Dennis. "Are Sarah and Kyle waiting for us?"

"They're meeting us at the restaurant," he explained.

Cassandra turned around to face Dennis, silently vowing to have a talk with Sarah. He was handsome, but not as attractive as Mac. He was also very nice and didn't deserve to be compared to Mac all evening. "Dennis, I owe you an apology. This wasn't a very good idea."

"Kyle told me about Mac, Cassie. I'm not trying to take his place. I just want us to go out and have a good time, nothing more."

"So you'll understand if I don't want to do this again."

"Why don't we wait and see how it goes? Is that fair enough?"

Cassandra nodded and the two set out on their date. They arrived at the restaurant and were seated with Sarah and Kyle right away. The four enjoyed a wonderful dinner together. Cassandra was beginning to relax and enjoy herself. As they left the restaurant, the group decided that it would be fun to go bowling.

Dennis opened the door for Cassie when they reached his car. She glanced behind her before climbing in and stopped when she saw him. Mac was watching her from his truck and the pain he felt was visible on his face. "Dennis, I…"

"Go. It's okay. I'll wait here just in case." Dennis had followed her gaze and figured out that the man across the parking lot was the infamous Mac.

Cassandra quickly walked across the parking lot to where Mac sat in his truck. "Mac…It's really not what you think."

Mac shook his head. "I should have known you would move on."

"No. I haven't." She was tongue-tied and couldn't think.

"It doesn't matter. You don't have to answer to me," he said coldly as he started to walk away.

"Wait, please," she called after him. "Mac." Cassandra started following him. "Mac, please listen to me."

Mac turned around and looked past Cassie at the man waiting in the car for her. "You better go. You're ruining your date."

"It isn't a date, not really." She paused. "I'm sorry. Can we go somewhere and talk?"

"I don't think that's what your date had in mind. Besides I have a meeting. Good-bye Cassandra."

Cassandra stood in the middle of the parking lot and watched him walk away. She couldn't make herself move. *What have I done? I've ruined everything. Lord, you tried to tell me not to do this and I did it anyway. Now I've made a mess of things.*

"Get in, Cassie," Dennis commanded, interrupting her prayer. She obeyed. "Do you want me to talk to him?"

"I don't think that's a good idea, but thanks for offering."

She tried to hold back the tears that threatened to fall. "Do you mind if I don't go bowling? I'd just like to go home."

Dennis drove silently to her apartment, not knowing what to say to comfort Cassandra. Kyle had told him about Mac, but conveniently left out that they were *still* in love with each other. Dennis could tell that the couple would get back together and suddenly realized why Cassie hadn't even wanted to go on the date. He dropped her off before heading to the bowling alley to have a talk with his friends.

Mac sat in his office thinking about Cassandra. He had just gotten back from a meeting and ran into Cassandra outside his office. He had managed to avoid her the entire week after seeing her on a date. After seeing her once, he couldn't concentrate on his work anymore. He missed her so much and it hurt knowing she had started dating again. Mac often found an excuse to drive by her apartment and her car was rarely there. She seemed to stay pretty busy. Mac, on the other hand, sat at home watching television and wishing he could call her. He was lonely and it made it worse knowing she wasn't.

When one of Mac's colleagues called to see if he wanted to go for drinks, Mac didn't give it a second thought. He was so bored that he probably would have done anything at that point. When the two men got to the bar, Mac had his first drink in a very long time. It didn't take long for him to have another and another. The next thing he remembered was his friend dropping him off at his house. That was the first of many nights that Mac spent drinking, trying to forget about Cassandra.

November 2000

Cassandra, Beth, and Sarah sat engrossed in the movie they had rented when the doorbell rang. "Who could that be? It's after midnight," Beth said. She looked scared. Tom had tried to contact Beth a few times since their breakup.

"I'll check. It can't be him. He doesn't know where we live, Beth," Cassandra said as she got up to see who was at the door. She heard Beth mumble something about that not stopping Tom as she walked away. "It's Mac," Cassandra whispered. Time had passed quickly after Cassandra made friends at church. She hadn't seen much of Mac. He rarely came out of his office anymore, at least while she was there. She thought that it made it easier for both of them. Her heart still ached for him, but she kept herself busy to dull the pain she felt.

"Aren't you going to answer it?" Sarah asked excitedly. By now Sarah knew the entire story of Cassandra's relationship with Mac.

Cassandra opened the door slowly. "Hello Mac."

"Can we talk?"

"Okay," she said, stepping out into the hallway, closing the door behind her.

"You're not going to invite me in?"

"We're watching a movie. What's wrong?"

"Cassie, I love you. I miss you so much. Can't we start dating again? Just spend some time together," he said as he caressed her cheek.

"Mac…" He leaned toward her then and almost kissed her, but she pulled away when she smelled the alcohol on his breath. "Have you been drinking?" She was shocked.

"A little." Mac had been drinking again for a couple of months now, but he wasn't going to tell Cassandra that. "What do you expect me to do? Sit around the house waiting for you?" he questioned defensively.

"No."

"What do you want from me, Cassandra?"

"I want you to turn back to God. Become involved in church again. That's what I want from you. I need to get back inside," she said, turning away from him.

"Cassie, wait. Come on…" Mac tried to stop her, but Cassandra ignored him and went back inside her apartment. He banged on the door again. "Cass, open the door!" he yelled.

She flung the door open and glared at him. "Mac, it's after midnight. You're drunk, and I'm certainly not going to talk to you when you're like this. Do you need me to call you a cab?"

Mac laughed. "Now you care about me?"

"You know I care about you…"

"I don't need a cab. I can get home," he said angrily as he stomped down the hall.

"Wait… I…I'll…I'll drive you," Cassandra offered reluctantly. She didn't want to be with Mac right now. He was acting like a jerk, but she didn't want him or anyone else to get hurt because he was driving drunk.

Mac stopped and turned back around. "Okay." Cassandra made Mac wait in the hall while she ran in to tell Beth and Sarah where she was going. She came back out with both girls in tow. "You need an escort?" Mac asked, rolling his eyes and started down the hall. The girls followed him and once they reached the parking lot, Beth and Sarah got into Sarah's car. "They're not riding with us?"

"No. How did you expect me to leave your truck for you?" she asked as she climbed into the driver's side of the truck. "Do me a favor and don't talk anymore. You're making me wonder why I love you," she said once he had climbed in the truck.

"I don't understand you."

Cassandra ignored him and drove silently toward his house. At one point he tried to put his arm around her. "Don't touch me," she snapped. Cassandra had never been so angry. When she pulled into his driveway, Mac was asleep. She roused him and walked to the door with him. She unlocked it and handed him the keys.

"Are you coming in?"

Cassandra turned when Sarah's car pulled into the driveway. "Good-bye, Mac," she said simply before leaving.

"What'd he say? What'd he say?" Beth and Sarah asked when she climbed into the car.

Cassandra sat silently for a moment before speaking. "I think I've made a mistake. He's further away from God now than when we broke up and it's my fault. I was so certain that it was God's will for us to break up," she said, shaking her head. "Maybe I should go try to talk to him."

"Cassie, from what you've told me, you were right to break up with Mac. He was bringing you down spiritually," Sarah said wisely. "I mean, look at you now. You're more involved in church activities, you've started teaching in Sunday School, and you're in the ladies Bible study. Would you have been willing to do all that if you were still with Mac?"

"Probably not."

"I think I agree with Sarah. I know you love Mac and if it's meant to be, it will happen someday," Beth chimed in.

The girls drove back to Cassandra's apartment. Sarah could see that her friend was still very upset. "Let's pray about it," Sarah suggested.

The three girls knelt at the couch and prayed for Mac and Cassandra. Cassandra was pleased when Beth took a turn to pray. She had not yet accepted Christ as her Savior, but she was interested. She'd been to church with Cassandra several times since the school year had begun.

When the girls finished, they continued to watch their movie. Cassandra and Sarah didn't realize that Beth wasn't paying any attention. She was still thinking about the prayers that they had said. She had begun to admire Cassandra and Sarah for their faith, and she had just realized that she could have that too. She just needed to ask for it. When the movie was over, Beth shared her feelings with the other two girls and they prayed with her as she accepted Christ as her Savior.

Mac remembered enough about Sunday night to know that he did not want to run into Cassandra anytime soon. He spent the entire week hiding out in his office. As he sat in his office on Friday afternoon, he debated whether it was worth it to leave early if he had to see Cassandra on his way out. *How could I face her? I made an idiot of myself.* He was trying to think of a way to restore his dignity when his phone rang.

"Mac, it's Cassie. Can we talk after work for a few minutes?"

Mac nervously cleared his throat before agreeing. After he hung up, he let out a groan. *Great. Now there's no avoiding her. I wonder what she wants to talk about. Maybe she's taken pity on me after the way I acted.*

Five o'clock came and Cassandra knocked on his office door. "Come in." He watched her walk in and sit down across from him. She started to speak, but he interrupted her. "Before you say anything. I'm sorry about the other night. I was way out of line. It won't happen again."

"It's okay. I wanted to talk to you about that. You know I care about you, Mac. And I worry about you, especially after Sunday night. You haven't exactly reacted to our breakup the way I had planned, but I still feel like I did the right thing. I hate the idea of you drinking again. I just want you to know that I'm here for you if you need me. I'll always be a friend," she said compassionately.

"Cassie, there is no way I could just be friends with you. I'm still in love with you. It would be too painful. It's bad enough working with you."

"It's hard for me too."

"I find that hard to believe…" Mac began. "With all your new friends and everything."

"I have made some new friends at church. I teach the five-year olds in Sunday School and I've started to go to that Ladies Bible Study you tried to get me to go to right after you got saved. And Pastor and Richard ask about you a lot."

"What do you tell them?"

"What should I tell them, Mac?"

"I don't know," he said, shaking his head. "I miss talking with Richard."

"Why don't you call him?"

"And say what? That I turned my back on God when faced with the first trial after I got saved? I already know what he would say to that."

"It's not too late to change. God will still forgive you."

"Forgive me? For being angry because *He* allowed you to get hurt. You didn't deserve that, Cassandra. You didn't. You've stayed pure because that's what the Bible teaches and how did He repay you?"

"Thank the Lord that He *didn't* allow Tom to take my virginity from me. But I'm fine now and have grown spiritually because of it. And Beth got saved. You know that would have never happened had she still been with Tom."

"When did that happen?"

"Sunday after you left." The two were silent for a moment before Cassandra continued. "What is it about it that you can't let go of? I don't understand why if I've accepted it, you can't. Why don't you just give Him another chance? Start coming to church with me again and talk to some people there about some of the things they've been through." Mac was shaking his head no. "Please. Maybe it would help," she pleaded, with tears in her eyes.

"I can't right now. I just can't. Even if I did, it would be for the wrong reasons. I'd only be going for you. If I go back, I want it to be for the right reasons." As he said this, he approached her. "I think my biggest hang up is that God would allow something that terrible to happen to one of His own. I mean, what's next? Isn't He supposed to protect us?"

"You've always been willing to study something you've questioned, Mac. Have you searched the Scriptures? Read the book of Job or about the apostle Paul." Just mentioning the apostle Paul's name got Mac's attention. He had always been intrigued by the story of Paul. Cassandra silently thanked God for giving her the right words to say. "Paul suffered many times for the cause of Christ and he was still faithful."

Mac didn't say anything, but sat down in the chair next to the one in which Cassandra was seated. "You said you missed me the other night," she continued, "well, I miss you too. There's nothing I want more than for us to be together again." Cassandra stood to leave. "Please at least think about what I've said."

"Wait," Mac said quietly, grabbing her hand. Cassandra looked down at him and waited for him to speak. Instead he kissed the back of her hand and held it for a moment.

"I'll see you Monday," she said before leaving. Cassandra wondered if she had gotten through to him. She hoped he would take it upon himself to study the Scriptures. She knew if he did, there was no way he could continue to reject God.

Cassandra drove back to her apartment and told Beth how the conversation had gone. As they were talking, Cassandra realized that Mac probably didn't have any plans for Thanksgiving. She knew that he never visited his parents for Thanksgiving. "Should I invite him to come home with me? I don't want him to spend Thanksgiving alone."

"I think that is up to you," Beth said. "I can't tell you what to do."

"Thanks a lot. You're so much help."

"That's what friends are for," Beth said, laughing.

Cassandra retreated to her bedroom and spent some time in prayer about the issue. She decided that it wouldn't hurt to invite him and he'd probably say no anyway. If he did say yes, they would be going as friends, nothing more. She decided that she would casually invite him sometime the next week at the office.

It turned out that Cassandra never ran into Mac at the office the following week. She didn't know if it was intentional on Mac's part or not. The weekend came and she decided that it would be easier to call and invite him than trying to catch him at work. She was nervous when she dialed his number on Sunday afternoon. When he answered Cassandra could tell that he was shocked to hear her voice.

After the initial introductions were out of the way Cassandra got right to the point. "I was wondering if you would want to go home with me for Thanksgiving."

Mac was silent for a moment. Cassandra assumed that he was too shocked to speak. "As friends or…"

"As friends," Cassandra interrupted.

"Why?"

"Well, I know you don't usually go to Texas for Thanksgiving and I'm sure everyone would love to see you."

"Have you told them about us?"

"I told them we were giving each other some space," she paused, "and that I still plan on marrying you someday."

"Let me think about it. I'll let you know." Cassandra was satisfied with that answer and they said good-bye. Mac called her the next evening to say that he would go with her, and they made arrangements to leave Thanksgiving morning.

The three-hour drive was the hardest part of the holiday. It was hard to find things to talk about. Cassandra ended up doing most of the talking. Mac didn't think Cassandra wanted to know what he had been doing to pass the time since their breakup so he listened to her stories of church, school, and her new friends. Once they arrived at the Smith house, Cassandra helped in the kitchen with the meal and Mac played basketball with Chris and Michael.

While they finished the preparations for Thanksgiving dinner, Marlene and Shannon pumped Cassandra for information. "Are you back together? I didn't know you were bringing him for dinner," Marlene said.

"No. I just felt bad because I knew he would be alone for Thanksgiving."

"So you're just friends?" Shannon asked.

"For right now, anyway. I got a chance to talk to him the other day and he seemed somewhat receptive. I suggested that he study about Paul and how he suffered for the cause of Christ. He didn't say he would, but if I know him like I think I do, he will. I'm sure if he starts reading the Bible again, he will turn back to God."

Thanksgiving went well. Everyone acted like nothing had changed since the last time that Mac had been there. It was not awkward or uncomfortable. The only difference was that Mac and Cassandra barely spoke to one another. Mac had cornered her on Friday evening to request that they leave on Saturday because he didn't want to go to church on Sunday. Cassandra agreed. They left Saturday evening. Mac glanced over to see Cassandra struggling to stay awake.

"You can rest if you want."

She smiled at him. "I am tired."

Mac moved his arm so that she could lay her head on his lap. She thought about it for a moment before lying down. Mac hadn't counted on what being so close to her was doing to his heart. He tried unsuccessfully to think about something else. She slept the rest of the way home so there was no struggle to make conversation.

When he parked his truck at her apartment building he didn't wake her right away. He just looked at her and brushed the hair from her face. *Maybe she is right. There does seem to be some blessings that have come from the whole thing with Tom. Okay Lord, I'm going to read more about Paul. I'm going to try and understand how you could have let Cassandra get hurt.* He was content just to sit and hold her for a time. She started to stir.

"Cass, we're here."

She sat up quickly. "I'm sorry. I guess I was really out."

"Thanks for inviting me. I really enjoyed seeing your family again."

"I'm glad you came."

Mac was staring at her full lips wishing he could kiss her. "Cass..."

She recognized the look in Mac's eyes. "I better get inside." She turned to flee from the truck and the intimate situation they were in, but Mac laid his hand on her arm. Cassandra's heart thundered in her ears as she turned back to look at Mac. She knew if he tried to kiss her that she wouldn't stop him.

Mac searched her face for a sign that a kiss would be accepted. He noticed that her eyes were filled with tears and decided to leave things as they were. "Thanks again."

Cassandra said good night and made her way up the stairs to her apartment. She noticed that Mac watched her until she was inside. Once inside she let the tears slide down her cheeks. *Dear Heavenly Father, I know it's only been five months, but it seems like forever. I miss Mac so much. Please convict his heart. Give him the push he needs to turn back to you, Lord. I love You and I want Your will in my life, but my heart aches for him.* She was interrupted when the phone rang.

"Cassie, it's Jenna. Is your invitation still open to attend church? I think I'd like to go tomorrow."

"Of course, of course. Would you like me to pick you up?"

"No. I don't want to go for Sunday school. I'll just meet you there."

The two arranged for Cassandra to meet Jenna the next day just before the church service so that they could sit together. When Cassandra hung up, her heart was lighter. She had been praying for Jenna to get involved in church. *This just might be the first step.* Jenna was a sweet woman and had become very special to Cassandra. Jenna was saved, but didn't feel the need to serve her Savior. Cassandra didn't understand this, but didn't argue with her friend.

Monday afternoon, Cassandra was excited to go to work. She wanted to talk to Jenna about what she thought of the church services and was curious how Mac would act after their trip to El Dorado for Thanksgiving. She walked in to a smiling Jenna.

"Why are you so happy?"

"Well, someone seems to be a lot happier than I've seen him in months."

"Really? He didn't meet someone else, did he?"

"That's not funny. What happened over Thanksgiving?"

"Nothing," Cassandra said, thinking she wouldn't be able to explain the moment in the truck when they had said good-bye. "So, what'd you think of the services yesterday?"

"I enjoyed it. Everyone is really friendly."

"Do you think you'll visit again?"

"Maybe."

Cassandra could see that Jenna didn't want to discuss it further so she got right to work. She was disappointed that she didn't see Mac the entire afternoon. She wondered if he was avoiding her intentionally. She sat in her cubicle finishing up her work for the day feeling somewhat defeated.

Mac walked out of his office and stopped when he saw Cassandra. She sat in front of her computer typing furiously. She was concentrating so hard that she didn't notice him watching her. She paused a moment and looked at the papers in front of her before continuing. Mac wished she would look up and when she didn't, he decided against saying anything. He had to start accepting their relationship for what it was right now – a friendship. If he entertained thoughts of anything more it caused him more pain. Cassandra had made it clear that they were just friends and it was time he accepted that; at least for now.

Mac stood in an upstairs bedroom watching Pastor Wentworth and Richard Walker approach his front door. *What are they doing here?* He decided not to answer the door. He turned from the window. *What if something has happened to Cassie?* Mac rushed down the stairs and flung open the door. "Pastor, Richard…is something wrong?"

"No, we're just out visiting this evening," Richard said, extending his hand.

Mac shook both men's hands and invited them in. "I must apologize, Mac. I meant to come by sooner," Pastor Wentworth said.

"How are you?" Richard asked warmly.

"I'm okay." Mac led the way to the living room. "Have a seat. Would you like something to drink?"

Both men shook their heads. "We've missed you at church."

Mac looked down at his hands before nodding. He was ashamed and embarrassed. "Actually, I was having trouble accepting something that happened. I didn't understand how God could let one of His own be hurt like that."

"Do you want to talk about it?" Pastor Wentworth asked.

Mac shook his head. "I'm working on it. Cassie gave me a lot to think about a few weeks ago. She challenged me to read more about Paul and I've been doing that." He paused. "Can I just ask you to pray for me?"

"Of course."

13

December 2000

Cassandra and Beth slipped into the pew next to Sarah at church Sunday morning. Cassandra noticed that Beth looked around for Kyle's friend, Matthew, whom she had started dating. Some of the young men in the church had taken an interest in Cassandra, but she hadn't noticed. She was still very much in love with Mac. Keeping busy and making new friends had made the breakup easier for her, but she missed him terribly. Since Thanksgiving, Cassandra had rarely seen Mac. He seemed to stay in his office most of the time.

The services started and Cassandra focused on the sermon until Sarah poked her and whispered. "Isn't that Mac on the back row?"

Cassandra tried not to be obvious as she glanced in the direction Sarah had pointed. She nodded. *Thank you, Lord.* She didn't hear another word of the sermon. She couldn't take her mind off of Mac and why he had decided to come to church. She glanced back at him several times, but never caught his eye. The services couldn't end soon enough for Cassandra. After the Pastor dismissed in prayer, she immediately walked toward where Mac had been sitting, but she was interrupted by one of Kyle's friends that had taken an interest in her.

"Hi, Cassandra. Do you have any plans for lunch?"

"Yes. I mean no." She looked past him and watched Mac walk out the front door. "I mean yes. Look…I'm sorry. I've got to catch someone. I'm sorry, Jason." She rushed past the young man to find Mac. She reached the parking lot and looked around, but there was no sign of him or his truck.

Cassandra didn't know that Mac had spotted her the second he walked in the door that morning and was trying hard not to stare at her. She looked beautiful and he longed to be close to her. He noticed that she was sitting with Beth and another girl he didn't know. He also took notice of several of the young men sitting near Cassandra trying to catch her eye. He watched as she smiled politely at them not seeming to take much notice. His heart sank when after the final Amen he saw a young man approach her and the two began to talk. He wanted to talk to her. He had so much to say, but decided against waiting for her to finish her conversation with the young man.

That evening Cassandra glanced back toward where Mac had sat that morning. He was there again. This time he was looking at her. They smiled at each other. When the service was over Cassandra rushed from the church to the parking lot. Mac was already getting into his truck. "Mac!" Cassandra called to him. "Wait!" Mac left the door open and waited for Cassandra to approach. "You rushed out of here so fast this morning, I didn't get a chance to say hello. We haven't talked in awhile. How are you doing?"

"I'm okay."

"It's nice to see you here." Cassandra wanted to invite Mac to dinner, but decided she couldn't rush into anything. *Attending church one Sunday doesn't mean he's back on track.*

"You look beautiful."

Cassandra blushed slightly. "Thanks."

"Do you think we could go…" Mac stopped when he saw what might be his competition approach.

"Cassie, we're going for pizza. Do you want to come?" Kyle asked as he and the friend who had tried to talk to her that morning walked by on their way to Kyle's car.

Mac suddenly looked uncomfortable and his facial features turned cold. Cassandra hoped that Mac didn't think she was interested in Kyle. "I've got to go." Mac mumbled.

"Tell Sarah I'll meet you there." Cassandra made an effort to explain why two guys would be inviting her for pizza without actually saying anything to Mac. She turned her attention back to Mac. "I'm sorry. Were you going to say something?"

Mac shook his head.

"Maybe I'll run into you tomorrow at work," Mac barely said good-bye before driving away.

The next morning, Cassandra couldn't get to work fast enough. She was hoping that Mac would talk to her more about why he had been at church. She knew that he probably wouldn't discuss it until after hours, but she was hopeful. She was disappointed when she arrived and Jenna said that he wouldn't be in for the day.

"What do you mean he's not coming in? Why not?" she questioned, feeling defeated.

"He called from Texas. Apparently Nic was in a car accident and is in pretty bad shape. I guess he flew out there last night."

"So that's why he was at church yesterday," she said slowly as she took a seat at Jenna's desk. "I hope Nic is okay. Did he say he would call or anything?"

"He said he would," Jenna said and gave Cassandra a big smile. "He also said that he left you a note on his desk."

Cassandra jumped up and rushed into Mac's office. She tore open the envelope that her name was written on and started to read.

Cassie,

I'm starting to understand some of the things you've been trying to explain to me. I've been studying the life of Paul, like you suggested, and I was almost ready to start coming to church again. My father called me yesterday morning to tell me about Nic and said that it didn't look good. I realized that if anyone could help Nic, it was God. I guess the Lord was giving me a push to get in gear. That's why I went to church yesterday. I realized that I'm the only witness my family has and I haven't been doing a very good job lately. Don't misunderstand me, I know I'm not back to where I need to be, but I'm working on it. I know you have every right to see other people, but please don't give up on me.

Love,

Mac

Cassandra sank down in Mac's office chair and cried for a few minutes. This was what she had been waiting for: Mac's repentance. She said a prayer for Nic and Mac before going back to work. She hoped that Mac would call soon so she could talk to him. It was late afternoon before Jenna waved Cassandra over after answering the phone. Jenna talked to him for a few minutes before handing the phone to Cassandra.

"Mac? How's Nic?"

"He's okay, Cassie. He's okay. He was in a coma and I've been praying over him all day. They didn't think he would wake up, but he did. They say it's a miracle, Cass. A miracle!"

Cassandra could hear the excitement in Mac's voice and was excited for him. "That's great. How are *you* doing?"

"I'm okay. I had a lot of time to talk to God today. I asked him to forgive me for the way I've acted, but I think I need to ask for your forgiveness too. I wasn't the man I should have been for you those last few months. I'm sorry, Cass."

"It's okay. I'm just glad everything is going okay down there."

"I haven't told you the best part. Nic is asking how to get saved. He's really interested. I'm hoping I'll have the chance to lead him to the Lord before I have to leave."

"When are you coming home?"

"I'll be home the 26th." He paused for a moment before speaking again. "Listen, I know we're not committed to each other anymore, but something's been bothering me since Sunday. I know it isn't any of my business, but are you seeing someone else?" he asked timidly.

"No. Of course not. They were just friends, Mac."

"Good. I was afraid you'd given up on me. Can I call you later this week?"

"Yes. I want you to. Tell Nic I'm praying for him." They said good-bye and Cassandra reluctantly hung up the phone. She knew that the time between that moment and when she would see him again would seem like an eternity. Jenna sent her home early and Cassandra spent some time in prayer, praising God for answering her prayers for Mac.

"Cassandra, just relax," Marlene Smith scolded her youngest daughter.

"But Mom, I didn't tell him when I was coming here. What if he can't get a hold of me?" Cassandra defended herself. She had been worrying nonstop since she came home the Friday before Christmas. "He said he'd call."

"I'm sure he's busy, that's all. Now take this to your sister. Maybe it will make her feel better." Marlene handed Cassandra a Sprite and saltine crackers. Melissa and Greg had made the announcement that they were expecting, although they didn't really need to announce it. Melissa had been terribly sick every morning since they arrived.

Cassandra did as she was told. She knocked on the bathroom door before entering. Melissa was hovering over the toilet. "Mom thought this might help," she said, offering the Sprite and crackers.

"Thanks." Melissa took them and took a sip of the Sprite. "Just think, this will be you in a couple years."

"I hope not. You look miserable."

"I just keep reminding myself that in seven more months I'll have a baby to hold and that will be worth it all."

"That's a good way to look at it. Shannon was never sick with Matthew, was she?"

"No, but I think she's a little sick with this one. It's going to be neat having babies so close in age. They'll have lots of fun together."

"Yeah." Cassandra sat thinking about that for a moment. Shannon and Melissa were due within weeks of each other. Despite seeing her sister so miserable, Cassandra was actually looking forward to the day when she and Mac would have children of their own.

"Cassandra! Telephone!" Chris yelled.

"That's got to be Mac!" she said before rushing from the bathroom to the phone in her old bedroom. "Mac?"

"Hi. Sorry it's taken me so long to call. Things have been kind of crazy here."

"I was beginning to wonder. How's Nic doing?"

"He's improving. He accepted Christ last night."

"Mac, that's wonderful!"

"I know. I'm so happy for him. My mother isn't too thrilled though."

"I'm sure she's not. What about your father?"

"He doesn't say much. I think he might be interested, but reluctant to ask questions because of my mother. How's your family doing?"

"Everybody's okay. Melissa and Shannon are expecting. They're both due around my birthday. You should see Melissa. She is so sick, poor girl." Cassandra paused for a moment. "I wish you were here with me."

"Me too. I'm not looking forward to the big party tonight without you," Mac said. "Father said he was disappointed that you didn't come with me this year."

"He's nice. I'm sure your mother doesn't miss me at all."

"Why would you say that?"

"Never mind," Cassandra said quickly, regretting the slip of her tongue.

"Is there something you're not telling me?" Mac questioned.

"Maybe. But how did you put it the other day? We're not committed to one another, right? I think that means that I'm allowed to have some secrets."

"For now, for now," Mac said, chuckling. "I better go. I'm going to try to skip the party and spend the evening with Nic at the hospital."

"Please, don't go. I want to talk some more."

"We'll talk again soon, I promise. Tell Mel and Greg and Michael and Shannon congratulations for me."

"Mac..."

"Cassandra Rose Smith, I love you. Merry Christmas."

"Merry Christmas. Call me soon," Cassandra requested before hanging up. She hated being away from him now that she knew they would be getting back together. She put down the phone and lay on her bed thinking about Mac.

She must have fallen asleep because she woke up to her mother calling her name. "I'll be right there, Mom," she said as she got up and straightened her clothes. She combed her hair and freshened up her makeup before descending the stairs and joining the rest of the Smith family for their Christmas Eve celebration.

The family always celebrated Christmas on Christmas Eve because they spent Christmas Day visiting grandparents. Cassandra loved the family traditions that they had become accustomed to. After the dinner, the family would gather around the Christmas tree and Curtis Smith would read them the Christmas story. Then they would open their gifts followed by hot chocolate and desserts. Marlene Smith always made all kinds of desserts and candies for her family to enjoy.

This Christmas Eve was no different. The family enjoyed the dinner before moving into the living room and gathering around the Christmas tree. Cassandra wished that Mac could have been there with her, especially since all of her siblings had significant others with them. Even Chris had invited his new girlfriend, Macy, to join the Smith family for Christmas.

Cassandra watched as her mother handed out the first gifts. They all took turns, youngest to oldest, as they opened them. She was happy with the gifts she had received and excited that everyone seemed pleased with the gifts she had given them.

"Who are those for, Mom?" Chris asked, pointing to packages under the tree after everyone had finished opening all of their gifts.

"Those are for Mac," Marlene replied. "I guess Cassandra will have to take them to him," she said as she looked at her youngest daughter. Marlene felt bad for her. She had talked about Mac nonstop since she came home three days ago. Marlene reached for one of the gifts under the tree. "I guess this one does have Cassandra's name on it," she said before handing it to her daughter.

Marlene watched her daughter's eyes light up when she saw the handwriting on the tag. "It's from Mac!" Cassandra whispered before tearing open the wrapping paper. She opened the box and found a journal. She flipped through it and saw that Mac had written on the first page. Cassandra silently read it's contents.

My Dearest Cassandra,

Words cannot express the love that I have for you or how much I've missed having you in my life over the last few months. You have brought so many wonderful things into my life including Jesus Christ and your loving family. The love, warmth, and support I've received from you and your family is like nothing I'd ever experienced before I met you. You've shown me what a family is supposed to be and I hope that we will someday have our own family together. I know you like to write your thoughts and feelings down on paper so I thought this would be the perfect gift. I hope that you fill it with all kinds of stories of love, warmth, and support between us. I can't promise you that everything in our future will be wonderful, but I'm going to try my hardest to love and cherish you the way that God has commanded me to. I love you Cassandra and I'm anxiously waiting for the day that you become my wife, whenever that may be. Merry Christmas!

With All My Love,

Mac

As Cassandra read, tears filled her eyes.

"Read it out loud," Chris said.

"No way," she said as she stood and exited the living room.

When she was safe in her bedroom, she let the tears slide down her cheeks. *Thank you Lord for this wonderful man You've brought into my life. Thank You for drawing him back to You. Lord, my heart aches for him right now. I miss him terribly. If it is Your will, would You make it possible for us to get married soon? You know that is the desire of my heart, but I want it to happen in Your time, not mine. Give us Your guidance.*

Cassandra heard a knock at her bedroom door. "Cassie, Honey? Can I come in?" Marlene asked quietly.

"Yeah." Marlene walked in and sat down next to her daughter on her bed. "I miss him so much right now. It's hard to believe we've been apart for almost six months and I miss him now more than ever."

"Of course you do, Dear. I think holidays always make people long for their loved ones more than any other time. And it doesn't help that you're getting back together and you can't even see him. He's a wonderful man."

"I'm glad that you think so."

"Why wouldn't I? I knew it would take a special man to claim your heart."

"How did the gift get here?"

"He mailed it with instructions on when to give it to you. It came early last week. He wanted you to be surprised."

"Well, I was definitely surprised. He's supposed to call again soon. He's coming home the day after tomorrow. I wonder if he'll come here or if I should go home tomorrow evening."

"Why don't we just wait and see how things go?"

"I can't wait to see him."

"I know," Marlene said, putting her arm around her daughter and giving her a squeeze. "Are you going to come back down for dessert?" Marlene said before standing. "I made your favorite chocolate covered peanuts."

"Mom, do you think we're ready to get married?"

Marlene sat back down and looked into her daughter's eyes. "Cassie, that's between you, Mac, and God. Anyone can see that you love each other, but only you know your heart. I will tell you what I learned from experience with your father. He was ready long before I was because of our age difference. If I were going to place a bet, I'd bet that Mac has been thinking about marrying you for a very long time – long before he proposed. Your father made it obvious. He proposed every month from the time I met him." Marlene said giggling. "He didn't want me to get away."

"Well, I'm ready. If he asks me again I know I'll say yes. I shocked myself last time when I turned him down."

"But that was a wise decision. You followed God's will, even though it was painful for you. That is what the Lord wants from us. He wants us to seek out His will and in the end we will be happier because of it. God's plan is always the best plan."

"I know. I was just praying about it when you came in. I want to be in God's will for my life. I know from watching you and Dad that I'll be happiest if I follow His plan for my life."

"Oh, Cassandra," Marlene said, her eyes filling with tears.

"Mom, please don't cry."

"I'm just so proud of you. You had us concerned for awhile."

"I'm sorry." Cassie paused. "I let my pride keep me from admitting that I wasn't saved. Praise the Lord He didn't give up on me. Just like He didn't give up on Mac. He was so angry with God for what Tom did. I'm glad that when Mac was faced with this trial, Nic's car accident, he made the right decision. That gives me confidence that he will continue to make the right decisions when faced with a hardship. I want to know that I can count on him when we face trials in our marriage." Marlene didn't say anything for a time. She just thanked God for the way her daughter had turned out.

Marlene hugged her daughter. "I love you."

"I love you too," Cassandra said, returning her mother's embrace. "Well, I guess we should get back downstairs. Besides, candy will make me feel better," Cassandra said, pulling back and smiling at her mother. She left the journal on her nightstand and followed her mother back downstairs to the living room.

Later that night, when Cassandra went to her bedroom to go to bed, she wrote in her journal. She wrote pages on how she felt throughout her separation from Mac and the feelings she was experiencing that night. When she closed her journal that night, she felt better. Cassandra felt that the Lord have given her peace about marrying Mac. Now she wondered how long she would have to wait before Mac asked her to marry him again. She was afraid that he would be hesitant from the fear of being rejected again.

The next morning, the Smith family went to Curtis's parents' house. They ate Christmas dinner there before leaving to visit Marlene's parents. Cassandra was busy throughout the day, but still managed to worry that Mac was trying to call her and she was missing the opportunity to talk to him. They returned to the Smith house that evening and Cassandra debated whether she should drive home to Lawrence or wait for Mac to call her at her parents' house. Her father answered that for her when a snowstorm started and the roads began to get bad.

Cassandra went up to her bedroom and started reading a book. When the phone rang, she jumped to get it. "Hello?"

"Hi. How are you?" Mac asked.

"I miss you. I'm glad you called. I was afraid you'd been calling all day and I missed it. I wanted to go home tonight so I could see you as soon as you got home, but it's snowing here. Dad doesn't want me driving in it."

"I don't want you driving in this either. You stay put and I'll come to you as soon as my plane lands."

"Is it snowing in Texas too?"

Mac hesitated, not wanting to deceive Cassandra. "I'm not sure."

"What? You said you didn't want me driving in *this*, like you knew it was snowing."

"Did I? I just meant I think your dad made the right decision, that's all."

"Oh. Anyway, I got the gift you sent me. Thank you so much."

"I thought you'd enjoy it."

"What you wrote was very sweet."

"I meant every word."

Cassandra heard the doorbell ring. "That's strange. The doorbell just rang. I can't believe someone is out in the middle of this." She knew that someone would answer it so she kept talking. "Mac? Are you there?" she said. There was no answer. "Mac?" Cassandra reluctantly hung up, thinking they had got disconnected. She sat up when she heard a knock on her bedroom door. "Who is it?" she asked. There was no answer, but another knock on the door. She got up and opened the door. "Mac!" Cassandra threw herself into his arms. They held each other for a long time before she pulled away from him. "You tricked me."

"I wanted to surprise you."

"Well, you did. I can't believe you're really here," she said, hugging him again. "We do get to spend part of Christmas together! We've got to go tell everyone you're here!"

"I saw everyone on my way up here. Besides they already knew I was coming," he said smugly.

"What? I don't believe you!" she said, giving him a playful shove.

"I had to make sure this is where you would be. I wanted to be with you on Christmas," he said, grabbing her hands and pulling her toward him again. "I love you, Cassie. You have no idea how much I've missed you."

"I think I do. I know you thought that since I kept busy I didn't miss you, but that's not true. I did miss you and I love you, too." They embraced again.

They didn't let go of each other for a long time. Mac held Cassandra tight, enjoying being close to her again. He buried his face in her long blonde hair, enjoying the smell he had missed for so long. They were content to remain silent and enjoy the closeness for some time. When Mac did pull back, he caressed her face and knelt down and gave her a soft kiss.

"I missed you," he whispered.

14

Cassandra and Mac sat in the living room a few minutes after their initial reunion in her bedroom. Cassandra was glad that her family members had conveniently left them alone. She had heated up some of the leftovers from last night's dinner for Mac since he had not eaten anything.

"This is so good," Mac said, taking a bite of the turkey and gravy. "I left to catch my plane today before my Grandma's turkey was done."

"I'm sorry you missed it." Cassandra felt bad that he had not been able to enjoy what she knew was his favorite part of visiting his parents for Christmas.

"Don't be. I wanted to be here with you. We've been apart long enough," he said, returning to his meal. Cassandra watched him as he continued to eat. "You're making me a little uncomfortable, staring at me while I eat."

"I'm sorry. I guess I can't believe you're really here."

"Well, I am. Now go get me some more tea," he commanded playfully.

"You're so bossy." She did as she was told and returned a few minutes later to find two-year old Matthew in Mac's lap. She stopped at the door and listened to the exchange.

"Does your mommy know where you are?" Mac questioned. Mac watched as Matthew grinned and shook his head no. "I see." Mac noticed that Matthew had his eye on the slice of chocolate pie sitting on the coffee table in front of them. "Do you want some of my pie?" The little boy nodded. Mac was eager to please and started giving Matthew bites of the pie.

"Yummy," Matthew said.

"Yeah, it is, isn't it? What do you think about your mommy having another baby?"

"Puppy."

"I don't think your mommy is going to have a puppy," Mac said, trying hard not to laugh. Matthew smiled and nodded his head vigorously.

The little boy found his book on the end table next to the couch. "Book. Read."

Mac pulled the little boy into his lap. "You want me to read your book." Matthew nodded and Mac began to read aloud.

"Matthew Lane!" Shannon called from the basement. With this, Matthew jumped down from Mac's lap, took a bite of the chocolate pie, and rushed from the room.

He returned long enough to take one last bite of pie. "Bye, Mac," he said with his mouth full.

"Bye, Matthew," Mac said, shaking his head.

Cassandra returned with the glass of tea. "You're good with him, although I doubt Shannon would be giving him chocolate pie this late in the evening."

"You saw his face. He's irresistible," Mac said, accepting the glass. "Thanks."

"I would hate to see you with your own kids."

"You mean, *our* kids," he said, looking at her very seriously. "And I'm sure you'll catch me spoiling them now and then." His tone lightened.

Cassandra smiled shaking her head. "Let me take your plate. Do you want some more pie since Matthew ate most of yours?"

"No, that's okay." Cassandra took his plate to the kitchen and returned to the living room. "Come here." Mac patted the seat beside him on the couch. Cassandra retrieved the gifts under the Christmas tree that were for Mac and took a seat next to him. Mac opened the gift from her, but refused to open the ones from her parents for the time being. "I think we need to talk about our future," he said, looking into her deep blue eyes. She remained silent and waited for him to continue. "I need to know what you're feeling about us right now."

"Well…I guess I assumed we were back together," she said with uncertainty.

"I know, but beyond that. What are you feeling compared to when we broke up? Have your feelings changed?"

"You mean about getting married?"

Mac answered with a nod and he studied her face intently.

"A lot has changed over the last six months," she continued, "but my love for you and my desire to marry you hasn't changed at all. Before when I didn't accept your proposal, it was strange. I even surprised myself. I wanted to say yes, but I couldn't picture my future attending church and serving God by myself. I had peace that we would get back together, but I didn't know when. It was agonizing, but I knew it was God's will. And now... Now that I've seen you turn back to God when faced with another trial, I'm encouraged by it."

"Encouraged?" he questioned, searching her eyes. "What do you mean by that?"

"You made the right choice, Mac, and I'm hoping you'll continue to do that. I think it's time that you tell me how you're feeling. It might make things clearer for me."

"I was wrong. I know I was wrong and I've repented for my anger and the things that I did while I was running from God. He has forgiven me and I'm starting over again. Do you know Psalm 51:10?" Cassandra shook her head no. "It says *Create in me a clean heart, O God, and renew a right spirit within me.* I've prayed that very thing. I disappointed you and I'm so sorry. I'm ashamed that my faith was so weak that after one trial, I ran from God. You were an example for me. God has blessed me so much through you. I thank him every day for bringing you into my life. And now I plan on serving God with my whole heart for the rest of my life."

"Oh, Mac. That's exactly what I hoped you had to say."

"So, you would marry me if I asked again?"

"Yes, *if* you asked again."

"I'm glad to hear that," he said, taking Cassandra in his arms and giving her a warm hug. When they separated they talked about their future for a long time. They had been talking for a couple hours when Mac said something and got no response from Cassandra. She had fallen asleep in his lap. He sat there looking down at her and fingering her blonde curls when Curtis Smith peeked into the room.

"She fell asleep on you, huh?" Curtis whispered.

"Yeah. I don't mind though. Any time with her is better than being apart," Mac said, glancing at the older man before returning his gaze to Cassandra.

"That is exactly how I feel about Marlene. When do you plan on asking her?" Curtis questioned.

Mac's head shot up. "Does that mean I have your blessing, Curtis, even after the way I've acted?" he whispered. Curtis Smith had no idea how much this had been on Mac's mind. Mac had been debating about whether or not her family would accept him after his lack in faith. He had not uttered a word about his doubts, even to Cassandra.

"I don't know the whole story and I don't need to know it. But I do know that if you've asked God's forgiveness and Cassie's than I have no fault with you. I'd be happy to have you as part of the family."

"Thank you, Curtis. I needed to hear that."

"Your welcome, Son." Curtis Smith paused before adding. "I think I'll say good night now."

"Good night," Mac said quietly, returning his attention to Cassandra. *Dear Heavenly Father, thank You so much for bringing Cassandra and her family into my life. Thank You for Your forgiveness. Give me Your guidance as I take the next step. I honestly feel like You've given me peace about marrying Cassie. But when? When is the right time? I would marry her tomorrow if I thought that would be appropriate, but I want your will, not mine. Please give me Your guidance. Amen.*

Mac sat holding Cassandra a few minutes longer before reluctantly carrying her up to her bedroom. He would have held her all night if he could have, but he knew it wasn't a good idea. She roused up as he covered her with a blanket. "I love you," he said, kissing her forehead. Then he went to the bedroom that he always used when he stayed with the Smiths. He was able to fall asleep easily after what had seemed to be a long day.

The next morning, Mac woke up early and got ready to go home. He had been off work for a week and a half and needed to get things ready for the upcoming tax season. It was starting all too quickly for Mac. He knew that the coming weeks would keep him busy, far too busy. He also had some planning to do. After speaking to Curtis last night, Mac had decided that he wanted to propose to Cassandra again very soon.

When he descended the stairs and wandered into the kitchen, Marlene was at the stove making breakfast. "Good morning, Mac." She glanced down at the bag in his hand. "You came a long way to be leaving already."

"I know. I'd like to stay, but I've missed so much work already and with tax season just around the corner…Before Nic's accident, I was only planning to take a couple of days off for Christmas."

"Does Cassie know you're leaving?"

"Not yet. I know she'll want to come with me and there's no sense in her getting up and around this early."

Marlene glanced up at the clock. It was 5:30 a.m.

"For that matter, what are you doing up so early?" Mac questioned.

"With everyone out of the house, I don't cook breakfast very much. I was excited to have so many to cook for this morning. I don't have everything ready, but I could find something for you before you leave."

"No thank you. I think I'll just drink some juice," Mac said, taking the pitcher of orange juice from the refrigerator and pouring himself a glass. "I think I'll run up and say a quick good-bye, if you don't mind."

"That's fine, Mac, although I'm sure she'll jump out of bed to leave with you," Marlene said, smiling as she pictured the scene.

Mac slipped into Cassandra's bedroom and sat down next to where she was sleeping. "Cassandra," he said quietly as he gently stroked her hair. "Cassie." He watched as her eyes peeked open and she smiled at him before closing them again. "I've got to get back to the office."

"No!" she objected as she sat up, suddenly wide-awake. "I want you to stay."

"I can't, Babe. I didn't plan on missing work last week and I've got a lot of catching up to do before tax season starts."

Cassandra started to crawl out of bed. "I'm coming with you then," she said defiantly.

"No," Mac countered, stopping her from getting up.

"But Mac…"

"It's 5:30 in the morning, Cass. There's no reason for you to rush around when I'm just going to work. I want you to go back to sleep and this afternoon when the roads have cleared you can come home." Mac could see that he had disappointed her, but she remained quiet. "Call before you leave and come by the office when you get into town."

"Okay," she said slowly. "But I don't like it."

"I know. I know. I love you and I'll see you soon," Mac said before leaning down to kiss her cheek.

"I love you too." Mac tucked Cassandra back into bed before saying good-bye and exiting the room. He let Marlene know he was leaving before starting the trip home. The three-hour drive gave him plenty of time to pray and think about the plan he was forming.

Mac arrived at the office in good time and was able to work in peace, since the firm was closed. He was the only one working and it reminded him of past years that he spent working through the holidays to avoid the trip to Texas to see his family. He determined in his heart that this would be the last Christmas break that he would be working through. When the next Christmas rolled around, Mac Lugot planned to have a family of his own.

Cassandra called around lunchtime to let him know that she was on her way. Mac worked furiously on the reports in front of him. He wanted to be able to spend the evening with Cassandra. It had been far too long since they had been on a date and Mac intended to make the evening special.

The time passed quickly between Cassandra's phone call and her arrival. She knocked on the open door before entering. Mac stood to greet her. "Hi, Beautiful," he said before hugging her.

"Those *flowers* are beautiful," she said, noticing the arrangement on his desk.

"I'm glad you like them. They're for you."

"You're so sweet," Cassandra said before picking them up to smell them.

"You think I'm sweet now. Just wait until we have dinner," he said with a mischievous grin.

"What are you up to?"

"It's a surprise," Mac said, returning to his office chair. He knew Cassandra wouldn't give up until he revealed his secret, so he changed the subject. "Now sit down and categorize these receipts for me. Here's the categories I need." Mac handed Cassandra a huge pile of receipts.

"I see what's going on here. You're buttering me up so I'll do your dirty work for you," she joked.

"I just want to get out of here in plenty of time to take you to dinner before church."

"I forgot it's Wednesday! We're going to church together! Is that the surprise?" she questioned. Mac frowned at her. "Fine, don't tell me. I don't care," she pouted. Mac laughed at her, shaking his head. Cassandra could tell she wasn't going to get any more information about the surprise so she started the job Mac had given her. "I want you to meet my new friends at church."

"That's a good idea. Be sure and introduce me to all those guys who were falling all over themselves trying to talk to you the other day," Mac said smugly.

"What? What guys?" she asked innocently.

"You've no idea, do you? That's one of the things I love about you. You have no idea what you do to a man's heart." Cassandra started to object but changed her mind, deciding to accept the compliment without argument.

Mac and Cassandra worked until five that afternoon before going their separate ways to freshen up and change for dinner and church. Mac had made reservations for six that evening at one of the finest restaurants in town. It just so happened that it was also the one restaurant that Cassandra had always wanted to go to, but thought it was too expensive.

When they drove into the parking lot, Mac watched Cassandra's face light up. He was hoping she'd be pleased and not worry about the expense.

"Mac! We're not really going to eat here, are we? It's too…"

"Cassandra Rose Smith, I haven't spent money on you in over six months so I don't want to hear a word about it," he said firmly. Cassandra opened her mouth to object again. "I mean it."

Cassandra shut her mouth and allowed herself to be led into the restaurant. It was beautiful. Cassandra assumed that Mac was probably used to such extravagance from his upbringing, but it was entirely new to her. She was thankful she had chosen to wear one of her nicer dresses.

They were immediately taken to their table and after they looked over the menu, Mac ordered for them both. Several times during the course of the meal, Cassandra had to remind herself not to mention the price of the food. She really did enjoy herself although she felt out of her element, much like she had felt at the Lugots' Christmas Eve party the year before.

After their meal, they attended church together. When Cassandra and Mac got there, they slipped into the pew next to Sarah. Cassandra was amused by her friend's look of surprise when she introduced Mac.

"It's nice to finally meet you, Mac. I've heard a lot about you," Sarah said, shaking Mac's hand. Sarah hugged her friend and whispered, "Call me *tonight*!"

Cassandra had not spoken to Sarah since the Sunday evening that Mac had attended church before he left for Texas. She had no idea what all had transpired.

Cassandra also introduced Mac to several of the other young people she had met after her increased involvement in the church. She noticed that Mac made sure to put his arm around her when she introduced him to any young man. It made her feel good that Mac wanted everyone to know they were a couple again.

They settled into their pew when the music started playing. The congregation sang a few hymns before the sermon started. Pastor Wentworth gave an interesting sermon out of I Corinthians. Cassandra was pleased when during the invitation, Mac took her hand and led her to the alter. They knelt and Mac led in a prayer for the future. When he finished, Cassandra said a short prayer of her own before they stood and waited for the service to end.

"Mac, it's good to see you again." Richard Walker approached them with an extended hand.

Mac shook it. "It's good to be back. I was going to try and catch you before we left. Are you still doing the men's Bible study?"

"Yes. In fact, we're starting a new study about Moses next week. You're welcome to come."

"Oh, I'll be there. You can count on that. If you'll excuse me, I need to see Pastor Wentworth for a moment," Mac said before leaving Cassandra and Richard.

Mac approached the Pastor slowly. He hadn't really decided what he wanted to say, but he knew he wanted to say something to the man. Pastor Wentworth stood with his back to Mac reading something. "Pastor Wentworth."

The man turned to face Mac. "Mac! It's good to have you here."

"Thank you, Sir. I'm glad to be back. I…I…I need to apologize to you, Pastor, for the way I've acted over the last few months. I was wrong and I wanted you to know that I've asked God's forgiveness and I plan to serve Him with my whole heart for the rest of my life. Can you forgive me, Sir?"

"You don't need my forgiveness, Mac. But I'm glad to have you back. Do you mind if I asked what made you turn back to God?"

Mac told the Pastor a short version of the story beginning with the things that Cassandra had said shortly before Thanksgiving and ending with Nic's unexpected recovery, leading to his salvation. The church was clearing out and Cassandra decided to join Mac and Pastor Wentworth.

"I'm not interrupting, am I?"

"No, of course not. I was just telling Pastor about everything that brought me back here."

"I'm sure you're happy to have him back, Cassandra."

"Very happy," Cassandra said, smiling shyly.

Mac slipped his arm around Cassandra's slim waist. "Well, I guess we need to go. I've got to get back to the office." Cassandra's disappointment was evident.

"Don't work too hard," Pastor Wentworth said before Mac and Cassandra walked away.

"What do you mean you have to get back to the office?" Cassandra complained when they were in the parking lot.

"I'm sorry, Babe, but I have to go. I want to get caught up so I don't have to go in at all this weekend. You know we're closed Monday and Tuesday for New Year's," Mac said as he opened the truck door for her. He knew that she was upset but decided that she would be more understanding once she knew his intentions for the weekend. He shut the door for her before going around and getting behind the wheel. "Cassie?"

"What?" she snapped.

"I'm sorry that you're upset," Mac tried again.

"I wouldn't be upset if you were putting me before your work. Please, Mac, just spend time with me tonight. I've missed you so much." Her voice softened and even in the dark, Mac could see that tears were threatening to fall.

Mac's heart constricted. The last thing he wanted to do was make her cry, no matter how happy he knew she would be this weekend. "Please don't cry," he said, reaching out to caress her cheek. "Do you want to go to my house for awhile?" Cassandra nodded and they silently drove to Mac's house. By the time they reached his house, Cassandra had relaxed and they were able to enjoy their time together. Mac ended up taking Cassandra home around midnight and heading straight for the office.

"Jenna, I'm so glad you came," Cassandra greeted the older woman the next Sunday at church.

"May I sit with you and Mac?"

"Of course! We're right over here," Cassandra said as she led the way to a pew in middle of the sanctuary. "Mac, look who's here." Mac greeted Jenna warmly and made room for her next to him in the pew.

Now that Cassandra and Mac had been inviting Jenna to church, she could no longer refuse. She knew deep in her heart that she should be attending church, but after her husband died years ago it had been easy to get out of the habit. It caused her tremendous pain to lose her husband and she still struggled with God on why it had to happen.

Jenna really did like the church and the pastor. She found that each time she visited, she left feeling convicted. Today was no exception. Only this time she couldn't ignore it. Pastor Wentworth spoke of God's sovereignty and when the time came for the invitation, Jenna nudged Cassandra and asked her to pray with her.

They knelt at the alter and Cassandra waited for Jenna to speak. "Cassie, I've realized something today. I am still angry with God for taking Trevor from me. That's why I've been disobedient by not attending church or even spending time with Him like I should. I felt He had no right to take Trevor, but He had every right. He had every right," Jenna repeated as she shook her head, tears streaming down her face.

"Would you like to pray and ask for God's forgiveness? Or I could pray first if you want." Jenna didn't answer, but bowed her head and started pouring her heart out to her Savior. Cassandra prayed silently with her.

Houston, Texas

Nic Lugot sat in his hospital bed reading from the Bible that Mac had bought for him before he went back to Kansas. He felt a little overwhelmed by it and had lots of questions. Nic was disappointed that he couldn't leave the hospital before Sunday so that he could attend the church Mac recommended. Nic remembered going there a year ago with Mac and Cassandra. He remembered that day like it was yesterday. He had sat in the pew next to his brother, critically watching everything around him. When the Pastor spoke about salvation, he had become convicted. He had stood holding onto the pew during the invitation, his knuckles white. At the time Nic had thought about what he would have to give up rather than the happiness he'd seen in Mac since his decision for Christ. Nic felt like God had spared his life in the car accident to give him a second chance, and now Nic knew that where he would spend eternity was much more important than parties, drinking, and girls.

"Nic, what are you doing?" Mrs. Lugot questioned when she walked into the room.

"Just reading my Bible."

"Why? You can quit the act. Your brother is gone. Can you believe that he left before Christmas dinner to go see that girl?" she said angrily.

"Mother, it's not an act. I've made a big change in my life by accepting Christ as my Savior. I hope over time you'll see what I'm talking about. As for Cassie, I think you would do well to accept her because I'm certain she is about to become your daughter-in-law," Nic said, trying to remain calm.

"Ha!" Katherine Lugot let out a sarcastic laugh. "I will never allow that to happen. Mac deserves better than that."

"Personally, I think Mac is very lucky to have Cassandra. She's a very sweet young woman. And seeing how he is twenty-seven years old, I don't think you'll have much say in the situation."

"We'll see about that," Mrs. Lugot said hotly. Nic didn't like the way she sounded and was about to say so when she continued. "And about this religion thing. I don't want to hear another word about it. If you think you need this, that's fine, but your father and I don't." Mrs. Lugot's final words were said so harshly that Nic had no idea what to say. His new-found Christianity left him with little knowledge of God's word to counter her remarks.

15

Cassandra dressed carefully for her date with Mac. They were supposed to have dinner before going to a church activity to bring in the New Year. She knew this would be one of the last dates they would have for a while because tax season was starting up again. Mac had been working extra to get caught up so that he could spend the entire weekend with Cassandra. They had spent three wonderful days enjoying one another's company and Cassandra was excited that they would also be spending the next day together. They would both be going back to work on Wednesday.

Mac picked Cassandra up at six o'clock and surprised her by returning to his house. "I thought we were going out to dinner," Cassandra said, getting out of his truck.

"I wanted to cook for you. Come on," Mac said, taking her hand and leading her inside.

Mac led the way to the dining room and helped Cassandra take her seat. Then he brought out the meal that he had prepared for her. It was her favorite, the very same dish he had made for her birthday. Mac had tossed around several ideas on how he wanted to propose to Cassandra for the second time, but he had always came back to his original plan. He didn't think that there was anything more romantic than enjoying a quiet dinner in the home that they would soon share together.

Cassandra didn't put the similarities in the two evenings together and did not suspect that she was about to be proposed to again. It wasn't until after she was finished and Mac knelt next to her chair that she realized what was going on. Tears filled her eyes and threatened to fall.

"Don't cry, Baby. I haven't even said anything yet," Mac said softly as he took her hand in his. "Cassandra Rose Smith, I've never been so in love with anyone in my life. I want to spend the rest of my life with you. Would you do me the honor of becoming my wife?" Mac slipped the ring on her finger and kissed her hand.

Cassandra smiled through her tears. "Yes." She put her arms around Mac's neck and the couple shared a sweet kiss. "I love you."

"I love you too." Mac stood up and took Cassandra in his arms. They held each other for a long time before separating. "How long does it take to plan a wedding?" he questioned. Cassandra responded with a laugh. "I'm serious. I've been looking at the calendar and I want to get married the first Saturday after tax season ends."

"That's not even four months away!" Cassandra exclaimed.

"I don't see any reason why we should wait any longer, do you?" he asked seriously as the two left the dining room and sat on the couch in the living room.

"Well, no. I guess not."

"I'd marry you tomorrow if I could, but I want you to have a wedding and all that."

"I can't believe this. It just doesn't seem real. There's so much to be done. Have you told anyone this?"

"No. Who else needs to know?" Mac joked.

"My parents, your parents. Oh no." Cassandra sighed as she thought about how Mac's mother would respond to the news.

"What is it?"

"Nothing. We just have a lot of work to do," she said simply.

Mac and Cassandra went ahead with their plans for the evening and attended the church activity. The next morning, Cassandra phoned her parents to tell them the news and they congratulated her. Marlene was already making plans by the time that Cassandra hung up the phone.

Houston, Texas

The news was not as well accepted at the Lugot household. When Katherine Lugot hung up the phone after Mac made the announcement, a plan was already forming in her mind. She was disgusted with how happy her husband and Nic were about the upcoming wedding. Katherine wondered why they didn't see that Cassandra Smith was completely wrong for Mac. She had not let Mac know of her feelings, but she planned to do everything in her power to stop this wedding.

"I think it's time I give Abigail a call," Katherine said to herself before picking up her address book and finding the phone number she was looking for.

Cassandra was sitting at Jenna's desk working on a report when Abigail Saxon stepped off the elevator. Cassandra noticed the woman immediately because of her remarkable looks. She tried not to stare as the woman walked toward her, but Cassandra couldn't help herself. The tall woman who approached her had long dark brown hair and deep green eyes. She was dressed in a gorgeous lavender suit that hugged her curvy figure. The short skirt and three-inch heels made her legs seem miles long.

"Is he in?" the woman asked approaching the door to Mac's office.

Cassandra was suddenly very curious about the woman who thought she could barge into Mac's office unannounced. She knew that it probably wasn't any of her business, but she was going to find out who this woman was. "Um. Excuse me. Can I tell him who's here to see him?" she asked as she stood .

The woman gave Cassandra a cocky smile. "Just tell him it's Abby."

Cassandra knew that she could use the intercom system to announce Abby's arrival, but she wanted to find out who this woman was so she decided to go in his office. She shut the door behind her. "There's a woman here to see you."

"Who is it?" Mac questioned impatiently. His annoyance wasn't towards Cassandra, but towards yet another distraction from his work.

"She said just tell him it's Abby."

"Ab...Ab...Abby?" Mac questioned as his head shot up. Cassandra could see that mentioning the woman's name had gotten his attention. "Abby's here?" he asked again. This time he was visibly frustrated as he stood and looked in a mirror that hung on the wall.

"Who's Abby?" Cassandra asked, now more curious than ever. She found it odd that he needed to check the mirror at the mention of her name. Mac's hand went to the back of his neck and then to his temple. "Mac?"

"She's...uh...one of my ex-girlfriends. I haven't seen her in three years. I wonder what she wants." Mac looked as if he were in agony.

"You've never told me about her." Cassandra pointed out the obvious. "Why haven't you told me about her?"

"Cassie, we'll talk about this later. I can't leave her waiting out there," he said sitting back down at his desk. "Send her in," he ordered.

"Mac..." Cassandra stopped when Mac glared at her. "Fine. Fine." Cassandra was not happy about the situation. Mac had been completely open and honest with her about all of his ex-girlfriends, but he had never mentioned anyone named Abby. *Why didn't he tell me about her? And why did he get so flustered at the mention of her name? What is he not telling me?* Cassandra's mind was racing as she led Abby into Mac's office. She watched as the woman hugged Mac and gave him a kiss on the cheek. It was all she could do not to slam the door as she returned to Jenna's desk.

Cassandra became more and more infuriated as she sat listening to the muffled voices and laughter coming from Mac's office. By the time Mac and Abby emerged from the office, Cassandra was completely angry. They were getting married in less than three months and one of Mac's extremely attractive ex-girlfriends had resurfaced. And Mac had spent the last half-hour talking to her.

"So, I'll be by later for dinner," Abby said as she turned toward the elevator.

Cassandra was shocked and shot Mac a dirty look. "I'll see you then," Mac said coolly, not even glancing in Cassandra's direction. Cassandra watched Mac watch Abby until the elevator doors closed.

"You're having her over for dinner?" Cassandra questioned.

"I was going to invite you too," Mac said finally turning his attention to his fiancé.

"I would think so!" Cassandra said rather loudly.

A young woman across the room looked up and stared. Mac noticed and quickly led Cassandra into his office. "What is your problem?" he asked after shutting the door behind them.

"What is *my* problem? I'll tell you what *my* problem is – you," Cassandra said angrily.

"Cassie, you need to calm down," Mac said carefully.

"You're right. I do need to calm down. But I want some answers," she said, taking the seat he offered.

Mac sat down in the chair next to hers. "I was wrong not to tell you about Abby. I was waiting for the right time and well...I'm not sure there is a right time. Abby and I dated for three years while we were in college." Mac paused. He wanted to leave the next part out, but knew it was important to be completely honest with his future wife. "We were engaged." Cassandra's mouth dropped open. "Honey, I told the truth when I said that I never loved anyone the way I love you. My relationship with Abby was nothing like our relationship."

Cassandra wondered if Mac thought that his last statement was supposed to make her feel better about him keeping this from her. She sat in silence for a moment trying to calm down and talk rationally. "Why didn't you tell me?"

"I was afraid of how upset you would be. I'm sorry."

"I can't believe you. You're the one who has always told me to be honest no matter what," Cassandra said, staring into his eyes. "I'm getting out of here," she said as she stood.

"Cassie, wait." Mac put his hand on her arm, but she pulled away. Cassandra rushed to the door and started to open it. "Well, are you coming for dinner?" he called after her.

Cassandra was enraged. "I wouldn't miss it!" She turned back long enough to scream. This time, Cassandra slammed the door without hesitation.

Cassandra had taken some time when she got home from the firm to pray and try to calm down before getting ready to go to Mac's house for dinner. She took extra care getting ready. She chose to wear jeans and the cashmere sweater that the Lugots had given her for Christmas two years before. She knew it would be a failed attempt to look more sophisticated than she was, but she felt the need to try and fit in with Abby.

She had calmed down considerably and even made her way to Mac's house early, hoping they would have time to talk before Abby's arrival. Cassandra let herself into Mac's house and walked toward the kitchen. She stopped short when she heard a woman's voice followed by Mac's laughter. Anger overtook Cassandra again as she stopped in the doorway between the kitchen and the dining room, and watched Mac and Abby cooking dinner together. She watched for some time before Mac finally noticed her.

"Cassie, I wondered when you'd show up," he said warmly, crossing the kitchen and taking her in his arms. "I was worried," Mac whispered. He introduced the two women. Cassandra tried to put her anger aside and be polite.

"Aren't you the secretary?" Abby asked, amused.

The woman's rudeness caught Cassandra off guard. "Well, I do work at the firm. I'm studying accounting at the University."

"You're a student?" Abby continued, and Cassandra nodded. "Did Mac lie about his age or something?" Abby didn't expect an answer. She was already laughing at her own joke.

Cassandra looked at Mac and he returned her gaze. He could see the hurt in her eyes and wished they could be alone. Mac knew he had messed up by not telling Cassandra that he'd been engaged before, but he really hadn't figured out how to tell her.

His relationship with Abigail Saxon had been completely physical. It was based on physical attraction and outward appearances. Mac's parents and Abigail's parents were close friends and had arranged their meeting. Mac had been blown away by Abby's looks and he had become infatuated with her. Looking back, he knew that he had never been in love with Abigail. It had been lust. Now he was left wondering how to explain that to his future wife, who had not yet experienced that type of relationship.

The evening continued with Abby trying to make Cassandra feel inadequate. Cassandra was fuming by the end of the evening. Abby was succeeding in getting under Cassandra's skin. "Could you give me a ride to my hotel, Mac?" Abby asked innocently. "I still can't believe you won't let me stay here. You have such a big house."

Cassandra could not believe what she had just heard. Did Abby really expect to stay with Mac? She watched carefully to see how Mac would handle Abby's comment. Mac glanced at Cassandra before he spoke.

"It wouldn't be appropriate for you to stay with me."

"Oh please. We've done far more than sleep in the same house together," Abby stated, looking at Cassandra. Mac also looked to his future wife, but his was a look of compassion. He was beginning to think that Abigail was purposely trying to hurt Cassandra's feelings. "Your mother told me about your new-found morals," she continued dryly, looking back at Mac.

When Abigail mentioned Mac's mother, Cassandra figured out what was going on. She was certain that Katherine Lugot had sent Abigail to Lawrence to cause trouble.

"It's not just morals. I've accepted Christ as my Savior, Abby," Mac said seriously.

"Whatever. It doesn't matter to me." Abigail stood and took her coat from the nearby closet. "Are you going to give me a ride or not?"

Mac looked at Cassandra. "Do you want to ride along?" He hoped she would say yes so they could talk as soon as he dropped Abigail off.

"I don't think so. I've got some things I need to do at home," Cassandra said. She had no desire to spend anymore time with such a mean-spirited person. She did wonder if she was making a mistake by allowing Mac to drive Abigail to the hotel alone, but pushed the thought away.

They all prepared to leave and Mac walked Cassandra to her car. "Can I come by later?" he asked. Mac planned on visiting Cassandra whether she liked it or not, but he decided to ask anyway. "I'd like to talk."

"Me too," Mac leaned down and gave her a soft kiss before wrapping his arms around her. "I don't think you need to walk her to her room," Cassandra said calmly before he released her.

"I love you."

"I love you."

With that, Cassandra proceeded to get in her car and drive back to her apartment. She kept a close eye on the clock to see if Mac was taking longer than needed just to drop Abigail off. She was thankful when the doorbell rang just twenty minutes after they had separated. Cassandra let Mac in and they settled in the living room before either of them spoke.

"I'm sorry, Cass. I'm sorry I never told you about her. I was wrong and I know that. I'm not going to make excuses as to why I didn't tell you because none of them are good enough. It's just complicated." Mac looked into Cassandra's eyes, trying to read them. He gave up and looked away.

"I guess I don't understand. What makes it so complicated?" Cassandra asked calmly, still not giving away her feelings.

"I told you that my relationship with Abby was nothing like our relationship. I guess it was sort of arranged and expected. I knew I wasn't in love with her, but…Well, she's very attractive. Looking back I think I was just infatuated with her body. I didn't know how to tell you. I was afraid of what you would think of me. I'm ashamed that I stayed with her for so long for the wrong reasons. But like I said before, those are just excuses. I should have told you."

"It's strange that she would show up now. Is she in town on business or something?" Cassandra couldn't shake the feeling that Katherine Lugot had something do with this.

"No." He shook his head. "She's a model in New York. She said she just wanted to visit me."

"Don't you find that odd?"

"Yeah, I guess so."

"I don't like it, Mac. Something is not right here." Cassandra stood up, shaking her head. "How did your mother take the news of our engagement?" she tried again.

"What? What does my mother have to do with this?" Mac asked, shocked by the change in conversation.

"Were Abigail and your mother close?"

"Well, yes. But I don't see what that has to do with why Abby's here." Mac stood up and looked down at Cassandra.

"She said she had talked to your mother. Katherine has never liked me and I'd be willing to bet that she has something to do with this."

"That's ridiculous! My mother has never given me any reason to think she doesn't like you," Mac said, sitting back down on the couch.

"Ask Nic if you don't believe me."

"What does Nic know about it?" Mac took Cassandra's hand and pulled her to a sitting position again. "And why would he know when I don't?" he questioned as he put a finger under Cassandra's chin, forcing her to make eye contact.

"Just forget about it. That's not really the issue. I don't want her around you, that's the issue."

"You don't need to feel threatened by her, Baby. I love you. You know that."

"But you said yourself that you're attracted to her," Cassandra said with tears threatening her eyes.

Mac thought for a moment before he spoke again. "Aren't you attracted to other people?"

"That's different. I've never been intimate with anyone. You spent three years of your life sexually involved with Abby. I'll admit that I'm jealous, Mac. She's shared something with you that I haven't." Cassandra wiped at the tears that were trickling down her cheeks.

Mac took Cassandra in his arms and held her as she cried. He didn't know what to say. He knew that she was right. *Dear Lord, thank You for Cassie. Thank You for her purity. You know that I regret my past and I've repented of that, but I see now that I still have to suffer the consequences of my actions. I've hurt my future wife. She suffers with this every day. I didn't even know Cassie when I was doing those things, but it still affected her. I'm so sorry that I hurt her, Lord. Give me the words to say to ease her mind and the wisdom and guidance on how I'm to handle Abby.*

"Cassie, I won't say that I know what you're feeling because I don't. But I was just praying and thanking God for your purity. I can imagine how I would feel if you had been with other men. I don't want you to worry about Abby. I'm sure she's not planning on staying long."

Cassandra wanted to request that Mac make Abigail leave town, but she knew that Mac had no right to do that. Abigail could travel and visit where she wanted, but she was hoping that Mac would make himself less available to Abigail while she was in town. Cassandra didn't think she needed to request that no more dinner invitations be given, so she just enjoyed being in Mac's arms.

When Mac arrived home that evening, the first thing he did was call his brother. He wanted to get to the bottom of the issue between Cassandra and his mother. Cassandra always changed the subject when he asked her about it and he wondered why she would have opened up to Nic instead of him. Nic answered the phone and Mac didn't waste any time getting to the point.

"What is it that makes Cassie think Mother doesn't like her?"

"Well, what has Cassie told you?" Nic asked. He didn't want to tell Mac anything that Cassandra didn't want him to know. Nic didn't feel that it was his place.

"She said that I should ask you if I didn't believe her," Mac said. "It's not that I don't believe her. It's just that Mother's never said anything to me."

"Well, that time you came for Christmas I overheard Mother say some pretty cruel things to Cassie. She didn't want me to tell you. She said that she would tell you."

"Well she didn't. What did Mother say to her?"

"Something about you being through with Cassie soon enough and that she wasn't suitable for you to marry." Nic knew that Mac was going to be angry with their mother, but he wasn't going to lie to him either.

"What? I can't believe I was never told!"

"I don't think Cassie wanted to ruin your visit. There's something else you should know Mac. Mother has expressed to me that she will do whatever it takes to keep you from marrying Cassie."

"Did she say why she doesn't like Cass?"

"No. I think it has to do with her faith. She's not too happy with me right now either."

"I hadn't thought about how difficult it would be for you. Are they giving you a hard time about your salvation?"

"Mother is, but Father doesn't say much. I have so many questions, Mac. This is all so new to me."

"Is the pastor at the church open to questions?"

"Yes. I think so."

"Give that a try. I've been fortunate to make some friends at the church here and Cassie's family has been great." Mac paused. "I'll try and answer any questions right now, if you want."

Nic took advantage of the opportunity to pick his older brother's brain and started asking all the questions that had come up since he had received Christ as his Savior. He shared with Mac how things were going for him and told about his church involvement. Mac ended the conversation by telling Nic about Abigail Saxon showing up and how Cassandra thought that their mother was involved. Nic noted that he wouldn't put it past her before they hung up.

Mac thought a lot about what his brother had told him and wondered what he should do. He couldn't decide if he should confront his mother or not. Mac was still thinking the situation over when he went to sleep that night.

Mac planned on asking Cassandra about the confrontation between her and his mother before work the next morning, but a fellow partner at the firm approached him as soon as he arrived. Mac was needed in a meeting so he would have to wait to talk to Cassandra. He waved to her before turning to enter the conference room. She smiled at him warmly. Mac found himself counting the days until their wedding as the meeting dragged on.

Cassandra wished she could have at least said hello, but went back to her work. She answered the phone and immediately recognized Abby's voice when she asked to speak with Mac. "I'm sorry, Abby. Mac's in a meeting right now," Cassandra said politely and confidently. She had done a lot of praying the night before and decided that she was not going to let Abigail Saxon intimidate her anymore.

"You wouldn't be trying to keep me from talking to him, would you Cassandra?" Abigail asked pointedly.

"No, Abby. It's obvious that you don't know me very well," Cassandra was shocked by the accusation. "I have no problem with Mac talking with you," she continued honestly. *It's more than talking that worries me.* "I can leave a message for him if you'd like."

Abigail did leave a message for Mac to call her as soon as possible before hanging up. Cassandra wondered what she had planned for Mac this time.

16

Cassandra handed Mac the message that Abigail had left as soon as he approached Jenna's desk. Mac took it as he whispered, "Come with me." He led the way into his office and closed the door behind them. Once they were alone, he pulled her into his arms and hugged her. "I was just counting the days until our wedding. I can't wait to make you mine," he said before kissing her sweetly.

"Mac! We're in the office," she teased as she pulled out of his grasp. Mac didn't usually show her any special affection while they were at work.

"I don't care. I love you," Mac said, pulling her close again.

"What's gotten into you?" Cassandra teased him while escaping his grasp again. "Look at your message," she added. Mac read it and smiled. "What are you smiling at?" Cassandra was annoyed by his look of pleasure.

"You. You could have kept it from me but you didn't."

"I wouldn't do that. I did a lot of praying last night and I'm not going to let her intimidate me anymore." Cassandra's chin rose.

"I'm glad to hear that." Mac glanced down at the note in his hand. "I wonder what she wants now. I guess I should call her." Mac smiled hugely as he looked at Cassandra, who was now trying to look busy so he wouldn't dismiss her.

He picked up the phone and dialed the hotel number Abigail had left. "What do you need, Abby?" Mac questioned easily. Cassandra wished she could hear what the woman's response was, but settled for listening to Mac's end of the conversation. "I don't know," Mac said as he glanced Cassandra's direction. Mac was silent again for a time. Cassandra noticed his hand going to the back of his neck and then to his temple. It was the gesture he always made when he was frustrated. "Well, I guess that would be okay. I'll be there to pick you up." Mac looked at Cassandra as he said this, taking in her reaction.

"What now?" Cassandra questioned as soon as he hung up.

"She wants us to go to lunch."

"Us or you?" She knew the answer, but wanted to hear Mac say it. "Did she invite you or us both?"

"Well, me, I guess. But I'm sure she meant to include you," Mac said lamely. Cassandra rolled her eyes. "I started to decline but she reminded me that she came to visit me and had no other reason to be in town."

"Exactly."

"What do you want me do, Cassie? Let her sit in the hotel by herself?"

"That wouldn't be so bad. Mac, if you didn't make yourself available to her, I'm sure she would be on her way. I know she's here to try and break us up – thanks to your mother - and if you leave the door open, she'll keep trying until she succeeds." Cassandra was successful in remaining calm.

"I'm glad you mentioned my mother. I was going to ask you about that. Why didn't you tell me what happened?"

"You talked to Nic?" Mac answered with a nod. "I just didn't want to ruin your Christmas with your family. Besides, if I didn't say anything I could pretend it didn't happen. She was so mean, Mac. Saying I turned you into a religious nut, prude, and not suitable to marry. I…"

"What? Nic didn't tell me all that. What did she say?"

"It really doesn't matter now. It was so long ago." Cassandra tried to get around recounting the conversation. The truth was, she didn't like to think about it anymore than she knew Mac would want to hear about it.

"Cassandra." The firmness in Mac's voice made her continue without argument. She remembered every detail of her conversation with Mrs. Lugot and relayed it to Mac. She watched as his face grew more red with anger with every sentence. "I can't believe her! I'm going to call her as soon as I get home from work and give her a piece of my mind."

"Mac, I'm not sure that is the best thing to do. Think about your testimony." She stood behind Mac now, rubbing his shoulders as he sat in his office chair.

"You may be right. But I think I should stand up for my future wife, don't you? Maybe I need to think about what I can say and still be respectful to my mother." The last sentence was spoken softly, almost to himself.

"I need to get back to work," Cassandra said, starting to walk away.

"Wait. Are you coming to lunch with Abby?"

"I really don't feel like being insulted today," Cassandra replied.

"Well, what am I supposed to do? I already told her we were going."

"If I remember right, you said you would be there to pick her up. You didn't say anything about me coming along. Do whatever you want to do." Cassandra was surprised at her calmness. She knew that Mac could call and cancel the lunch, but she also knew that he wouldn't do that. "Just don't come back here apologizing, claiming things got out of hand." Cassandra turned to leave, but turned back to continue. "That is what she's after, you know."

Mac raised his eyebrows. "I don't think *that's* what she wants."

"Don't be so sure," Cassandra said before turning to leave Mac's office. She surprised herself with how she had handled the situation. She knew she had God to thank for her calmness. Although she wasn't happy that Mac felt he needed to entertain this woman, Cassandra had decided that she wasn't going to allow herself to get overly upset about it either.

Mac sat in his office staring at the door Cassandra had just disappeared through. He couldn't believe how calm she had been and she practically gave him permission to go to lunch with Abigail. He wondered why Cassandra felt like Abigail wanted to get him into bed. He hadn't even given that a thought. He decided that he would ask Cassandra about it later. Right now he had work to do.

Mac came out of his office at noon to go to lunch. "What are you going to do for lunch?" Cassandra responded by pulling out a brown paper sack that contained her sandwich and chips. "Please come with me."

"I don't think so. I think you need to see what she's trying to do and that's only going to happen if you're alone," Cassandra said confidently.

"Why are you so sure that is why she's here?" he asked kneeling down next to her chair.

"Because I think your mother sent her here to cause problems between us and that would *definitely* cause problems between us."

"Do you really think that my mother is involved in this?" Cassandra answered with a look. "I think you've got this all wrong," Mac said, shaking his head. "I guess I should go. I love you."

"I love you too." Mac stood and crossed to the elevator. He looked back at Cassandra before getting on it. "Just remember what I said before," she added before taking out her sandwich.

Mac drove to Abby's hotel hoping she would be waiting in the lobby. He sat in the lobby for awhile before finally approaching the front desk and asking to call Abigail's room. "Are you coming down?"

"I'm not quite ready yet. Come on up."

Abigail gave Mac no chance to argue so he reluctantly boarded the elevator and made his way to her room. He knocked quietly wondering what Cassandra would think about this. There was no answer so Mac knocked again a little louder. Abigail came to the door and invited him in to wait. "I think I'll just wait out here," he said swiftly.

"Oh, please, Mac. Are we not friends?" Abigail Saxon was obviously annoyed. Mac looked at her nervously. "Get in here."

Mac walked in and sat down on the sofa. Abigail disappeared through some double doors. Mac assumed it was the bedroom. She made light conversation with him from the other room. When she was ready, she came out and sat on the couch next to Mac. "Are you ready?"

"Why are you so scared to be alone with me?" Abigail paused for a second before guessing. "You're afraid that Cassandra will find out. I won't tell if you don't."

"I'm not scared to be alone with you, Abby. I just don't think that it's necessary, that's all. It doesn't look good." Mac stood up and walked toward the door.

"When did you start caring so much about what things looked like? You really do care too much what people think. Is that Cassandra's influence?"

"It's not that." Mac had his hand on the doorknob, but turned back toward her again. "Since I got saved, I have a responsibility to be a good witness to others." Abigail rolled her eyes. "Why are you here?"

"What do you mean? I came to visit you." Abigail stood and sauntered toward him.

"But why? It's been more than three years. Why now?"

"Well, I guess I found out you were getting married and didn't like it." Abigail placed her arms around Mac's neck and leaned toward him.

Mac placed Abigail's arms back at her side and took a step back. "Did my mother send you?" The shock in Abigail's face gave him his answer. "She wanted you to cause problems, is that it? What exactly was your plan, Abigail? Surely you think more of yourself than to come down here for a one night stand." Mac was angry now. He was angry with his mother and the woman who stood in front of him.

"It's not like I wouldn't have enjoyed it." Abigail attempted to touch Mac's face, but he evaded her move. "Look, I'm bored with this. It's obvious to me that you are in love with this Cassandra person. And she seems nice enough if you like that wholesome thing." Mac started to interrupt her, but she continued. "I don't think your mother realizes how serious you are about her. She fully expected me to be able to come here and steal your heart away. And I must say that I'm surprised that you've resisted me. Things have definitely changed since the old days."

"You're right about that. *I've* changed." Mac turned and grabbed the doorknob again. "Good-bye, Abigail," he said before exiting the hotel room. He drove back to the office in a rage, anxious to call his mother and let her know how he felt.

He stepped off the elevator and Cassandra's head shot up. She could see that he was angry and followed him into his office. He sat down at his desk in a huff. "You were right about them both."

Cassandra knelt down in front of him and remained quiet for a moment before speaking. "Do you want to share my sandwich?" Cassandra asked. Mac looked surprised, but he knew she wasn't the type to say 'I told you so.' "I have a little left," she continued.

"I love you," Mac said, shaking his head, his anger toward his mother and Abigail temporarily forgotten.

"I'll get my sandwich," Cassandra said, exiting Mac's office.

"Oh, Cassie. I'm glad you're here. I must speak to you and Mac," Jenna said. "Is he available?"

"Yes. Go on in. I'm trying to find something for him to eat."

"I'll wait for you. I have some news." Cassandra was all ears. Jenna had gone to lunch with Mr. Deerborn from church. The two seemed to be getting rather friendly. Jenna noticed Cassandra had stopped and was staring at her. "Go on. Hurry."

Cassandra quickly found her sandwich she intended to share with Mac and bought him some chips out of the snack machine. "Let's go."

"You're back early, Jenna," Mac said as he greeted her.

"And she has news," Cassandra said teasingly.

"Now you just stop it, Cassandra," she said before turning back to her boss. "Joe and I have decided to get married." Jenna ignored Cassie's gasp and continued. "We will marry next Wednesday at the court house. I want you two to be there."

"Oh, Jenna, that's wonderful!" Cassandra exclaimed.

"I'm very happy for you," Mac said. "But why the rush?"

"Well, we've both had a big wedding in our life. We decided we didn't need another one. A quiet, simple ceremony is what we both want."

"This is so romantic. It has happened so fast," Cassandra added.

"I know, but we've been praying about it." The three of them were silent for some time before Jenna found the courage she needed to continue. "I knew you would be happy for me. But there is something else."

"What is it?"

"We'll be moving to Florida. I will finish the tax season with you and then we'll be leaving."

"Oh." Cassandra's face fell. "I will miss you so much."

"I will miss you too, Dear."

Jenna looked at Mac, waiting for him to respond. She had been his secretary since he started at the firm several years ago. In many ways, she felt as if Mac were her own son. He had always confided in her and sought her advice. "Are you upset, Mac?"

"No," he said slowly. "I'm very happy for you. I just can't imagine this place without you here. You haven't just been a wonderful secretary to me over the years, but so much more." This was an understatement and Mac knew it. Jenna was his other mother. "Cassandra and I will just have to plan on visiting you."

"Mother…I want to talk to you about Cassandra."

Mrs. Lugot sighed.

"I love her very much and it's time you accept that. She will be your daughter-in-law in a few months whether you like it or not." Mac paused. "She told me the things that you said to her when we visited. And I can't even believe that you sent Abby here. What were you thinking?"

Mac had waited a few weeks before calling his mother to discuss the situation with Abby. He had decided that he was just too angry to call as soon as he'd found out about her involvement in sending Abby to Lawrence to cause trouble.

"That you could do better, of course. Cassandra is so…so…"

"Don't. I don't want to hear it."

"Mac, I just hope you've thought this through."

"I spent a lot of time in prayer about this."

"Don't start that again."

"I'm sorry you can't accept that I've changed, but I hope that you will eventually." Mac silently prayed for the right words to express his feelings without destroying his Christian testimony.

"Don't worry. I won't bother Cassandra or you anymore."

Mac and his mother said good-bye before ending their phone call. He hated leaving things on such bad terms, but felt that his mother had given him no choice. Mac knelt down beside his bed and prayed for his mother and Cassandra. He wanted his mother and future wife to love each other. He was interrupted when the doorbell rang.

"Hi Baby," Mac said as he opened the door and hugged Cassie. "I just got off the phone with my mother."

"You confronted her?" Cassandra pulled back and looked at him.

Mac took her hand and led her into the living room. "Yes, but I don't know that it did much good. She did say she wouldn't bother us anymore, but she didn't apologize. I was just praying for her. I want you two to love each other." He said the last sentence as they sat on the couch and looked at one another.

"I know. I'm sorry."

"It's not your fault." Mac sat silently, thinking of his future for a few moments. "How many children do you want to have?" The couple had talked about having children before, but had not gone into the details.

"What? That is certainly a change in subject." She laughed lightly. "I'm not sure. At least two."

"I want to start trying as soon as we're married. What do you think?"

"Well…that would be okay. But I wouldn't mind a couple of years to ourselves."

"I'm not getting any younger, Cass," Mac said seriously. Cassandra couldn't help herself and let out a laugh. "I'm 27."

"I know. I know," she said after she had stopped giggling. "That's fine, Honey. We don't have to wait."

"You're sure?" Cassandra nodded and he let out a sigh. "Two more months."

"Two more months," she repeated.

Mac decided that he needed to shift his thoughts before his mind went on to inappropriate things. He looked at the clock. "We better get started on supper. Richard and Debbie will be here in about an hour."

The couple had invited Richard Walker and his wife, Debbie, to dinner. They were becoming good friends. Cassandra began the preparations by thawing chicken. Mac had wanted to make spaghetti, but she had volunteered to help him make something different. They had decided on fried chicken, mashed potatoes and gravy, stuffing, corn, and homemade rolls.

Mac watched as Cassandra prepared the meal, occasionally asking him to help with something. His mind was wandering to the future again. Seeing her cooking in their future kitchen was doing things to his heart. He found himself thanking God for how busy he was with work. God knew how difficult the weeks leading up to their wedding would be for him. He thought back to the day when Cassie had told him that she was saving herself for marriage. At the time he had hoped she would eventually give in to him, but now he thanked the Lord they had waited. Their wedding night was going to be something special.

Richard and Debbie arrived a short time later as Mac was setting the table. "Come in. Have a seat. I'll check with Cassie to see if dinner is ready."

"Mac, let me do that. You and Richard just sit here and talk," Debbie offered.

"Thank you," Mac said, taking a seat in a chair across from Richard.

"Something smells wonderful," Debbie said as she entered the kitchen. "Can I help with anything?"

"I don't think so. Everything is just about ready."

Debbie took a seat on the barstool as Cassandra started making the gravy. "How're the wedding plans going?"

"Okay. I haven't really done too much. My mom is helping a lot since Mac and I are so busy. The only thing I've done is choose my dress. I just tell her what I want and she's taking care of the details."

"It's getting close. You must be very excited." Cassandra nodded and continued stirring the gravy. Debbie sighed. "My wedding seems so long ago. It's hard to believe we've been married seven years."

"So you waited awhile before starting a family. Isn't Tim turning four this month?"

"Yes. That's hard to believe as well. Thomas will be three soon. And little Jennifer started taking steps today."

"They could have come tonight."

"I know. But Richard and I needed a night out. They are spending the night with my parents. They were so excited."

"Well…I think we're all set." Cassandra started carrying the dishes of food to the dining room and Debbie followed with the rolls and corn. When the four of them were seated around the table, Mac said a prayer before they started eating.

"This is wonderful." Mac was the first to comment. Richard and Debbie agreed. "Why haven't you cooked like this for me before?"

"I'll be cooking for you for the rest of our lives. Why would I want to start sooner than I have to?" Cassie teased.

"You're a smart woman," Debbie said as she laughed.

They enjoyed the dinner and fellowship for a time before the women started clearing the table. Cassandra tried to refuse Debbie's help with the dishes, but she insisted. Mac and Richard made their way to the living room to continue visiting.

"Two months is going to feel like forever," Mac sighed.

"I remember those days. Debbie and I dated for years before we married. We were high school sweethearts. Waiting those last few weeks were torture." Mac nodded knowing what Richard meant. "The best advice I can give you is not to spend too much time alone."

"Sometimes I think I don't deserve her, Richard. She is so special…and pure." Mac looked down at his hands thinking about his past.

Richard knew exactly what Mac was thinking. "Does Cassie know?"

"Yes, of course. I'm just sorry that I don't have that gift to give her. Does that make sense?"

"Perfect sense. Sin is a terrible thing. Even if it's been confessed and God has forgiven us there are still consequences for our actions."

"Looking back I can see how foolish I have been. It's just like the Bible says in Hebrews. *'Sin brings pleasure for a short time.'* Now I see that while I may have enjoyed myself at the time, I've sinned against God and against Cassie." Mac paused before continuing. "That's it. I've asked God to forgive me, but I've never asked for Cassie's forgiveness."

The men continued to talk for awhile after Mac's realization, but Richard could see that his friend was preoccupied. When Cassandra and Debbie returned, Richard waited a few minutes before turning to Mac and Cassie. "I hate to eat and run, but it's not very often that I have my wife all to myself. The meal was delicious. Thank you." Debbie took her husband's lead and stood and followed him to the door. They said good-bye before leaving.

Cassandra started for the kitchen to unload the dishwasher. "Cass, come here. I need to talk to you."

"What is it?" she asked as she joined him on the couch. "Is everything okay?"

Mac took her hand and kissed it. "I realized something tonight when Richard and I were talking. I need your forgiveness."

"My forgiveness? For what?"

"Cassandra, I'm sorry that I didn't save myself for marriage. I sinned against God, but I also sinned against you. It's bothered me for some time now and it just dawned on me that I've never apologized to you or expressed how much I regret my decision. I'm so sorry."

"I forgave you a long time ago. It does make me feel better to know that you regret it." She paused. "I try not to dwell on it." Cassandra couldn't stop the tears that pooled in her eyes. She turned away from Mac and attempted to gain her composure.

"Cassie." Mac waited for her to look at him, but she refused. "Cassandra, look at me." She obeyed. "I'm sorry."

"I know." Her voice squeaked as she tried not to cry. "I know that you're sorry and I *have* forgiven you. It just…It still hurts." The last words were said in a whisper before she broke down and cried.

Mac took her in his arms and held her as she cried. *Lord, I've caused this pain. I didn't even know what I was doing at that time would cause Cassandra so much pain, but I'm sorry. Please help me to be the man she needs me to be. Help me become the man of God you've commanded me to be. Thank you for blessing my life with Cassie. I love her so much.*

17

The next few months were very busy for Mac and Cassandra. Mac hadn't thought about how difficult it would be to make wedding plans during tax season. He was thankful for Marlene Smith and her help in the preparations. The couple had not heard another word from Abigail Saxon since that day Mac was going to go to lunch with her. She had not even said good-bye, which proved to Mac what he already knew: that she didn't care about him at all and certainly hadn't come to visit him. Now the wedding was just a week away. Mac and Cassandra had just arrived at the Smith house where they would be staying until the wedding.

Mac had not spoken to his parents since he had confronted his mother. He sent messages about the wedding to them through Nic who was happy to help. As the couple pulled into the driveway, Mac let out a groan.

"What is it?" Cassandra asked. She followed his gaze and saw the limousine sitting in front of her parents' house. "Are they here? I thought they weren't coming until the day before," Cassandra questioned, referring to Mac's parents.

"Who else do you know that would have a limousine in this town?" Mac asked. He pulled his truck to a stop and grabbed their bags. "Come on. Let's get this over with." They started to walk toward the door, but Mac stopped and turned toward Cassandra. "Cassie, I've never told you that I'm sorry for the things my mother said to you. I'm sorry she hurt you. And I don't want you to worry about her at all. Just be yourself." Mac had put the bags down just long enough to hold Cassandra's face in his hands. "I love you."

"I love you too," Cassandra said before Mac released her and picked up the bags again. They walked to the door and Cassandra opened it. "Hello? We're here," she called.

"In the kitchen, Cass," Marlene called to her daughter. Mac and Cassandra entered the kitchen to find Marlene and Katherine sitting at the kitchen table with some iced tea. "I thought you'd never get here. We have some last minute planning to do." Mrs. Smith stood to hug her daughter and Mac. Mac and Cassandra greeted their mothers before Mac took their bags upstairs.

Cassandra wandered to the backyard looking for Nic. She hadn't seen him in so long. "Nic! Nic!" she called when she spotted him. He was in the far corner of the yard playing fetch with the Smiths' Labrador retriever, Rocky. Curtis Smith and Mr. Lugot sat on the deck talking.

Nic jogged easily up to Cassandra. "Hi Cassie," he said, hugging her warmly.

"If I remember right, that was far better than the last time you hugged me. Have you been practicing?" Cassandra teased.

"I see how I rate," Mr. Smith interrupted.

"Sorry, Dad. It's been a long time since I saw Nic. How are you?" she said crossing the deck to give him a hug. She turned to Mr. Lugot. "It's nice to see you again, Damon," Cassandra said, extending her hand.

"Since we're going to be family, I think it would be okay to hug," Mr. Lugot said as he hugged Cassandra.

She turned her attention back toward Nic. "It's so good to see you. You had me worried there for awhile. Are you completely recovered?" The two walked back out toward the yard and Cassandra greeted Rocky and tossed his ball for him some more. They talked easily. No one would have known they hadn't seen each other in over a year.

Mac took his time putting the bags away before joining Cassandra, Nic, and the older men in the back yard. He felt sorry for Marlene being stuck in the kitchen with his mother. He could only guess what subtle ways she was finding to insult the Smith family. Mac hadn't been outside for long when Chris showed up. After the introductions were made, the four young people decided to play a little basketball.

"I'll get your brace out of the truck," Cassandra offered.

"I don't need it."

"Think again. I won't have you hobbling up the aisle on Saturday. You *will* wear the brace."

"Yes, Dear," Mac said as he watched her walk away. *Is it possible that she will be my wife in only one more week? I've been anxious for so long and she will finally be mine. Thank You, Lord, for Cassie. Help us to place you at the center of our marriage. Help me to love her...*

"Are you ready?" Chris asked.

"No. Cass is making me wear my brace. Hold on a minute."

When Cassandra returned and Mac had his knee brace in place, the four began a game. Cassandra was having so much fun that she allowed herself to forget about Katherine Lugot sitting in her mother's kitchen. In the first game, Mac and Cassandra teamed up against Nic and Chris. It was a close game, but Mac and Cassandra pulled it out in the end. Then they mixed it up a little and put Nic and Cassandra on the same team. This game ended quickly as Mac and Chris won with ease.

They had just sat down for a break when Marlene peeked her head out and called for Cassandra to join the women as they looked at the wedding dress and bridesmaids' dresses. Cassandra glanced at Mac and he gave her a look of compassion. He hoped that his mother would have enough tact to show no disapproval of the preparations Cassandra had made for the wedding.

Katherine, Marlene, and Cassandra climbed the stairs to the bedroom where the dresses hung and the flowers were stored. "Why don't you try on your dress, Dear?" Marlene asked.

"Oh, Mom. You've seen me in it a thousand times. Besides I'm all sweaty." She glanced at Mrs. Lugot. Cassandra could see the disapproval on her face. No doubt she was thinking that a lady didn't play basketball with the men.

"That's true. We'll just have to wait to show Mrs. Lugot until you've cleaned up." She paused. "Here is her bouquet," she continued, handing it to Mrs. Lugot.

They continued looking over the flowers and other decorations that were going to be used for the wedding until Marlene thought she needed to start dinner. "You will join us for dinner, won't you?" she asked, turning to Katherine.

"We don't wish to intrude."

"You're more than welcome," Marlene said before standing and exiting the room.

"Very well," Mrs. Lugot said as she followed her hostess from the room. "How can I help?"

Cassandra stared at Mrs. Lugot's back, wondering if she even knew how to cook. She went to the closet and looked at her wedding gown. As she fingered the white satin she thanked the Lord for the Godly man He had given her. She couldn't believe that by this time next week she would be Mrs. Mac Lugot. Her thoughts shifted to Mrs. Damon Lugot and how much *help* she was being in the kitchen. Curiosity got the best of her and she made her way downstairs and joined her mother and Katherine in the kitchen. To her surprise, Katherine was bent over a mixing bowl with flour covered hands.

"Shocked?" she questioned when she noticed Cassandra's gaze. The younger girl didn't know how to respond. "I *can* cook, Cassandra. It's just not my favorite thing and I usually arrive home late from the law firm."

Marlene looked at her daughter. Mrs. Lugot's tone hadn't been very pleasant and she could see that Cassie was still fumbling for words. "Cassie told me that you have a full staff at your house. That must be wonderful," she said, effectively rescuing her daughter. *If you like being waited on hand and foot*, Marlene wished to add. *Dear Lord, forgive me. I'm wrong to judge this woman's lifestyle. We are from different worlds and that doesn't make mine better. This woman is about to be a big part of my daughter's life and she has no idea how special she is. Help these two to learn to love each other.* Marlene continued her prayer as Katherine explained her staff's duties.

Cassandra took the opportunity to exit through the patio door to the backyard. The men were gathered on the deck. "Hey…Come sit with me," Mac said when he saw her. There were no other chairs so Cassie took a place in Mac's lap. He looked into her eyes and could see the hurt she was feeling. "Are you okay?" he whispered. She nodded and turned her attention toward the men's conversation. Damon was explaining what Lugot Industries was and she found this very interesting. Mac had never gone into details concerning his family's business.

A short time later, Marlene stuck her head out and called for them to come in for dinner. As they filed in, Mac held Cassandra back. "Are you sure you're okay?"

"No." She paused. "I don't want to talk about it though."

"Remember I love you." Mac took her hand and led the way inside.

When everyone was seated around the table, Curtis thanked the Lord for the food and the special reason they were gathered. During dinner the conversation turned toward attending church the next day.

"We would love for you to join us." Curtis invited.

"Count me in," Nic said.

"Katherine and I would also like to come," Damon surprised everyone by saying. He ignored the look of horror he received from his wife and continued. "What time shall we be there?"

"I can't believe they are really here," Mac whispered to Cassandra the next morning as the services began. His parents were sitting on the end of the pew next to Marlene Smith.

"I know. I've been praying that the Lord will work in their hearts, Honey," she said before turning her attention back to Pastor Allen.

"I'm trying not to get overly excited, but it *is* a start, isn't it?"

"Yes, Dear. Now let's be a good example for them and pay attention," she said as she winked at the man she loved.

Mac smiled and looked down toward his parents. If he had known their thoughts, he wouldn't have been so excited. Katherine Lugot had put up a fight about attending church the night before and the couple had yet to make up. Damon was infuriated with his wife. By the time they were ready to leave the hotel, he didn't even want to go. However, being the stubborn man that he was, he was not going to allow his wife to have her way.

He now stared blankly at the pastor, his mind elsewhere. *How have I allowed things to get so out of control? Kat thinks she can bully me and get her way. It didn't used to be this way.* Damon's thoughts shifted to the Smith family and how different they were from his own. He glanced at his wife.

Her thoughts were running along that same line, only she wondered what had gotten into her husband. It wasn't like him to force her to do something.

The services couldn't end soon enough for either of them and they politely refused an invitation to dinner at the Smith household.

"Cass, why don't you try it on?" Marlene questioned Monday afternoon when Mrs. Lugot came for a visit while the men golfed. She saw the hesitant look that crossed her daughter's face. "Maybe Mrs. Lugot would like to see it," Marlene suggested.

Cassandra stepped into the walk-in closet and put on the dress she had chosen for her wedding day. She wondered what Mrs. Lugot would think of the fairly simple dress. When she opened the door and stepped out, Katherine Lugot gasped. Cassandra's cheeks flushed with anger. Marlene looked at Katherine and then to her daughter. "Isn't it beautiful?" Marlene questioned, trying to relieve the tension in the room.

Katherine Lugot cleared her throat before she choked out. "Yes. It's beautiful."

Cassandra had told Marlene about the way that Katherine had treated her when she visited the Lugots in Texas. In the three days that Marlene had known Katherine, she was seeing it firsthand and she felt horrible for her daughter. *Dear Lord, my instinct is to lash out at this woman for her rudeness, but I know that is not what You want me to do. Please don't let this woman ruin my daughter's wedding. Help all of us to take advantage of the time we'll have with her and be good witnesses to her.*

"Can I change now?" Cassandra's question interrupted Marlene's prayer.

"I'm sorry. I was just praying. Is the fit still okay? We don't need to make any adjustments?"

"No. It's fine," Cassandra said before stomping back into the closet. Once she removed the dress, she sank down on the floor and cried. *Lord, please help me. I can't let Mac's mother ruin my wedding day. I think my dress is beautiful and I know Mac will like it. Why do I allow her to hurt my feelings? Lord, would You soften Mrs. Lugot's heart to You and Your Word. I realize that she's lost and Satan is using her as a tool to try and destroy my happiness. I won't let him though. I know this marriage is Your will. Help me to handle Mrs. Lugot in a way that will bring honor and glory to You. Help me to remain respectful no matter what. And above all else, put a love in my heart for her. Amen.* Cassandra wiped the tears from her eyes and dressed quickly.

Later that evening, Cassandra found herself alone with Mrs. Lugot in the living room. "I just want you to know that my feelings haven't changed. I don't approve of this wedding and I will never accept you as a Lugot."

Cassandra searched for words to say in return, but before she could think of a polite way to reply, Damon Lugot entered the room. "Katherine, I've had enough of this," he whispered through clenched teeth. "Excuse us, Cassandra. And my apologies." Mr. Lugot put a hand to his wife's elbow and led her out the front door.

Cassandra stood, wondering what Mr. Lugot would say to his wife and if it would make any difference. Mac joined her and took in her pale features. "What's wrong?"

"Oh…uh…your mother," she said, looking past Mac toward the door.

"What did she say this time?" he asked, his eyes alight with anger.

"Well, your father interrupted. They're outside." She finally turned her attention to her fiancé.

"What?" Mac was shocked. He couldn't remember a time when his father had stood up to his mother. Mac sank down on the sofa next to Cassandra and sat quietly thinking about what was going to happen. He wondered how his mother would react to being reprimanded. "This has never happened before. I don't know what she'll do," he said softly, lost in his thoughts. Neither of them spoke until the Lugots returned a few minutes later.

Mrs. Lugot entered the house and stood directly in front of Cassandra. "I'm sorry for the way I've treated you, Cassandra. I realize that since my son loves you, you are a very special person. I only hope that you will give me the opportunity to repair our relationship since we will be family."

Mac's mouth dropped open and Cassandra tried to find words to say in return to her future mother-in-law. "I would like that," she managed.

Mr. Lugot stood at the door taking in the scene. Nic had also entered the room in time to hear his mother's apology. The look on his face was identical to the one on Mac's face: complete shock.

"Cassie, I'd like to talk to my boys if you don't mind," Mr. Lugot said, entering the room. Cassandra excused herself and joined her family in the basement. When he was alone with his family, Mr. Lugot talked with them about the way things were going to change in the Lugot household. He apologized for his lack of leadership over the years. He also admitted his regret for the way he had not been there for his sons as they were growing up.

"Please. I want you to stay here," Cassandra pleaded with Mac on the night before their wedding. He had announced his intention to spend the night with Nic in the hotel room.

"No. I don't want to see you until you walk down that aisle tomorrow morning." He saw the disappointment in her eyes. "Look at it this way, this is the last night we will ever be spending apart."

Cassandra liked that idea and moved on to her next concern. "Are you going to tell me where we're going on our honeymoon?"

"I told you before. It's a surprise."

"Well, how am I supposed to know if I packed wisely?" she objected.

"I told you to pack for a warm environment. That's all you need to know."

Mac had made plans to return to the home they would be sharing for their first night together. The following morning they would fly to Houston and leave on a seven-day cruise to the Caribbean.

Mac put his arm around his bride-to-be. She was obviously flustered by his secrecy. "I love driving you crazy." Cassandra laughed, thinking she loved having him drive her crazy. She didn't voice her thoughts, but sat quietly enjoying being close to him. "I'm glad that this week with my parents has turned out okay," he said, his thoughts turning serious.

"Me too. I must admit I was shocked to have your mother apologize to me. What do you think made your dad stand up to her?"

"Well, I know he likes you a lot. He thinks you're one of the sweetest young women he's ever met. That came directly from him, by the way." Cassandra smiled, thinking about how nice Damon was. "From all he told us, I think maybe he was impressed with your family. Probably much like I was the first time I met them. My family life has not been anything like yours,

Cassie. You are very fortunate. You know, Dad used to attend church with my grandparents when he was younger. I wonder if he ever accepted Christ."

Cassandra noted that this was the first time she had heard Mac refer to his father as Dad. "You don't feel like you can ask him?"

"Not yet." Mac paused for a moment before continuing. "But maybe soon." He looked at his watch. "I better go. I don't know what the guys have planned for me."

"Nothing too crazy, I hope. I love you."

"I love you. Have fun with the girls." Mac kissed her cheek and opened the door to leave. Cassandra squealed with delight when she saw Sarah and Beth standing at the door.

"You're here! Come in. Come in." Mac took his leave then, laughing at Cassie's excitement. "I didn't think you were coming until morning."

"We couldn't miss the bachelorette party!" Sarah exclaimed, embracing her friend.

"Mel was just going to rent some movies or something."

"Oh no. I don't think that will do at all!" Beth said as she motioned to someone outside.

Cassandra was floored to see several of her friends file into her house. "What is going on?" she asked, noticing they were carrying gifts. Beth started to answer, but then stopped when she saw her friend's face as she noticed that she had been set up. Her mother, Shannon, Melissa and even Mrs. Lugot were the last to come in. "Melissa! You lied to me!"

"Technically, I didn't. I just said we would do something here at the house. I didn't elaborate."

Marlene and Shannon ignored the excited chatter and got right to work. They set up chairs in the basement and brought down the refreshments. The ladies enjoyed the cake and punch before Beth urged Cassie to start on her gifts. She opened them one by one, thanking everyone for the wonderful things she received. Katherine Lugot took her turn and handed Cassie a small package.

She was a bit surprised, but when she looked up at Mrs. Lugot and saw her warm smile, she tore into the wrapping paper. "These are beautiful!" Cassandra whispered as she fingered the pearl necklace and earrings. She stood and hugged Katherine.

The older woman returned the embrace. "I thought you could wear them tomorrow. But only if you want to," she said as she pulled back.

"Were they yours?" Cassandra questioned. Katherine nodded.

This did the younger woman's heart a world of good. *Maybe she is accepting me into her family. Thank you, Lord. Continue to work in both of our hearts. I want to love this woman as I should and I want her to love me.* "I think they will look wonderful with my dress. Thank you Mrs. Lugot."

"I think it's about time you call me Katherine."

Marlene waited patiently before handing her gifts to her daughter. She silently thanked the Lord that Cassandra and her future mother-in-law seemed to be making some progress in their relationship.

When Cassie had taken her seat again, her mother stepped forward and handed her a package. Cassandra gasped and her face heated with embarrassment as she opened it. Inside were two beautiful camisoles.

"Show us!" Sarah called from across the room.

Cassandra obliged, but not without her face heating again. She thanked her mother before accepting the next package. "Oh, Mom." She whispered as she pulled back the tissue paper to reveal a large family Bible and a devotional book for couples. "Thank you," she said as she stood to hug her mother. "I love you so much."

"I love you too. I'm so happy for you, sweetie."

The organ began to play at exactly ten o'clock, announcing the beginning of the ceremony. Pastor Allen, Mac, and Nic made their way to the platform and took their places. Mac watched anxiously as Melissa came down the aisle. He smiled thinking of her objection to being in the wedding with her round belly. Cassandra had convinced her though, and she looked lovely.

And then he saw her. She stood at the back of the sanctuary on her father's arm, waiting for her entrance. From that moment on Mac couldn't take his eyes off of his lovely bride. He watched her walk toward him and took in every inch of her. The dress she had chosen was perfect. It accented her features so well that Mac found himself prematurely thinking of the evening to come. He forced his mind back to the ceremony.

Mac and Cassandra stared into one another's eyes as they exchanged their vows. Mac could see that Cassandra's eyes were moist, but she managed to control her emotions. Then the Pastor announced them as man and wife and gave Mac permission to kiss his wife.

My wife. I like the sound of that.

He took his wife in his arms and gently kissed her.

*****